Fi

Story By

Thomas Knapp

Based on MegaTokyo: Endgames By

Fred Gallagher

Editor

Ray Kremer

Chapter One: What's in a Name?

Sunay stepped onto the deck, feeling the southern sun on her face, and found herself thinking something she never thought she'd ever think.

That she rather missed winter. At least the winter months of Navarre and the Versilles province... where the air got a little cooler, and the winds brisk. It was a nice change of pace from the heat of summer without the bone-chilling freeze found further north. There was a genuine seasonal shift from the refreshing cool to the green of spring to the heart of summer then the splendor of fall color before yielding to the nighttime glaze of frost that marked the winters in Southern Avalon.

In the southern seas, there were two seasons, sweltering humid heat and typhoon, and both were really grating on Sunay's nerves. It didn't help matters that after the initial flurry of activity, the south seas were a *really* boring job. Monitor the void far to the south, note that it hadn't changed, occasionally get intelligence from agents on shore reporting that Aramathea was planning absolutely nothing, repeat every month.

Hopefully this current trip to the coast would bring something that could at least take her attention off of the heat. Their course was set back for Beredon, in the Free Provinces, though Ahmin hadn't yet said why. The foxgirl understood thanks to her own dealings with land operations; the agents and administrators there hadn't told him, and probably wouldn't until the *Goldbeard* was getting the rowboats ready.

The Admiral emerged from below decks, his brows still furrowed angrily as he stared down the approaching port. "Sunay."

"Sir," the foxgirl replied.

He took two long breaths, as if trying to steady his anger. "Garth! Prep one boat on the port side."

The deckhand complied as swiftly as he was able, and Sunay asked, "Only you, I take it?"

Ahmin glowered, and replied, "No. Only you."

The foxgirl blinked rapidly. "Me? Why?"

"I have no idea," Ahmin answered. "Sensitive information, I am told. I don't know why they asked specifically for you, and I doubt you'll know why until it's too damn late."

"I don't have much a choice in this, do I?" Sunay asked.

"Comes from the Western Free Provinces administrator

personally. I would rather like to remain on good terms with as many of my fellow administrators as I can. I can understand all too well why you'd be reluctant, but I'd rather you complied, though."

Sunay exhaled with an animated flapping of her lips. "Understood. I'll do it."

"You *won't* spend hours in an Aramathean jail. I'll promise you that," Ahmin said sternly. "I'll break you out by force within twenty minutes if it happens, I don't care *what* plans I ruin."

Sunay could hear the admiral's sincerity, and appreciated the thought. "Thanks. I mean that."

"Boat's ready, sir!" Garth declared, snapping a playful salute as he stepped back towards the winch.

Ahmin nodded, and clapped Sunay on the back gently. "Good luck."

"Yeah," Sunay agreed dourly as her ears flattened. "I'll probably need it."

She climbed into the rowboat, and reluctantly took the oars only after the *Goldbeard* had long cleared. With a defeated sigh, Sunay began to churn her shoulders and take the little boat to shore. It occurred to her that it was the first time she had been alone on one of these missions.

At least, alone with land agents of the Gold Pirates... which by her experience meant she was running solo.

At the same time, if Ahmin wasn't comfortable with this administrator, he wouldn't have agreed to send her alone... right?

Perhaps if she repeated that in her head enough times, she'd be able to convince herself.

She pulled up to the dock, feeling extremely small as the wooden boardwalk was at eye level. She really hoped she'd get over herself quickly, she didn't want to have this "small fox in a big world" feeling for the entire course of the mission. She was a grown woman, she could handle herself on her own for a few days, for Coders' sake.

She jumped onto the dock, and hadn't even finished tying down the rowboat when she was approached by a man with a yellow scarf with white printed flowers around his neck. He was otherwise well dressed for a man in the Free Provinces, unstained button-up shirt and knee length shorts well suited for the heat of summer on the South Forever Sea.

"Miss Sunay?"

"Aye. What's it to ya?" the foxgirl grumbled. She might have stupidly agreed to this, but that didn't mean she was going to make it easy for *anyone* involved.

"I'm to escort you to the meeting location for your briefing."

She refused to look at him beyond that first appraisal, pretending to be *very* carefully tying the rope that would moor her rowboat to the dock. "And why should I believe ya, eh?"

"Because Admiral Ahmin would no doubt hunt me and my bosses down like a bloodthirsty hound if I put so much as one hair of your tail out of place?"

She had to admit *that* was a good answer. "How 'bout this? Ya tell me where to go, and I'll go there. No offense, but I'd rather not trust any o' ya until I absolutely have to."

She heard her would be escort sigh in resignation. "Very well. The meeting is taking place at the Towers Beer Hall, it's the second tavern in the row on North Street on your right as you are leaving the town center."

Sunay finally straightened, and tipped an invisible hat in the man's direction. "Thank ya kindly."

Beredon had changed quite a bit over the last two years, but that was hardly uncommon for Free Province towns. Even the most "permanent" of settlements had tremendous population turnover. City-states could disappear overnight in the Free Provinces for any number of reasons depending on the major political powers involved. While important mercantile towns like Beredon were much more stable, that still didn't mean that people wouldn't come and go frequently, taking their business with them if necessary.

Even the roads were different, having been switched from loose stone to red brick. While she had no doubt it was easier on carts and pack animals' hooves, that couldn't have been cheap to completely renovate. She worried that the leaders of Beredon would draw some unwanted attention by displaying such wealth.

The traffic was starting to pick up as the afternoon sun took its path towards evening, workers and customers shifting from the stores and towards restaurants and taverns, much like the beer hall she was approaching. Except this one was... oddly closed... considering the time of day.

Sunay looked up at the sign above the main doorway. Towers Beer Hall. This was certainly the place she was directed to. Looking left, then right, she set her jaw and rapped loudly on the door. It opened swiftly, and an elderly old man in black suit and a gold sash stood on the other side, with brown hair combed over a mostly bald scalp. "Miss Sunay of the Goldbeard, I assume. Come on in, come on in!"

"And how do you know I am she?"

"Not many foxgirls that wear the gold," he replied. "Not to mention the earring. It was told to me to be an indicator."

Sunay's eyes drifted to her old present from Laron, that on the advice of friends she had kept. "How... who among you *knows* of my earring anyway?"

"Ah! *There's* my little fire fox!"

Sunay froze in place, just at the entry to the main hall, her ears flattening. She knew that voice. Damn it, she knew that voice...

Rola appeared with a swish of her coppery tail and that same broad unsettling grin that Sunay had remembered, "Hello, little fire fox! It is so wonderful to see you again!"

"Like...wise..." Sunay whimpered, yanked forward as Rola grabbed her arms and pulled her fully into the main hall.

"We simply *must* catch up! The meeting won't be for a while, so we simply *must!*"

Rola spun animatedly, prompting Sunay to remark, "Yer tail was gray last time we met."

The wolf spirit sighed loudly, "You saw me in the transition from winter to spring. During the winter months, I am a most boringly dreadful gray. As spring comes around, my hair starts to turn, starting from the top and working the way down. Then I am this delightful color until the winter!

"So, how have you been, my little fire fox? Has life on the seas been pleasant?"

Sunay's eye began to twitch. "Why are you calling me that?"

Rola grinned again and chirped, "Well, since you are a pirate and all, I figured you simply *must* have a true pirate moniker. Something that invokes fear and respect! Something that reflects who you are and grants you notoriety!"

Sunay's left eye was now in full twitch. "Please... don't."

Rola had already moved on, clapping her hands. "I'm *so* glad that you accepted this request. For there... is something we really need to discuss face to face." Her lips turned downward to a frown, and she added, "You will be so mad at me, and I deserve it."

"What did you do?" Sunay asked flatly.

The wolf spirit bit her lower lip. "Well, Law and I were in Vakulm last fall, and I tried to relay the news that you wanted me to tell your dear Laron... but..."

The foxgirl's eyes bulged. "Rola... you... *didn't*..."

6

Rola's ears turned backward, and she said, "I *tried...* but he looked *so sad...* and he was oh so happy when I told him the truth!"

"I'm sure his current paramour appreciated that news," Sunay grumbled.

Rola's grin returned, "Oh, it was of little concern. He and Sulia had a bit of a falling out last year at some point. He wanted to be a merchant, whereas she had assets in Avalon that she couldn't afford to abandon for a life on the road. He's actually apprenticing under a friend of mine nowadays."

Sunay chided herself for the happy twitch in her ears. Even *if* Laron was now unattached, she had important duties herself, and she wasn't going to abandon them. "So I take it all this means you're a Gold Pirate after all?" the foxgirl asked, eager to change the topic.

The wolf spirit bit her lower lip and said, "Well..." Rola then jerked her head toward the front door and shouted, "Law! The rest of the party is here!"

Rola's husband emerged, looking rather dour. "About time."

"Salvador!" Rola said, flipping her hand towards the front door, "Do be a dear and let him in."

"Provided he is who we think."

Rola huffed, "I know his smell, Law."

A knock on the door followed, long after the steward of sorts had already moved to the entry. "So that's how he answered so fast," Sunay noted.

"I have a very good sense of smell," Rola replied, glaring daggers at her husband.

The butler returned with the final member of their party, a very large Avalonian man with black hair and a light tan. Sunay had initially thought that the slight slouch in the man's back was due to clearing the low door frame, but when he didn't straighten out suggested it was a chronic condition.

Rola skipped to his side, reaching up to pat the man on the shoulder, "This is Pierre, he is a continental merchant, which is someone who takes the long roads from coast to coast. Anywhere from Avalon to Reaht, this fellow can go there. Quite handy really, I'm rather jealous."

"I think you'd trade for your familiar roads quickly," Pierre replied.

"I'd rather we get this meeting *on* the road so that we can all get back to ours," Law grumbled, taking a seat at the long end of the table.

Rola gave Law a stern glare, but conceded, "He's right. Time might not exactly be our enemy, but it's not exactly our friend, either. Gather 'round, have a seat, and we'll start the briefing."

Sunay dropped down across from Law, Pierre taking the seat to her right, and Rola next to her husband. "I'm not sure how aware you are about Administrator tomes, Sunay..."

"Aware enough," the foxgirl answered. "I assisted a mission with landlubbers in Grand Aramathea that indirectly dealt with one."

Rola nodded, ignoring Sunay's slur for land agents. "Good, then you don't need a primer. We are dealing with one such tome that has bounced just out of reach of our agents for about three years. And it's finally resurfaced... in the possession of the Venerated Citizen Torad of the Gold Coast."

Sunay's head tilted. "The Gold Coast is in Aramathea. Shouldn't our assets in the empire be handling that?"

Rola and Law looked at each other, and the wolf spirit said, "We have unique assets that will allow us a better shot at the artifact. Our colleagues in the First Empire have conceded this to us. Most notably, we have Pierre here, and he's tied to us."

The foxgirl regarded their large companion. "And what angle does he have that no one else does?"

"An association with Dominus Socrato, who has taken considerable interest in the artifact Torad possesses," Pierre explained. "The Dominus has already approached my brother and me to trade for the tome, and declared money is no object."

"Torad is a very... difficult sort," Rola interjected. "He doesn't take visitors very often on his lands. Pierre and his brother are our way inside without the raid that our agents in Aramathea are ready to resort to. In addition, Dominus Socrato is a powerful mage who might very well be able to glean far too many secrets of our organization if he were to gain possession of the artifact. Our plan deals with two concerns at one time. Pierre, would you like to continue?"

The large merchant nodded. "My brother and I will presumably be making negotiations with Torad in his meeting room. While we are occupying him, Sunay and Rola will infiltrate his vault. Once that is done, you will swap the Administrator's tome with a replica. At that point, you get out while we close the deal. While Torad is exceptionally ornery, I wouldn't gamble on having more than thirty minutes before we either reach an agreement or he throws us out."

Sunay's eyes narrowed. "Okay... why are *we* important in this scheme?"

"Well, Rola is the one that managed to learn the combination to Torad's vault," Pierre explained. "Whereas *you* come highly recommended for your climbing skills, which will be needed if you're going to be scaling the south wall."

"And why am I doin' that? Pretend I have no idea what's goin' on. Actually, don't pretend."

Pierre unrolled diagrams and blueprints of Torad's manor. "The south wall looks directly over the beach. It has a lookout tower to watch out to sea, but directly underneath it on the beach is a massive blind spot. You can climb over the wall and once inside let Rola in through a service gate on the east side of the grounds."

This still wasn't adding up for the foxgirl. "I find it hard to believe that someone as disliking of guests as ya claim this Torad is would 'ave such a massive hole in his security."

Pierre nodded. "He doesn't, which is *another* reason why it's important that you and Rola have this duty."

"And that is...?"

The merchant offered a slight grin. "Surely you've noticed by now. You're invisible."

Sunay blinked repeatedly. Why is it working with land agents gave her headaches like this? "Uh... huh."

"What I mean by that is outside of Avalon, chimeras... don't seem to draw much attention. You're like an uncomfortable existence that others would rather not address or notice, so they don't. You can get a lot closer to people who would normally be wary. You can approach places that others wouldn't normally be allowed to approach. Like the guards posted underneath the south wall."

Sunay had to think about that, and then acknowledge that the merchant... was right. She couldn't figure out *why* that was true, but memories of walking straight up to a heavily armed Phalanx soldier in Grand Aramathea while having every reason to be a highly wanted suspect in a raid on Aramathean soil would suggest he was correct. "How many guards are we talkin' about?"

"Four, usually," Pierre said.

Rola tilted her head. "Two each. Sounds like fun."

"We're not talking about a 'gathering'," Law grumbled with a suspicious glare in his wife's direction.

"Only because you're never interested love," Rola shot back, then gave Sunay a suggestive grin.

That made the foxgirl shiver, which was clearly the wolf spirit's intent. Desperate to change the topic, she turned it back to business, "What if there's *more* than four?"

Rola's grin refused to fade, "Oh... I think once you learn *my* part of the plan, you'll discover that it wouldn't matter if there were *twenty* men standing guard."

This time, *both* Sunay and Law shuddered, though the wolf spirit's husband quickly set his jaw and refused to rise further to the bait. The foxgirl, however, did. "And what *is* yer plan, then?"

"Oh... that will be for later, after we part ways. Girl talk and all."

"*Anyway...*" Law interjected forcefully.

Rola waved him off, "Right right... we scale the wall, wind our way to the vault, swap the real tome with the fake, then get out. If all goes perfectly, Pierre and Law deliver the fake to Socrato, and we take the real one for proper disposal. At the worst, we at least get the real one off the market, if you will."

Sunay pursed her lips in thought, then asked, "Why go to these lengths anyway? Socrato said money was no object, didn't 'e? Offer the moon, get the tome, then swap it out after the fact."

Pierre shook his head, "Because there is a very real possibility that no amount of money or goods will be enough. Torad isn't always reasonable, and we need to make sure at the very least that we secure the Administrator's tome."

Rola added, "We'd rather not have to resort to a raid. Aramathea's still rather worked up about the operation on Sacili."

Sunay rubbed her forehead in exasperation. Climbing... sneaking around... if these people needed someone from the *Goldbeard* for this, this job was right up Juno's alley. "Okay... so why *me*? When there's a chimera *on my ship* who would be better suited fer this? Did you not *know* we have a *spider* chimera on board who damn near runs up walls or somethin', Rola?"

The wolf spirit looked surprised. "Oh, I didn't ask for you, dearie. Pierre did."

Pierre quickly gave a response, "Your crewmate Juno is subtle in a different way than we require. We're trying to *avoid* deaths. I'm not sure the spider chimera has that level of restraint, and it wasn't a gamble worth taking considering you are more than adequate for the job."

Sunay leaned back with a sulk, mostly because she didn't want to admit that Pierre was probably right about the spidergirl. "Very well. Guess I ain't gonna be able to back out at this point anyways."

"We leave tomorrow morning," Rola concluded, "So that gives

us the evening to drink and be merry! Salvador, do bring us a round of the house ale, would you?"

"You plan on having any food with your beer this time?" Law asked.

"Yes," Rola retorted bitingly, "There is apple glazed ham, apple sauce, and apple pastry as well. Nothing wrong with a round or two while the food is being prepared."

"And apple cider to drink, I assume?" Sunay said.

Rola shook her head, "Of course not. A lovely green tea from Reaht that Pierre here has gotten me hooked on. Why would you think that anyway?"

Salvador emerged from the kitchen with a tray of four mugs, and Law was the first to claim his, the tray passed along counter clockwise from there.

"To a painless mission," Law offered in toast. "For once."

There was something Sunay could agree with after all, as she and the other clinked their glasses together. Sunay quite happily downed her first mug, then a second, by the time their dinner arrived. Then three more both during and after the meal.

This caught Rola's approval. "Oh ho, the little fire fox has gained the ability to hold her ale."

"Ain't quite up ta where yer at, ah'm sure," the foxgirl replied, pleased with how little she slurred, even though she knew she was slipping into old speech habits. "But ah'm gettin' there."

Pierre blinked rapidly, shaking his head as if to clear it. "Frightening that ladies half my size are handling their alcohol better than I am."

Law shrugged, dabbing his upper lip with a yellow handkerchief that he tucked back into the front pocket of his shirt. "Now you know why I don't even try to go past two anymore. My wife could drink a party of Daynes under the table."

Pierre poked Sunay in her side while she was in the process of sipping, which caused the foxgirl to sputter. "What?" she grumbled after coughing twice.

The merchant replied, "Just have a few questions, if you don't mind me asking."

She eyed him with suspicion, but nonetheless said, "Well... go 'ead, but ah reserve th' right ta tell ya ta buzz off."

He regarded her carefully, like he was closely examining her face for any tells of a lie. "You always gone by the name of Sunay?"

"As long as ah can 'member."

"I assume you were born in the north?"

Sunay shrugged, "Ah think so. Ah was way too young t'member anythin' before mah time in th' orphanage outside Navarre. I know Domina Morgana used th' red fox as 'er curse's inspiration, but she claims she wasn't tha only one who did. Git somethin' straight... I ain't no bastard princess, even if ah *was* the king's daughter."

Pierre laughed, "Not what I wanted to know, honest. Does the town of Lourdis mean anything to you?"

Again she shrugged indifferently, even though every time she heard the name, it sounded like something she *should* remember. "Ah know *of* th' place. Ah know it kinda close t' Navarre, but that 'bout it."

"Do you remember *anything* about your mother?"

The foxgirl shook her head, "Not really. A li'l bit, here 'n there, mebbe. Ah think she 'ad green eyes? Mebbe? I guess? Dunno. Blond hair... brown... ish... kinda?" she then crossly asked, "Why da ya care anyway?"

Pierre rubbed his temples, "A sister of mine had a daughter that we were told she was taking to our family in Lourdis just before the Revolution. But neither I nor my brother found either of them. When I learned of a red fox chimera in the Gold Pirates... I thought perhaps... but I knew it was a long shot. The King had many illegitimate children with more women than I could count... and that's assuming you're even the King's daughter to begin with."

"So even if'n ah was... we'd never be able ta know," Sunay said glumly.

"Sounds that way. I apologize. Just the curiosity of an older man daring to hope after almost two decades."

"Ah, it ain't a bother. Can't blame ya fer thinkin'." Her eyes narrowed again, and she snarled, "Unless dat's why ya dragged me here and not Juno."

"If that was all I wanted, I could have easily sent the request to your commanding officer through any number of contacts."

Sunay still flattened her ears and stared him down warningly. "Well... 'kay. Ya better not be lyin' t' me."

Rola interjected, sliding another mug in front of Sunay. "Less accusing, more drinking!"

Sunay accepted the mug, took a long pull, then asked Pierre, "What was yer niece's name?"

"Lauren, allegedly... but I'm not even certain of *that* much. See, my sister earnestly believed the King loved her... and she pushed my brother and me out of her life. I'm honestly a bit astonished she listened to my brother long enough to escape before the Revolution tore down the palace gates."

"Well, if Lauren is still out dere, all ah can tell ya is dat she didin' come to mah orphanage, and dat was tha only refuge fer chimeras in da whole damned province. I was da only fox in da whole place."

"Sometimes knowing what isn't is as important as knowing what is," Pierre recited from some old wisdom he must have picked up on the road.

"But not in dis case, ah bet."

Pierre shook his head. "No."

Sunay pushed away the empty mug of what had been her sixth pint. The corner of her vision was starting to get hazy, and she knew that she didn't dare go any farther tonight. "Okay, I dun wanna be hung over come th' mornin', so ah'm gonna call it quits 'ere."

Rola sat down her mug, and declared, "Oh yes... and we must do our planning as well!" The wolf spirit jumped to her feet, vaulted the table, and grabbed Sunay's arm, "We shall let these gentlemen iron out what other details. Come, come! We don't want to be out shopping too late!"

Rola was stronger than she looked, able to easily pull Sunay from her chair. The foxgirl stumbled, but caught her feet quickly enough to prevent herself from face-planting. "What... whar ah we goin'?" Sunay sputtered as she found a stride that matched Rola's, stepping out of the beer hall and into the early evening streets of Beredon.

The wolf seemed to know exactly where they were going, and the fox knew that any further questions were going to fall on deaf ears. There wasn't much to be done other than get swept away by the force of nature known as Rola, especially since Sunay was too tipsy to do much more than keep pace.

The muggy summer evening air didn't exactly increase her alertness any, so it wasn't until she was pulled into the tailor's shop that she processed where Rola had been taking her. "Wha... why're we gettin' clothes? Wha fer?"

"We might be 'invisible', but we still need a reason to be on the beach!" Rola explained cheerily as she approached the sales desk. The wolf spirit tapped the desk to get the clerks attention and said, "I'm Rola, I believe my order should be ready."

The woman at the desk was a slight, pretty Aramathean girl with her beautiful carmel skin and chocolate brown hair that looked oh so adorable and exotic and made Sunay all sorts of jealous when inebriated. A slender index finger ran down an open brown leather book though open orders, and stopped after two pages. "Ah yes, two sets of Gold Coast swimwear, I believe?"

"That would be right!" Rola chirped with a smile.

Sunay didn't like it when Rola smiled like that. Why was Rola smiling like that?

"It is ready for you, Madam Rola. I shall retrieve them for you."

With the clerk out of earshot, Sunay began to air her concerns. "*Two* suits, eh?"

Rola hushed her. "Be grateful for the gift, and leave it at that."

"Feh. E'rey word ya utter tell me ah won't 'preciate it one bit," the foxgirl said.

The wolf spirit gave Sunay that hungry grin again. "I never said anything about *your* appreciation."

Sunay had to hold her tongue as the clerk returned with two folded cloth squares that were far too small for Sunay's sensibilities. Rola took one, and handed the other to Sunay. "I already know mine will fit, and while I'm reasonably certain as to your measurements, I could be wrong. Dressing rooms are on the north wall. Hurry now. If it needs alterations we need to know quick-like."

When the foxgirl didn't promptly reply, Rola applied more of her surprising strength to give Sunay a spin and push in the right direction. Sunay stumbled, gave Rola a nasty glare, regretted the quick head motion, then with a groan locked herself in the first dressing room.

She dropped the cloth bundle on the bench, then carefully pulled apart the folds to get her first look at the contents. She didn't like what she saw. "An' where th' rest o' it?" She called out, knowing that Rola had to be right on the other side of the door with a broad, mischievous smile.

Sunay wasn't wrong, either. "Just try it on!" the wolf spirit said happily.

The foxgirl slowly released her breath, then reluctantly undressed, dropping her clothes unceremoniously in a pile behind her. She then uncertainly picked up the halter top by its extremely thin shoulder strap, eyeing the white material dotted with orange distastefully. Contrary to how she dressed normally, Sunay didn't particularly like showing off too much skin... but there was only so many times she was willing to sew buttons back on.

14

As a result, she was not the slightest bit comfortable with this. "Rola, ah'd..." she began, before closing her eyes, taking a deep breath, and focused on not slurring her words, "I'd probably pop outta this thing if I so much as breathed too heavy."

"Not if it fits right!" Rola countered. "Which is why we need to find out! Hurry it up!"

"I'm not leavin' dis damn store if I don't, am I?" Sunay guessed.

"I will stand vigil at this door all night if I have to," the wolf spirit confirmed.

The foxgirl yielded, sticking her head through the loop, properly adjusting it to cover her breasts, at least the most essential bits, then tied it off in the middle. She had to admit that it clung to her so tightly that even some extremely energetic turning and twisting wasn't enough to dislodge herself. "It fits!" she shouted.

The wolf spirit remained undaunted. "And what about the bottoms?"

Sunay exhaled again, picking up the other narrow-strapped, barely there material that in theory would cover her butt and naughty bits. Much like the halter, it wasn't entirely effective at that, but it left the bare minimum to the imagination at least.

The foxgirl spun around, and caught a look of herself in a full length mirror helpfully mounted on the northeast corner of the changing room. She froze in place, not being used to seeing herself from an outside perspective. She didn't... look bad at all. She wasn't exactly fond of how much cleavage the top displayed, and the waistband hung so low that a generous portion of butt was visible, but the low rest had the advantage of not chafing or pinching her tail.

A life on the seas obviously hadn't whittled her down... she looked every bit a well developed young woman. A pretty young woman, at that.

"Okay, I have to admit... I'm looking pretty good," she muttered.

Unfortunately, it was still loud enough for Rola to hear. "Oh! I must see! Come out!"

Sunay froze again, this time in dread. There was *no* way she was stepping out in public wearing less than she normally would while sleeping.

"The whole beach is going to see it when we get to the Gold Coast," Rola reminded. "No sense being shy about it now!"

Rola was right of course, and Sunay had already stupidly

agreed to this whole scheme. It would look terrible to back out now because she was being prudish. Not like she hadn't already shown more to a fellow who was barely more than a stranger for the sake of an objective, either. Sunay was being silly, and she knew it.

The foxgirl took a deep breath, flung open the door to proudly display herself to the world... or at least the people in the store, when a voice that should not have been present reached her ears.

"Madam Rola, you told Mister Law that I was supposed to meet you here, but I don't know why you would... oh... my..."

Sunay's ears flattened in terror and her eyes bulged in a mix of fright and embarrassment. The light brown hair, the blue eyes that were as blue as blue could be... he wasn't as tanned as she remembered, and the smooth cheeks had weathered a bit, no doubt from the stress of the last two years, but this was a young man she remembered all too well.

The foxgirl shrieked as her cheeks flamed bright red, covering her cleavage as she grabbed Rola and yanked the wolf spirit into the dressing room, slamming and locking the door shut soon after.

Rola had a broad, toothy, teasing grin on her face as Sunay hissed angrily, "What is he doing here?"

"I told you Laron was apprenticing under Law," Rola replied innocently.

"You told me Laron was apprenticing under 'a friend!'"

Unrepentantly, Rola retorted, "Law's a friend."

Sunay clenched her eyes shut, her entire body red and trembling with embarrassment. She shoved Rola out the door, and shouted, "Lemme change and I'll be right out!"

Rola called back cheekily, "I do agree, I think it fits you very well! Although I do think you'll need to... trim... between your legs a bit!"

Sunay flushed bright red even though she was alone. She hastily pulled off her suit, balled it up in the original cloth, then wrapped herself and slid back into her shirt and trousers, rolled her stockings onto her feet, then thrust her feet into her boots and laced them up tight. She tried to steady her breathing to try and get the accursed color out of her neck and cheeks, though a quick look at the mirror told her that wasn't very successful.

Sunay knew she couldn't hide in there forever, blushing or not, and so she stepped outside to meet the pair waiting outside. Rola quickly snatched the bundle from Sunay's hands and dashed off, presumably to pay, and left the foxgirl alone with Laron.

16

It helped the foxgirl's embarrassment that Laron was blushing just as vividly as she was. "I... I'm sorry." she said in apology. "I... jus' wasn' expectin' ya, is all."

"I know Madam Rola is a terrible prankster. She didn't tell me you were here, either," he replied. "So... you are helping them, I assume?"

Sunay kept her head down bashfully. "Yeah. Kinda already regrettin' it."

"You shouldn't!" Laron protested. "I mean, you looked *great!*" The poor boy went bright red again. "I mean... oh Coders... I... I..."

Sunay didn't want him to die of fright. "You look pretty good too," she said, gently punching him on the arm, then blushing when she felt just how firm his bicep was. Gently rubbing over where she had punched she said, "Really... good... actually."

"Mister Law has me doing all of the loading nowadays," Laron said sheepishly. "I guess it builds... muscle."

"I'll say," Sunay mumbled.

"Goodness, if you two get any more red, you might both just faint!" Rola chirped, a cloth bag slung over her arm, flashing that ear to ear grin that drove Sunay batty.

"Ya did this all on purpose, didn't ya?" Sunay growled at the wolf spirit while maintaining eye contact with Laron.

"Laron, dear, why don't you show Sunay where she'll be spending the night?" Rola suggested, patting him warmly on the shoulder as she spun about and left. "Do try not to be up too late. We leave early. See you in the morning, my little fire fox."

"Of course," Sunay replied, trying not to show her clenched teeth.

The wolf spirit disappeared into the late evening streets, and Laron regained enough composure to offer Sunay his hand and say with the charm she remembered him for, "Shall we go, my lady?"

"Yeah, we better. We mus' look like fools right now."

She took his hand, and perhaps not too subtly ran her fingers up his forearm before settling in his elbow as he dutifully began his task. Sunay leaned into him, but if he had any problem with the closeness, he didn't say anything. Even his body language didn't change, so she took that as permission to maintain her position snugly against his side, matching his steps as they took a *very* slow, but not unwelcome, pace.

"I am so very glad you're okay," Laron finally said, breaking the comfortable silence. "I spent no small amount of nights worrying about you after you left my company in the family palace. It was such a relief when Madam Rola told me the news that you were well."

"*Yer* relieved?" Sunay replied. "Do ya know how long *I* worried mahself sick, knowin' what happens to people who 'disappear' in Avalon?"

"It was extremely fortunate, for both me and my family, that I had caught the interest of Gold Pirate agents. Without that influence, I probably *would* be digging the ditch that I would then be buried in."

"And now you're under Rola and Law's care," Sunay said. "I'm not sure yer better off."

"Mister Law and Madam Rola are wonderful teachers," Laron objected. "They're both excellent merchants with their own unique talents. Law has such incredible knowledge of how markets shift and how best to manage inventory, personnel, and supply. It matches perfectly with Rola's natural charisma and keen skills of observation."

"Charisma, eh?"

"Charisma is just as much the ability to sweet talk your way into a good deal as much as it is applying pressure and intimidation or twisting a sequence of events in your favor. Like, for example, having me show up on her order just as you are trying on a remarkably fetching set of swimwear."

That got her to blush again. "Well I'm glad *you* liked it at least."

Laron was back at full charm, and Sunay found she didn't mind the flattery at all. "At the risk of sounding too bold, I enjoyed the view tremendously. You were pretty before, and you've only grown more lovely the last two years."

"Don't stop now," the foxgirl teased, basking in the attention, playfully dancing her fingers along his delightfully toned arm. "Go on..."

"I'm afraid this is where I have to stop," Laron said with a regretful tone, pointing ahead of them to a two-story red brick building with a sloped roof of black shingle. It was decently maintained, with yellow flowers in full bloom at each side of the single red door, and a "Red Roof Inne" sign hovering above a covered walkway.

Laron said with a hint of disappointment, "You'll need to check in with the innkeeper, obviously, but it's already been reserved and paid for. And despite Madam Rola's suggestion, and as much as I would desire it, I don't think it would be terribly proper to be spending the night. Perhaps if our paths were to cross again and we didn't have quite as many duties to perform?"

Sunay reluctantly broke away, and stepped back towards the inn door. "Maybe. We'll see."

She hurriedly slipped through the door of the inn, fanning herself in an attempt to cool her heated cheeks. But the stupid grin lingered through check-in, entry into her room, and even as she pulled the covers over her body and fell asleep.

Maybe this mission wasn't going to be so terrible after all.

Chapter Two: Honor Among Thieves

Sunay emerged from the changing stall reluctantly, even though she had seen what passed for suitable clothing on the Gold Coast, and that she wasn't the slightest bit out of place. The Aramatheans clearly had no such thing as modesty. Or shame.

"Ya know..." Sunay said to her mission partner, "Ya coulda told me I'd be the only one paradin' like a fool."

Rola's suit was not nearly as revealing, a single piece offering in cherry red with a pink translucent sarong. The wolf spirit was predictably unrepentant. "I don't have your... charm, you could say. I'm jealous, honestly."

"Uh huh."

Rola picked up a leather satchel, eyes turning towards the northwest. "I do believe this portion of the beach is just too crowded. Let's find something with more space, shall we?"

The pair began their walk up the beach, towards what would be normally reserved for wealthy beachfront owners. As Pierre had claimed, Sunay and Rola easily walked right past guards for neighboring lots that normally would have immediately intercepted any trespassers and either had them arrested by local Phalanx or at best tossed off private property.

Sunay said in genial conversation. "Ya know, you could have also told me that Laron was your apprentice."

"Not *my* apprentice, Law's," Rola corrected, then smiled. "But where would the fun have been in that?"

There was a long pause, then the wolf spirit said, "I was rather surprised to see him return before morning. I couldn't have been more clear what I was expecting unless I had outright *ordered* him to have some fun with you."

"Laron's a gentleman," Sunay replied.

"Yes, I know. He's far too much like Law in that regard," Rola said with distaste. "I was hoping seeing you half naked would break him of that annoying behavior."

"I'm more than *half* naked," Sunay grumbled. "And some girls *like* gentlemen."

"Gentleman is just another word for wasting time," the wolf spirit said. "But whatever suits you, I suppose. I do think this is more suitable, don't you?"

Sunay didn't look directly at the wall that served to separate the beach from Torad's estate, but got enough of a look to see six guards holding position. "What kinda person buys a beachfront estate, then builds a wall in front o' it?"

"The sort of person who cares more about status than enjoying life," Rola said with disdain, staring at open contempt towards the wall and the guards. "Be ready to distract them, will you?"

For a moment, Sunay was worried that would stir the armored men holding position at said wall. But the six guards seemed almost hellbent on avoiding eye contact, like they would rather pretend that the foxgirl and wolf spirit weren't there. "An' how am I supposed to do that?"

She dropped her satchel, then opened it and pulled out a wrinkled ball of... something, colored blue and red and yellow. Sensing Sunay's curiosity, she said, "A new toy that Law got for me from Aramathea. It's going to be all the fashion for beach goers, I'm told."

There was a clear nub on the material, which Rola started blowing into, causing the ball to expand into a smooth orb about a foot in diameter. Once fully inflated, Rola pushed the nub inside the ball with a popping sound, and held it up for Sunay's appraisal.

The foxgirl wasn't particularly impressed. "What... is it?"

Rola responded by throwing the ball into the air, where it took what seemed like an unnatural ascent then descent, far too slow for something of its size. It dropped onto the sand in front of Sunay, bouncing twice and spinning to a stop. The wolf spirit sighed exaggeratedly, and said, "You were *supposed* to bump it back into the air."

Sunay cocked an eyebrow questioningly.

"Just throw it," Rola said.

The foxgirl bent over and picked up the ball. It didn't feel nearly as slick as the shine on its surface would suggest, a really odd sensation rather unlike anything she had experienced before. "This is... so weird."

"Throw it!"

With a resigned sigh, Sunay tossed the ball with an underhand motion in Rola's general direction. The wolf spirit settled under the descending toy, linked her hands together, then bumped the ball back into the air with her forearms. Sunay attempted to replicate the motion, though her attempt at returning the bump led to an awkward tumbling ball that spun into the sand a depressing two strides from Sunay's feet.

Rola laughed, and that stirred Sunay's pride. What had been

disinterest turned into a rather heated competition very quickly. The ball bounced back and forth with increasingly intense bumps, both girls grunting and snarling as they chased down their quarry before it hit the ground.

Sunay had actually somewhat forgotten they were supposed to be on a mission in her desire to get the better of the wolf for once, and initially crowed in victory when Rola stumbled backward, only able to get one arm on the ball, and send it careening towards the wall of Torad's estate as the wolf spirit fell face first into the sand, her coppery tail twitching comically after the pratfall.

The ball came to rest at the edge of the sand, mere feet away from where the ground turned into more stable sandstone and where the guards to his estate were in position. All of them were focused on the ball, like they didn't know what exactly they were looking at or what they were supposed to do with it.

At least Sunay's part in Rola's plan became clear. She jogged towards the ball, watching as the guards eyes uncertainly slid towards her on their approach. They looked like their duty to be alert was warring with their discomfort at acknowledging her presence.

Well, at least keeping them distracted wasn't going to be difficult. She picked up the ball, clutched it to her stomach, just under her breasts, and said happily, "Hi!" while adding an animated swish of her tail for effect.

It was almost insulting to the foxgirl that her tail was what captured all the attention, the eyes of all six guards quite visibly following the full circle path her tail had taken. That would be a funny story to share with Rola later, Sunay mildly irked by men not ogling her. The wolf spirit would no doubt take great humor in that.

The awkward silence that followed was more due to Sunay deciding that anything she was going to say would fall on deaf ears. She instead let her tail do the talking, at first swishing randomly before turning into a little game where Sunay started drawing letters with her tail.

"Y-O-U-A-R-E-I-D-I-O..." She recited, then yelped in fright as a very cold, very wet sensation nudged her in the small of her back, "YAAAH!"

Sunay spun around to identify the source of the interruption, finding herself looking at the muzzle of a very large, copper wolf with a white underbelly, unusual not just in its coloring but in its size, easily able to look Sunay in the eye. Even having never seen Rola's natural state, it wasn't hard to identify the wolf spirit.

Rola butted the foxgirl to the side, then charged, spooking the guards who had been so entranced moments before. They scrambled in all directions, forgetting any and all training while the clearly magical creature harried them, and giving Sunay a clear, unguarded path to the wall.

"And I needed t' be a distraction for what again?" Sunay grumbled, sprinting to the wall, and taking as strong of a hold as she could. Sea air had pitted the brick and ate away the mortar, which made for an easy ten foot climb for even a novice climber. For Sunay she needed one good handhold then was able to vault herself up and over.

She found herself in a garden of exotic plants, or at least what Aramatheans would consider exotic, as she quickly identified a row of giant sunflowers common in Avalon, and assumed that most if not all of the others were imported from other lands as well. She ducked down behind one row of hanging bulb plants when she heard the sounds of other guards approaching, and stuck her head out as they ran past her to the west.

She might be "invisible", but she somehow doubted *anyone* would overlook her trespassing within the manor grounds itself.

Sunay went east, according to the plan, leading her towards what was the rear veranda of Torad's manor. The sound of raised voices caused her to freeze and duck at the bottom of the stairwell that led to the large covered deck. An armored man dressed like a guard had his back to her talking to a smaller, trim middle-aged man in a white toga with silver sash.

"What is the meaning of this racket?" the toga clad man demanded.

The guardsman answered, "We're not sure, Master Torad. The guards claimed they were being attacked by a ghost wolf."

Not surprisingly, Torad didn't buy that explanation. "A ghost wolf."

"*Something* panicked them, Master Torad."

"Well, until you find this 'ghost wolf', tell them to keep it down! I am entertaining guests, and I don't need any more vile rumors about me, especially that I've hired drunkards for guards!"

Torad spun about, and the door slammed angrily. Sunay used that opportunity before the guard turned around to sprint across the path and back into the relative cover of the garden. She kept out of sight, slowly working her way east, until she reached the gate she was looking for, conveniently abandoned due to the panic outside.

She popped the door open, expecting to have to wait for Rola to show. Instead, she walked in straight in, her bag over her shoulder, and more than a little irritated. "Took you long enough," the wolf spirit grumbled, casually closing the door behind her.

"Well excuse me for ya kicking the hornet's nest in here with that display!" Sunay hissed.

"Had to cause enough panic to get you inside," Rola answered. "It worked, didn't it?"

At that point, Sunay clenched her eyes shut as Rola dropped the bag and bent over to dig through it. "And why... are ya *naked*?"

Rola pulled out a small black bikini set and pulled it on quickly. "Well, I can't exactly change while clothed. Messy that, getting your paws all tangled in shredded material, especially something as skintight as a swimsuit. One claw gets caught in a hem, and I might as well be powerless while I'm tumbling around like a newborn pup."

Sunay, on the other hand, was more focused on the wolf spirit's new attire. "Ya had that tawdry thing the whole time? Why didn't ya wear *that* out in public?"

Rola shook her head. "Oh goodness no. Far too embarrassing."

Sunay grit her teeth as Rola grabbed her by the hand, and ordered, "Come along now, my little fire fox. There's a job that needs doing."

Rola didn't exactly take cover. In fact, she brazenly led Sunay right down the middle of the paths, right past several guards, who paid them no mind. Sunay boggled, but Rola silenced her as they approached the veranda Sunay had slinked past minutes before.

The guardsman looked annoyed at their presence, but not much else. "Ladies, Master Torad is entertaining business."

Rola smiled. "I understand. But the master told us that we were to entertain ourselves in the sauna."

"The sauna is to the north, along the exterior garden path," he replied. "I apologize if I don't show you there myself. There's been a bit of a panic outside."

"I was wondering what all the shouting was about. Well, thank you, dear sir. We can find the way on our own."

"The master will attend to you shortly, I am sure."

Rola stepped back, took Sunay's hand again, and led her to the north. "Not the best scenario, but not the worst," she said thoughtfully.

"Wait... wait... wait!" Sunay protested, forcing Rola to stop.

"You mean to tell me I could 'ave walked around as I pleased?"

"Once you were inside, most certainly. Torad entertains all sorts of foreign ladies, especially chimeras. It's one of his little fetishes. Coders, Torad himself might not even think twice about seeing you considering how many ladies he invites."

"And none of you thought to inform me of this until now?" the foxgirl demanded angrily.

"No one else on the team knows I'd wager," Rola said, her voice turning somewhat guilty. "Truth be told, this isn't my first time here."

"Say wha?"

"Law doesn't know, and I'd rather he not ever know," Rola said with a surprising determination. Sunay couldn't remember the wolf spirit ever looking so serious before. "I did many things to help the man that became my husband before we were married. I'm not entirely proud of all of them."

Sunay really didn't need the details spelled out, but she did want to confirm one thing... "Is this... previous meeting... how you came about learning the combination to his vault?"

Rola narrowed her eyes in warning, but still admitted, "Yes. And that is all I will say on the matter from this point forward, am I understood?"

Sunay nodded.

"Good. Now come along. I think I know how we are going to proceed."

The sauna was effectively part of the garden as far as Sunay was concerned, enclosed on three sides by panels of glass, plumes of steam billowing out from the open side, with a pool of bubbling water surrounded by a border of polished and carved volcanic stones.

"It's a completely artificial hot spring, for what it's worth," Rola noted. "There's an underground vent that blows hot air from a furnace in the manor itself. Still looks pretty, though."

She then looked up towards the manor, pointing to the third level. "Here is where your climbing expertise comes in handy, my little fire fox. See the fourth window from the west on the third floor? That is the room right next to the vault."

Sunay did note that there was an odd gap between that window and the next one to the east.

"The vault is locked by a three bar system. You pull each bar out to its correct length according to the correct notch, and that will unlock the vault. From the top down, it is 7, 3, 1. I'm not exactly sure where the administrator's tome is, but I can't imagine it would be hard to find. It's a black book with a red eye on the cover. Very old."

Rola then handed Sunay the satchel. "The fake is in here. Swap it out with the real one, then get out as fast as possible. Good luck."

Sunay nodded and plotted her ascent. Each floor had an overhang that could potentially be a nuisance, but coming from the forests of Navarre, not particularly challenging. In fact, she cleared the first overhang by jumping to grab it and pulling herself up.

The second jump was slightly more risky, due to the slope of the overhang she was on and the less sturdy footing, but not a particular danger either. A final pull up brought her through the open window, and into what appeared to be a cleaning closet, filled with brooms lining the west wall and two buckets of tepid water that Sunay almost knocked over because they blended in well with the gray stone floor.

Avoiding that potential disaster, she slinked out into the hall, made sure no one else was in the vicinity, then quickly hopped in front of the vault door. As Rola said, the vault was closed by three bar locks which extended across the length of the solid iron door, and overlapped several feet onto the wall. The actual latch was hidden by an iron box so that a thief couldn't simply line up the door properly, and thus requiring the proper combination.

7-3-1.

Sunay then grabbed the loop on the latch box, pulled... and nearly dislocated her shoulder as it stubbornly refused to move, a metallic clang reinforcing her failure.

The bastard had changed the combination.

The foxgirl panicked, jumping back into the cleaning closet and shutting the door, forcing her breathing shallow so as not to give away her position any more than she already had. She initially feared that the attempt had failed, as she heard heavy boots that had to belong to a guard.

The footfalls came closer, then stopped short, followed by the clanking of the vault door loop being pulled, and then the creak of the door opening. Sunay stepped back out into the hall, thinking that depending on how large the vault was she could slip in, hide, and do her business once the guard vacated.

She peeked around the open door, and instead found the guard changing a book that matched the description she was given with a copy. What fresh hell was going on here? How many levels of duplicity were layered in this damned manor right now?

26

Regàrdless of the answer to that question, Sunay knew she couldn't let this man walk away with the tome. But at the same time, she couldn't make too much noise and alert the whole damn manor with a fight. But as the man turned around and forced her to retreat... she knew she had to do *something*.

Then she had an idea. An extremely risky one, but at this point she thought the risk was necessary.

She jumped out of the closet, charging after the guard, then intentionally throwing herself into him, shouting, "Oi! Gotta go gotta go!"

The pair collapsed, and sent the tome sprawling out of the guard's grasp. Sunay quickly swapped the tome on the floor with the one in her satchel, then put on as innocent a face as she could as the guard jumped to his feet and leveled his spear at her.

"Who in the black hells are *you?*" the man demanded. He was a younger fellow, an Aramathean with reddish brown hair, quite the oddity among their kind from Sunay's experience. "How did you get in here?"

Sunay whimpered, "I... I was out in the sauna, but I needed to... uh... freshen up. Then... I got lost... and I don't know where I am... and... and..."

"Damn furry whore," the guard muttered under his breath, forcing Sunay to bite her tongue. He violently snatched up the now fake tome, and threw out his arm angrily to the west down the hall that Sunay had come from. "Stairs on the west side. On the next floor down, take a right. It is a white door three doors down. If you miss it, you're as dumb as I think you are. Now get out of my sight before I throw you out and report you to the Phalanx for being a nuisance."

Sunay dashed away like she was obeying orders, while in reality she jumped back into the cleaning closet, and out the window. Rola was waiting eagerly, snagging the Administrator's tome with a twinkle in her eye. "Brilliant work, my little fire fox! Now, let's get out of here and get properly dressed before we rejoin our kin, shall we?"

The foxgirl hadn't heard a more blissful idea in her life.

~ ~ ~ ~ ~

Sunay had wanted to tell Rola about exactly what had happened in the manor, but Rola had told her to wait until they rejoined the crew in Beredon for the debriefing. "No sense telling me now what

27

I'm gonna have to hear again."

Law had been waiting eagerly for the report, and regarded it grimly, holding the Administrator's tome in his left hand, turning it about in appraisal. "Sounds like Torad had his own little bait and switch planned. That's... concerning."

"Why's that?" Sunay asked.

"It tells us Torad understands that there's something special about these tomes, rather than just being some collector of old books," Rola explained as she plucked the book from her husband's grasp. "We're going to have to have eyes on him and his purchases. It might be nothing, and that he just likes what he thinks are old magic books, or he might know more than we're comfortable him knowing. Either way, our agents on land are going to be spread even thinner watching this latest potential threat."

Pierre brandished the fake that he had acquired. "Well, we'll find out soon enough. I'm sure he'll eventually figure out the copy he has is a fake, and we'll see where it goes from there."

Rola grabbed that one too, comparing the two as she looked back and forth. "He'd have to know intimately how special the tome is, the handiwork in this copy is remarkable."

"But *that's* our brethren in Aramathea's problem," Law declared. "We've done them a favor, and that's all we're able or willing to do. Now, if you don't mind, Rola and I have some other things to discuss..." he glared at his wife, "So if you'd excuse us momentarily... Pierre, you're dismissed. Sunay, stay for a bit."

Law stood, and gestured for his wife to follow him into a side room. and Laron took that as his opportunity to enter as his teachers exited. "I take it the important details are all settled?"

Sunay shrugged. "Guess they got a few things' fer me, but yeah, I suppose so."

Laron violated what Sunay would have normally considered her personal space. He reached under her ear, and hefted the earring he had given her. It felt like a lifetime ago at this point, a promise made between a boy and girl who didn't even understand the promise they were making.

"I'm... rather amazed you kept this," he said tenderly.

Sunay blushed, and didn't go out of her way to hide it. "I... someone very smart told me to keep it. That they were memories I shouldn't discard. I'm glad I didn't."

Laron reached into his left trouser pocket, and revealed a black box. "I... still have the other one. It's still yours if you want it."

Sunay had come to learn exactly what those earrings signified from Bolin about a year back. They were part of an old Avalonian marriage proposal. Before rings became commonplace, *any* jewelry of value were used to signify an engagement of a young woman... earrings being popular way back in the early days of the land. She had wondered since if Laron understood the significance. This suggested he did.

"I... have responsibilities now, Laron," she replied. "I have a crew that is counting on me, and I can't turn away from them. Not now. Not yet."

The young man shook his head. "I didn't mean *now*. A merchant's apprentice wouldn't make a good husband. But I want you to know that my feelings have not changed. And the offer I made then is still there when I have the means and the stability to be a proper spouse. I'll wait as long as I have to, Sunay."

The foxgirl surprised him by lunging onto her tiptoes, and driving her tongue past his lips as they met. "Keep that earring safe," she advised. "Ya never know when I'm gonna want it."

Pierre waved, a tome tucked under his left shoulder. "I need to be getting back to my brother. He's no doubt wondering where I got off to, and we've got to get this to Dominus Socrato."

"Your brother ain't a member?" Sunay asked.

Pierre shook his head with a laugh. "Coders, no. He's far too free with his love and his information. Reliable, sure... a great salesman, absolutely... but discreet, not in the slightest. Good work, fire fox. You might have just saved a lot of people when all is said and done."

"Don't *you* start," the foxgirl growled as Pierre patted her on the shoulder. It was bad enough Rola started with that, the last thing she needed was for it to start spreading around.

There was a moment of raised voices from the side room, though not loud enough even for Sunay to pick up any distinct words. Not that she felt the need to guess; Law was no doubt extremely displeased to learn of Rola's... association with Torad, and most likely hadn't been told the entire truth about that association.

Laron looked back at her, his eyes twinkling. "Ya know, my dear... those two might be arguing for a while. I can think of a few things *we* could do in the meantime..."

Sunay grinned back, and gladly took Laron's hand as he led her out of the beer hall in a sprint.

Rola was visibly annoyed when she hunted down the pair an

hour later, most likely because they were at an open air cafe sipping lemonade rather than in the nearest inn tumbling in sheets. "There you are, my little fire fox," she said cheerily, though her expression did not relay cheer.

"Everythin' okay?" Sunay asked.

Rola's voice then matched her face. "No, but it will be. All couplings have their bumps in the road. Law is overreacting, and he'll understand that in time." The wolf spirit then clicked her tongue and said in parting as she retreated, "Well, if you aren't having proper fun, I suggest you get back to your ship, because I won't be covering for you."

Sunay sighed, finished her glass in one gulp, grabbed her satchel, and slung it over her shoulder. "All right, I guess this is parting for now."

Laron stood to meet her and gave her another kiss. "Now that I know where you are, I can keep in touch."

"Merchant's Guild Hall in Grand Aramathea is probably th' best place to send letters," Sunay said. "The Goldbeard tends to swing by there every couple o' months or so. I'll be looking forward to it."

Sunay hastily stole one final kiss before she took off in a full sprint towards the docks. The *Goldbeard* was waiting right off shore, and the foxgirl hoped it hadn't been waiting long. She knew they had went on a short patrol while she had been on loan, and she hoped they hadn't rushed back.

If they did, it had likely been on Juno's behest, as the spidergirl was the first one waiting for Sunay as the foxgirl hopped over the railing. "This is fer you. Take it. I don't wanna have it no more."

"This" was referring to the duty clipboard that Juno had been put in charge of as acting first mate while Sunay was away. The spidergirl could no doubt see the writing on the wall, that she was next in line for a promotion, either on the *Goldbeard* or some other ship, and wasn't entirely certain she liked the idea.

Sunay took the clipboard slowly between thumb and forefinger, a broad grin across her face. After a week of getting torqued about by Rola, the foxgirl was happy to be on the tormenting end for once. "Ya sure? I'm sure you did so amazin' that the Admiral would like ya to keep doin' it."

"An' he could ram the center mast straight up his..."

Ahmin appeared, throwing open the door below decks, his face unreadable as he said sternly, "Sunay. Down here. Now."

An uncomfortable silence fell on the deck as Ahmin ducked

down below again, Juno regarding the first mate with worry. Sunay was equally unnerved. Had she done something wrong? And if so... what?

The foxgirl left Juno's company with a nervous nod, and went down the steps to the lower decks. She already knew where Ahmin wanted her to go, Ahmin's cabin was the only place below decks the admiral willingly went, which didn't help her concerns any. It meant whatever he had to say was something he didn't want anyone else on the ship to hear.

Sunay knew the drill, go in, close the door behind her. Ahmin was already at his desk, hands in front of his face. He said grimly, "I already got the report from the Administrators about the mission to the Gold Coast. Our Aramathean agents aren't happy."

"Rola and Law kinda expected that," Sunay admitted, "I guess they moved in without entirely clearin' things with our guys in the empire."

"That's not what they're angry about," Ahmin replied, then corrected himself. "Or, I should say that's not what they're angry about that I'm inclined to listen to. They're upset because the tome that Law and Rola turned in for destruction was a fake."

"Say wha?" Sunay gaped.

"The tome wasn't real. It was a forgery. Very well done, but a fake nonetheless. Our Aramathean agents insist that Torad purchased a legitimate Administrator's tome off the black market, and they don't like the insinuation that their intelligence was flawed."

While Sunay had plenty of reason to doubt the intelligence of their kin in the First Empire, the foxgirl wasn't inclined to doubt them on this score.

"I personally don't have any skin in this, but it would ease my mind immensely to sort out exactly who had what tome and when and how. Is there anything you can think of that might not have made it into the report?

Her mind raced back to the mission. The guard she had swapped books on must have thought it was legitimate... why would they bait and switch a fake? The one she had when she left Torad's manor must have been the real thing.

From there, the tome had always been in either her or Rola's possession... until...

Sunay's eyes flashed open. Both tomes, the copy and the real one, had been on the table during the debriefing. Rola had remarked how similar they were. Then she and Law had their disagreement, they

31

had left... then Laron came in... and... then Pierre had left... with what she had assumed was the fake in hand.

Had he taken the *real* one?

Her mind raced farther down that thought. Pierre had specifically chosen her for the mission, Rola had claimed. She had figured it was because the merchant had been curious about a foxgirl who might have been his niece. Wait until Rola and Law left, then when Sunay was preoccupied with Laron, snatch the real tome out from under everyone's nose.

But how would he have known he'd have that opportunity? He would have needed someone else to set the stage... but why would Rola and Law go with such an insane scheme that would no doubt get them in trouble?

What if she was wrong about all of this?

Sunay shook her head, her temples starting to hurt as her mind tied itself in knots trying to *untie* the tangled mess presented to her. It was making too little sense to *not* make sense... which didn't make *any* sense.

Ahmin noticed the visible strain in her brow. "Sunay?" he asked, mildly concerned.

Sunay shook her head again, this time to reject the thoughts percolating. It wasn't right to cast aspersions off of unsubstantiated recollections. "I can't think of nuthin', sir. Whenever I get involved on land, it always goes sideways 'bout four different times. I can't ever make heads or tails of it, and I'm just givin' mahself a headache tryin'."

Ahmin nodded. "Do your job, get out. I understand that. And don't worry, from this point on, I'm not accepting any requests for you to be involved in land missions. You've done your time."

Sunay bit her lip. "Well... I don't wanna rule it out in the future *entirely...*"

"Oh?"

Sunay blushed, and wanted to slap herself. "Laron is Rola and Law's apprentice now."

Ahmin remembered that name, and she could see his mask shift as he grinned. "I see. Well, I'm sure I can coordinate some appropriate shore leave with those two in Beredon or the Gold Coast without subjecting you or any of my crew to further nonsense."

Sunay finally fought back the color in her cheeks. "Thank you. Appreciate it."

Ahmin then said playfully, "I guess if anything good came of this it's that we know Rola and Law are Gold Pirates after all, eh?"

Sunay nodded silently, and turned to leave, when she abruptly froze.

She remembered Law's yellow handkerchief... and that he had that same handkerchief poking out of his pocket the first time she had met him. But Rola... Rola never had such an indicator at any point. A Gold Pirate *needed* that indicator as a starting point for verification.

Rola might *know* about Gold Pirate maneuvers through her husband, but *she* wasn't a member herself.

And that was when everything fell into place. Everything that had happened had been Rola and Pierre's machination. *She* had left the tomes, *she* had already demonstrated using Laron as a tool of distraction... but why? She was a prankster, but she wasn't malicious. She wouldn't have stabbed her own husband in the back without good reason... at least, Sunay didn't think so.

"Sir... what would happen if Dominus Socrato actually got a hold of an Administrator's tome?" Sunay asked. "Would it be *that* dangerous?"

Ahmin shrugged. "That's hard to say. There's no indication whatsoever that he knows what to do with the one he already *has*."

"Wait... we *know* the Dominus already *has* an Administrator's tome, and we haven't done anythin' about it yet?"

Ahmin shrugged in exasperation. "Not my authority. He's managed to fudge some things through what amounts to brute force, but nothing that compromises Gold Pirate activities. We have eyes on him, and those eyes tell us he's far different from the militant he was earlier in life, and that his focus is entirely on stopping the spread of the Void."

"That'd be a noble goal. Kinda in tune with ours, really."

Ahmin nodded. "True. But there's also good reason to believe our eyes in Kartage have been... compromised, and aren't accurately relaying the situation within the Dominus's sphere of influence. I don't like it, but the Administrators don't want to raise a stink about it. We'd have to expose a *lot* of assets and put a *lot* of people in harm's way for a raid of Kartage to be successful... and as long as our agents *in* Kartage are saying there's no harm, no one is going to move."

"Are they still gonna think that way if he has *two?*"

Ahmin grunted in disdain. "I think they're content to believe that Torad had a fake, and that we swapped a fake for a fake. It makes our kin in Aramathea look bad, but let's be honest, they didn't look too good to begin with, and it's not like Dominus Socrato is going to be any more or less dangerous with a second book like the one we already know he possesses."

Sunay brought the discussion around to its conclusion. "Well then, I don't see any reason to believe otherwise."

Ahmin clearly didn't like the conclusion, she could see it in his eyes. "No, I suppose not."

"Is it *that* 'ard to believe that Dominus Socrato ain't a power-hungry monster seekin' to expand the dominion of Aramathea?"

Ahmin leveled a glare on her darkly. "Socrato's weapons decimated hundreds of ships fleeing the collapse of Scheherazade sixty years ago. One of his ballistas sank the refugee boat right next to mine. Tens of thousands *died* because of *his* weapons and *his* word suggesting we were an invasion force. So pardon me if trust and forgiveness are hard to come by."

"Don't ya think you might be letting personal opinion cloud yer judgment here?"

Ahmin dropped his head, hovering just above his desk. "I know I am, which is why I'm not going to voice any objection to what Law and Rola found. I'm going to say you confirmed their sequence of events. I just hope this doesn't bite us square in the backside later."

A nagging dread built as she left Ahmin's cabin and back to the deck. If her theory was correct, Laron's timing had been impeccable, and at just the right time. Either Rola had amazing foresight and knew *exactly* when Laron would be needed to provide a distraction, or he had been part of the scheme.

She *really* didn't want her trust to be misplaced.

Chapter Three: Whispers in the Dark

Dear Sunay,

> *I'm sure you're busy, which is why you're not answering my letters, but I hope you reply soon. Events on this continent are starting to worry me, and I don't know how much longer the trade lines will be safe for messages or any travel at all. It will do me no end of good to know you're still well before then.*
>
> *One thing that has happened is that Vakulm is out on an island, metaphorically of course, especially for my family. Avalon won't give them sanctuary, and southern towns have already been filled to overflowing with refugees fleeing the threat of Daynish raiders. My family has yet to move, and I'm increasingly fearing that it's now too late.*
>
> *Maybe I'm worrying over nothing, like Madam Rola says. But I know Mister Law is growing increasingly concerned, and I know a lot of the Gold Pirate resources are being moved south along with other refugees. The northern provinces might have survived this winter... but I'm terrified next winter is going to bring more than snow.*
>
> *I'm scared, Sunay. Scared for my family. Scared for myself every time our road takes us north. Please tell me that I don't have to be scared for you. Please tell me that the south seas are safe and secure.*
>
> *Please... just write to me.*
>
> *With love,*
> *Laron*

Sunay had read that letter, and all those before it, a hundred times. It wasn't that she didn't want to write him, or that her duties kept her too busy. It was that she didn't know what to say. She still was struggling with the trust issues that stemmed from the whole Torad's estate mission... putting a powerful artifact in the hands of a dangerous man.

She couldn't write to him and pretend everything was well

until she was certain he hadn't used her... no matter how much it was obvious he was hurting.

And she was going to have plenty of time for those thoughts to run through her mind as she prepared for night watch.

Night watch was arguably the most important duty on an open seas vessel. You needed a sharp eye, a keen ear, and the ability to remain focused through stretches of time where most people were already sound in slumber.

At least, that's what Sunay told herself.

In truth, it was a mind-numbing chore, especially in southern waters. In the north seas, the threat of ice was real enough that you had to pay some real close attention. In the south, the biggest worries were typhoons and other large storms, none of which were exactly subtle.

All of this meant Sunay was in a battle for consciousness as she stood at the *Goldbeard's* bow, arms on the railing, leaning forward with her chin in her hands. As the first mate, she actually had no obligation to this duty. Jacques never did while she had been on the crew, for example, but it was one of the ways that Sunay 'made it up' to the others for jumping so abruptly into a command position, wanting to maintain she was just as much a crew member as anyone else, and not snatching every bit of privilege she could.

"Quiet night, ma'am," Mally declared.

Sunay grunted tiredly. "Just 'ow I like it."

Mally was one of the newer crew, hired on a month ago as the night helmsman to spell Bolin after the previous night man, Carinsi, was given a job as a primary helmsman on a different vessel. She was used to night duty, she claimed, and more than capable of handling a ship the *Goldbeard's* size. For the most part, she had been right, though she didn't quite have Bolin's finesse.

Evidence of that came as a wave clapped solidly against the *Goldbeard's* starboard side. The movement rattled Sunay and startled her to full alertness. Though it proved to be fortunate, as while the foxgirl was about to turn and chide Mally for being so rough on the wheel, the sound of human voices from overboard caught her ears.

She couldn't quite make out everything that was being said... something about rougher waters in the open sea... how they should have waited.. something about it was for a better purpose. The foxgirl didn't need to hear much else to get the gist of it: novice sailors out on the open sea in the dead of night.

The Gold Pirates had no set policy on how to handle civilians in distress, something left entirely to the individual ships. The

Goldbeard, as a rule, was willing to help provided they weren't doing something time sensitive, though Ahmin *was* known to give a pass on people in distress due to their own stupidity depending on how sour of a mood he was in.

Sunay, on the other hand, hadn't been embittered enough for that yet. "Mally, turn us heading... ninety," the foxgirl ordered, then up to the rigging, "Michel, raise the sails to half. I wanna take this slow."

If there was one thing Sunay really liked about Mally, it's that she didn't talk back or question Sunay's orders like Bolin was wont to do. Michel was the same way, even if he wasn't nearly as quick to the job as Juno. But they got the job done, and the ship took Sunay's heading and speed towards the voices she had caught on the wind.

She kept her eyes low, squinting through the faint light provided by the waning moon, expecting and eventually seeing a smaller craft bobbing in the waves. While these would be considered calm seas by most standards, for the small schooner, it was no doubt a struggle just to keep the craft from capsizing.

As the *Goldbeard* turned alongside the craft, Sunay could make out three distinct figures, one of them a child, which boiled Sunay's blood to no small degree. It was one thing to be stupid and get yourself killed. It was entirely another to drag a kid to death with you.

"Oi!" she called out. "I ain't gonna ask what the black hell yer all doin' out here in that li'l dinghy! At least not until yer all up here where I can yell at ya proper like!" She turned her head back to the deck and continued issuing orders. "Michel, git down here, and help me lower some rope fer these folks!"

Sunay insisted that the child be raised first. The foxgirl was a bit surprised to see that the child was an Avalonian girl with bright auburn hair and green eyes, but not surprised to see that she was emaciated from several days, if not weeks, on survival rations. Her hair was a mess and her knee length dress had definitely seen better days. It stirred pangs of sympathy from the foxgirl, and further anger for the adults aboard.

It was two men, equally haggard... though not apparently related, at least no family resemblance she could see. It made sense; had a mother been present, they wouldn't have been in this mess.

Sunay paced in front of the trio, eyes glaring daggers made of fire. "I'm only going to ask this once, and yer answer better be damn good, or I'm tossin' every single one of you maggots overboard and takin' the child somewhere your stupidity can't infect 'er. What did ya'll think ya were doin' goin' out in the open sea in *that*?"

The three exchanged nervous glances, and gestured towards each other animatedly before the one in the middle, a mostly bald, short Avalonian man barely above Sunay's height and in a threadbare vest, finally spoke. "We... we were seeking the blessings of the next world."

"Say wha?" Sunay asked increduously.

"The land of gold... the second life promised to those who follow the new word."

"Yeah, that explains jack squat."

The man to the left spoke next, a lanky tall middle aged man with sandy brown hair flecked with gray. From the way the child was clinging to his leg, most likely the father. "Beyond the Void. The land of gold lies beyond the boundary. A paradise beyond measure, in a world beyond this."

"My mommy is waiting for us there," the girl finally said meekly, grabbing tighter to her escort's pant leg.

"Folks, I hate to break it to ya, but the only thing 'beyond' the Void is more Void. Ya risked yer lives just to die."

"But that's not what the Minister said..." she whimpered. "He said Mommy was across the Void. She was waiting for us, he said."

The younger man added, "We didn't want to be separated from Alice. The Minister wanted the kids and the adults on different ships... so we left early."

"The rest o' them?" Sunay asked.

"The congregation. We assembled on the coast, away from the eyes of those who wouldn't understand, the Minister said."

"How many people are we talkin' about here?"

He looked at his father-in-law for confirmation. "About a thousand, at least, right?" he said, more confident when he saw the older man nod.

Sunay's face went pale, and she said as her eyes narrowed to dots and her ears flattened. "Michel... wake up th' Admiral. I think he's gonna need to hear this..."

~ ~ ~ ~ ~

Ahmin might not have been happy to be woken in the middle of the night, but he certainly understood why once he had his own opportunity to question the three refugees. "Like ripples in a pond when a stone is cast..." he mumbled, opening the door to his cabin then issuing his orders. "Sunay, wake up Garth. Have him find... someplace... for these three to sleep tonight. Then have Mally plot us a

38

course for the nearest settlement, Coders if I know where that is right now, and have Michel set us to full sail. Then wake up Juno and both of you meet me here for the briefing."

After Sunay complied, and despite an exceptionally grumpy Juno, they settled in for what was no doubt going to be their next mission.

Ahmin rolled out a continental map, and drew a circle with finger along the northern section that was considered Daynish territory. "Well, here's the deal. As you might now, the Daynes are stirring up north. There's been no large scale raiding... yet... but the smaller scale raids are happening with increasing frequency, and that's sending everyone else scurrying."

Ahmin's finger went south through the Western Free Provinces. "Avalon's gearing up for another Daynish Campaign, and that's forcing people south. They're either being denied sanctuary and forced further south, or they're strong enough to displace current settlers, and forcing *them* south."

"But eventually, they run out of places to flee," Sunay noted.

"And where this 'Minister' has stepped in," Ahmin added, "promising these people who have been drug backwards across a continent a life of paradise if they just sail out with him across the Void. This is where it gets weird. This fellow has apparently separated the 'pilgrims' onto two separate boats. One for all the adults. One for the children."

"Why?" Juno asked.

Ahmin shook his head. "I have no idea. But what we do know is that they are getting ready to launch, and we might not be able to save both ships. Obviously, we need to focus on the children, but what good will it be saving them when there's no place for them to go?"

A knock on the door caused Ahmin's head to jerk upward. "I'm in a briefing. Who is it?"

"Your helmsman," Bolin said. "I was just a little curious why ya had Mally head us straight for Kartage."

The admiral nearly exploded. "*What?*"

He burst out of his cabin, stomping up the steps towards the deck, Sunay and Juno and Bolin right behind, worried about the prospect of having to calm a raging tiger chimera on a boat. Once Ahmin hit the deck, and came into the dawn light, he saw the domed tower of Kartage reflecting a dull gray. "*Why* in the Coder's name are we *here?*" he hollered at Mally.

"Ya told Sunay to have us travel to the closest settlement!"

Mally replied in defense.

Sunay tilted her head towards the night helmsman, and said, "Well... ya did."

"Shut. Up." Ahmin growled, forcing the foxgirl to snap to a rigid attention and gulp nervously.

"Missa Ahmin?"

The foursome turned back to the deck where little Alice, the child of the three they rescued, was in the doorway, nibbling on her thumbnail. "Is all okay? Are you angry at us?"

The tigerman released all his tension in one defeated groan. "Kartage is on a flood plain, we won't be able to get too close. Sunay... prep a rowboat. You and I are going to appeal to the Dominus for sanctuary for our stowaways."

"Why me?"

"Because your old friend Daneid is the Phalanx Captain here in Kartage, and I'm not going to be the only one to suffer. I figure if you can keep your composure, it'll inspire me to keep mine."

Sure enough, Sunay's blood started boiling at the very mention of the lieutenant that gave her so much grief. "And if'n I can't?"

Ahmin shrugged. "Well, then we get to go out in a blaze of blood and fury. I figure it's a win/win."

Sunay could do flippant too. "Ya make a strong point. Let's get goin'."

Juno helped Sunay lower the boat and said, "Listen... you both better come back. I don't wanna be a captain, and I sure don't wanna be one *yet*, ya get me?"

Sunay helped Alice into the rowboat, where her father took her, then the foxgirl hopped in herself. Ahmin took the oars, and the hour-long trek to the walls of Kartage began.

The keep itself was actually surrounded by water. "Pretty common in the spring," Ahmin said, his eyes narrowing. "There's a lift that will take us to the top of the wall on the south side. From there, that's where events could get real fun."

The rowboat sided up to the wall, Ahmin gently nudging it along until they found what they were looking for. A white sign invited them to hold position, then a voice from the top of the wall shouted, "State your name, your civilian status, and your business."

Ahmin answered, "I am Ahmin, this is Sunay, and these are three refugees that we found on the sea. Sunay and I are part of a merchanter vessel, the Goldbeard, that sails between Beredon and Grand Aramathea, and we are here to appeal for sanctuary for these refugees."

"You'd need the Dominus's approval for that."

"We're aware. We're ready to appeal to him personally if need be."

There was a long beat of silence, then he said, "Move your ship to the lift. We'll let you wait at the top of the wall while word gets sent to the Dominus... because it might take a while."

Ahmin complied, gently nudging the boat forward, and over a large wooden square that sat several feet below the water level. Instead of a pulley system Sunay was expecting, it was a genuine lift, a sloped wooden grate caught the bottom of the boat and carried it up to the top of the wall. The entire process looked completely automated as far as Sunay could tell... if there was someone pulling the crank, she couldn't see it.

"Why don't we have anything like this?" Sunay asked.

"Because this mechanism quite possibly weighs as much as the Goldbeard in whole," Ahmin replied darkly, "And I rather like giving my crew something that needs a little manual labor now and again."

Sunay chuckled, then comforted Alice who was more than a little unnerved when the boat went places boat should not go. At the top of the lift, guards grabbed both ends of the rowboat and slid it off the grate and into a rest position on the side. As the five disembarked, Ahmin was handed a small token made of white stone with the number "7" engraved in it and colored with black paint.

"If you *do* get an audience with the Dominus, he'll meet you in your keep," the guard explained. "When you come back, give one of us that token, and we'll retrieve your boat for you."

"Assuming the Dominus is willing to hear your appeal," a second guard grunted. "Figures that a bunch of foreigners stumble on us while Captain Daneid is away, so that *we* have to deal with them."

"Yer captain ain't here?" Sunay said, not sure whether she was happy or sad to learn that.

"He got held up by family business in Grand Aramathea, then the spring flood hit the delta and the Dominus gave him an extended leave. Why? You know him?"

Sunay had to force her voice to remain cordial. "We've met, yes."

The guard summoned a messenger, writing down Ahmin's request for sanctuary, and sent the young boy off. "Now we play the waiting game. Hope you don't have anywhere to be."

"This is more important," Ahmin said, and Sunay could agree with that sentiment. While there were a thousand people that *might* be sailing out into the Void very soon, there were three people right now that they *knew* needed help. She just hoped it didn't take *too* long to provide that help.

Morning turned to afternoon, and Ahmin grew impatient. He growled incoherently, though Sunay knew exactly what was on his mind. Every hour spent here waiting was another hour that the "Minister" could be using to get a head start. He leaned against a parapet on the wall, eyes seething angrily.

That's when Sunay had an idea. She leaned next to him, and said, "How about ya git back to the Goldbeard, sail out to where that whole 'pilgrimage' is going down, and ya can just swing back and pick me up later?"

"What if the Dominus won't meet with you or provide sanctuary?" Ahmin asked.

"Somehow I doubt they're just gonna dump us out into the ocean. I think I, or the four o' us, could rough it fer a few days. We *do* have to stop that pilgrimage, and we probably ain't got a lotta time to do it in. Besides, if that ass captain ain't here, it ain't fair for only you to face yer anger, right?"

Ahmin wasn't simply going to take Sunay's word for that. "Is that acceptable?" he asked the now four guards that had assembled, no doubt out of concern of the increasing agitated tigerman.

The guards conversed among themselves, and their lieutenant replied, "I think that's suitable. One of us can even escort them to the high ground if it comes to that."

Ahmin didn't *like* the arrangement, but at least he saw the wisdom in it. He presented his token, then slapped a telepathy stone into Sunay's right palm. "I'll keep in contact. Let me know what happens the minute you sort it out."

"Aye aye," the foxgirl promised.

Ahmin made his leave, presenting the numbered stone that corresponded to the rowboat, and she watched him set out back towards the *Goldbeard*. As fate would have it, the admiral was still in sight when another messenger returned, relaying word that Dominus Socrato had approved sanctuary for the three refugees... but he still wished to speak with those who had brought them in.

"Guess that's you, girl," the lieutenant said with a sympathetic expression.

"Yeah... I guess it is..." the foxgirl replied. "Where do I go?"

The lieutenant pointed to the tower. "Footman Athas will lead you," he said, gesturing to one of his guards to escort the outsiders. The Phalanx guard saluted, and opened metal gate to allow access to a stairwell on the inner side of the wall leading to the outer keep. Sunay fell in behind the guard, her three charges nervously taking up behind.

Despite at least fifteen feet of water surrounding them on all sides, the people of Kartage were going about their daily business as if nothing was amiss. People clearly can adapt to *anything*.

Well... except for the Void.

The inner keep and the tower were effectively the same structure, and the main hall served as the intermediary point between both. That was where Sunay met the man that caused so much anguish to her admiral.

Socrato certainly didn't *look* like a powerful mage that inspired such strong emotions. She had expected something similar to Morgana, who had an aura of might and unnatural power that the foxgirl could literally feel. This man didn't seem the least bit interested in such intimidation; he was just an old man in the dress of a Venerated Citizen of Grand Aramathea.

"Greetings, Miss... Sunay, am I correct?" he asked amiably, and when she nodded, he continued. "Very good. I was concerned my messengers didn't relay names properly." He then knelt before the child, and asked, "And what is your name, little one?"

"A... Alice..." the little girl said shyly, clutching her father's trousers tigher and burying her face in his hip. "This is my daddy."

"Simon," the younger adult added, offering his hand in a shake that Socrato took. "And this is my father by marriage Geralt."

"A pleasure. Captain Vasalm, have these three housed in the Steadly Inn for now, and have the bill sent to me. We'll arrange a more permanent place for them when the next ships come in or the waters recede, whichever comes first."

"So we're not gonna see my mommy now?" Alice said.

Sunay patted the child on the shoulder. "Not until you've lived a nice long life. She'll be waitin' for ya then. Ya don't need to cross the Void to do that."

"But..."

"You should listen to the lady, my dear child," Socrato said soothingly, even though his features were etched in concern. "I've seen many people in my day cross the line between life and death. It's not something you should seek out. Captain, do escort these three please. Miss Sunay, do stay a moment."

The Phalanx captain did as ordered, then Socrato declared, "Everyone else, do leave us for a time. I will summon you back in when you are needed."

Sunay knew enough about mages to know this wasn't exactly a welcome development, and once the main hall cleared, *then* she felt that overwhelming power that she had been expecting. It was one thing to face such power with her Admiral right next to her, like when she met Morgana. All alone... it was much more intimidating, and she was regretting telling him to leave.

Socrato's face went stern as he sat in the large central chair of the hall, upholstered in red velvet and trimmed with gold. He lowered his face down behind his steepled fingers and asked, "I wonder... what brings the Fire Fox, the scourge of Sacili, to *my* keep?"

The foxgirl gulped, and she tried to sent thoughts to Ahmin, but didn't receive any reply.

"I'm well aware of the telepathy stone in your ear, my dear," Socrato warned, "and have taken lengths to make sure that the answers I receive will be unfiltered by anyone you may wish to consult."

He dropped his hands, and his face lost some tension. "I am *somewhat* aware of the organization you serve. I know that your fellow Gold Pirates have an uncanny ability to be exactly where they need to be, and when your kind pops up, that means something of great importance is occurring nearby.

"So... I ask again, what brings you to my keep?"

Sunay gulped nervously. On one hand, Ahmin would probably kill her if she revealed too much to this man. On the other, Socrato could quite possibly kill her if she didn't reveal enough. She decided to cooperate with the near and present danger. She'd worry about the one in the future then.

"There's a big problem brewin' to the west of here, at a stretch of beach past the Gold Coast, I'm not entirely certain if the land is claimed by Aramathea or is part of the Free Provinces, but I'm guessin' the latter," the foxgirl explained, "because there's a whole bunch o' refugees from northern city-states gettin' displaced, and they all been convinced by some person calling himself 'The Minister' that there's a paradise waitin' for 'em out past the Void."

"And that is where your partner ran off to before our audience, I assume?"

Sunay nodded. "Aye. We're not entirely certain when this 'pilgrimage' is going to shove off. Just that we knew this 'Minister' has separated the adults and the children, and set them on two separate boats. Time is of the essence, Dominus."

"So it is," Socrato agreed. With a snap of his fingers, a map manifested from nowhere, and unrolled in front of Sunay, hovering in her air in front of her. "Indicate on the map exactly where you understand this pilgrimage to be taking place."

Sunay did so to the best of her ability, though the contact unnerved her... it felt there, but not there at the same time. The peculiarities only added when the map abruptly zoomed in for a closer view. It was a rocky shore line, no doubt why there were no settlements nearby, and definitely outside of Aramathea's official borders.

Socrato acknowledged that fact as well. "Hmmm... yes... that could be problematic to move one of our ships into free waters," the Dominus said, "and I suspect that their route would keep them in free waters as well, all the way through the Gibraltar Islands, and straight into the Void. If not for a trio of pilgrims trying to get a head start, it very well might have worked."

"It still might to some extent," Sunay said with a frown. "We're one ship. They're launchin' two. Our focus would be on th' children..."

"That is a noble focus, but it shouldn't be necessary," Socrato replied thoughtfully, staring down Sunay warily, "What do you say, Gold Pirate? Are you willing to set aside whatever issues you have with me to save the day?"

Sunay feared she would regret this, but said it anyway. "Yeah... let's do it, Dominus. But do you wanna risk maneuvers in the Free Provinces?"

"If I were planning to divert a nearby ship from the Imperial Fleet, it might. But two people shouldn't cause eyebrows to raise even in any nearby city-state, much less diplomats in Avalon."

Sunay cocked an eyebrow, and asked, "How do ya figure th' two o' us are gonna stop an entire *ship?*"

"You merely need to act when I need. I will handle the rest."

Socrato bellowed out to the south door of the hall, "Lieutenant Baraq!"

A woman in traditional Phalanx armor and her helmet tucked under her arm, stepped through the door and saluted. "Dominus."

"Inform Lanka that I will be gone likely today and tomorrow and miss my scheduled fitting. I have urgent business I must attend to. Do give her my apologies." The Dominus stood, and took a deep breath while straightening his toga. Then he ordered Sunay, "Now, come

45

with me."

He led the foxgirl through the rear exit of the main hall, and to a stairwell that he took up. Sunay's eyes narrowed as she climbed the steps. There was something... off... about them. "What is with these stairs?" she asked, not expecting an answer.

"Good exercise for people who spend every other waking moment reading or studying magic," he said. "Imagine if we were going to the twenty-third floor of my tower."

The foxgirl shook her head animatedly. "No thank you."

The fourth floor landing had two exits, one to the south, and one to the west. Socrato opened the door to the south, and it led to a balcony of sorts situated on the slightly sloped roof of the inner keep. "You need to completely cross through, my dear pirate," Socrato said, gesturing to Sunay when he saw she still had her tail inside the stairwell.

Sunay flicked said tail into the open air, and asked, "Why are we out here now?"

The dominus waved his right hand in the direction of the door, and the stairwell then turned a black darker than pitch. "What fresh hell did you do...?" Sunay asked, nervously stepping away from the door. It wasn't very strong, but Sunay knew that heavy weight in her gut and the chilling wave that made her feel sick.

"Step through, please," Socrato ordered, gesturing to the doorway.

Sunay shook her head rapidly, stepping even further back and hugging herself, like she could warm herself from the metaphysical chill.

"We don't have time for this nonsense!" the Dominus insisted angrily. "Get in there. Now!"

Sunay instead took another step back, and whimpered.

Socrato stared down the foxgirl, and his features softened as he came to grasp the fear she was displaying. "I see... you're one of the sensitive people, aren't you? You can feel this portal's connection to the Void, can't you? I am sorry. I do know about the connection between this particular technique and the silent terror that lurks in the oceans far to the south."

"I am loathe to use them as a result," he continued. "I... lost someone very close to me while using it, before I fully understood the connection myself. I only use them now out of absolute necessity and because I now take the precautions that make the travel completely safe. There isn't any other option, my dear. Not if we wish to be in time."

She had to make a quick decision to trust the man that her admiral had such an intense loathing for. She told herself that if Dominus Socrato had wanted to hurt her, that he could have done it much more directly than this. If he wanted to hold her prisoner, it's not like he needed some Void-touched magic. There was no reason to believe that he was being anything other than honest in his urgency.

She clenched her eyes shut, and dashed through the doorway... then fell onto her hands and knees and threw up. The first sensation she felt was the burning of bile in her throat, then slightly damp grass under her fingers, and her knees felt wet as well. She opened her eyes, and outside of seeing a pile of her own yellow-green vomit, she quickly discovered she wasn't anywhere inside.

"That unsettling, was it?" Socrato's voice came from above and to her left. She weakly turned her head in that direction as the Dominus replied, "Well, if it is any consolation, it gets easier the more you do it."

The foxgirl whipped her head back down to spit out another bubble of bile, then coughed. There wasn't going to be a "more" to it. Once was one time too many, as far as she was concerned. Her skin was still crawling and she felt dirty from head to toe, like she just jumped head first into the *Goldbeard's* latrine.

"Quickly now," Socrato said simply, offering his hand to the foxgirl, then helped her to her feet.

Sunay then started to process where they were as the clammy dread finally began to evaporate. They were just outside the doorway of a cabin in a heavily wooded area, quite unlike the usual landscape she had come to expect of Aramathea. "Where... are we?" she wondered as she fell into step behind the mage.

"Just north of the Gold Coast," Socrato answered, his pace surprisingly fast for a man his age, even Sunay found she had to move swifter than she normally would in order to keep up. "That little trick chopped off a good three days of travel for us. But we still have some distance to go."

He rounded the cabin as Sunay tried to contact Ahmin again, this time with considerable more success. *Admiral? Ya there?*

Ahmin's response was a mix of relief and anger. *Sunay! What happened to you?*

The foxgirl answered, *Dominus Socrato. He's drug me out to the Gold Coast. Dunno why or how, but he claims he's going to help us secure the pilgrims.*

He turned thoughtful at the news. *The Gold Coast? I see... you and the Dominus might just beat us there in that case. Can you ask him whether you'll be coming to the objective by land or by sea?*

"My admiral wants to know if we're comin' by the land or sea," Sunay relayed as they rounded the west side of the cabin to a covered stable damn near the size of the cabin itself.

Socrato look confused, then snapped his fingers, "Right. Your telepathy stone. I hadn't thought to continue blocking it once we left my main hall. Fortunate, really, as coordination *would* be helpful. Tell him we will be approaching by land. It will take us longer, but I have ready access to fast horses. Fast ships require manpower that would result in questions I'm not keen on answering."

The door to the stable was open, which Socrato took as a good sign. "Negri! Are you in here?"

Sunay had seen her share of stable-hands in her time as a Gold Pirate. Negri did not fit the mold. She was a slight thing with brilliantly blond hair and a remarkably full figure, accented by the very short, very tight denim trousers and a sleeveless cotton shirt that she had tied off to expose her midriff.

"A friend's choice," Socrato grumbled as Sunay gave him a sly look. "Get those perversions out of your head, young lady."

"What can I do you for, Dominus?" Negri asked, wiping oiled hands on a yellow rag with white flowers that she tossed flippantly into a bucket. Sunay's eyes followed said rag before settling back on the stablehand, wondering if these were the eyes that were watching Socrato.

"How many horses are ready for fast riding?" Socrato asked.

"Depends on where you're going, I'd wager."

"Northwest, along the coast, past Gourney, in the Free Provinces. Probably two days travel."

"Verti, Marti, and Swelter could get you there. Give me about thirty minutes. Need me to drive?" Her voice then trembled nervously as she added, "Or is this a...?"

"Oh, don't you start that nonsense too," Socrato growled. "I am not sowing these wild oats, I promise you. Those fields are *long* since barren. But it is of great importance that it be done quickly, and yes, I will need you to man the reins."

"Then give me thirty, sir," Negri declared. "We'll leave as soon as I've got them all hitched up."

The Dominus nodded. "Then I will return shortly. I need to send a message."

We're comin' in by land, the Dominus says, Sunay relayed. *We'd be about two days, I'm bein' told.*

Alright, that's good actually, Ahmin answered, *because I have the feeling our little 'Minister' isn't going to be on the ships with his pilgrims. Once you arrive, find him. Neutralize him, by any means necessary.*

"Neutralize?" Sunay reiterated.

Ahmin clarified the order. *Incapacitate him for questioning if possible. Kill him if you have no other option.*

Understood.

"So, coordinate with your crew?" Socrato asked knowingly.

"Not yet, really. It's gonna depend on a lot on what things look like as we all get there," Sunay answered. She wasn't entirely on board with this man being privy to all their plans, even if he was allegedly being helpful right now.

If Socrato was suspicious, he didn't show it. "Makes sense. It may be that we'll be entirely too late to stop either ship, and that would be something your superiors will need to know before committing to any strategy."

"Uh huh," Sunay replied flippantly, dropping down into a cross-legged position to wait for the stablehand to return with their transportation. It was a boring wait to be sure, but she wasn't keen on too much chatting with the Dominus.

Socrato picked up on this. "It's going to be a very dull two days if you're not willing to talk to me."

Sunay was fine with dull. Life of the high seas wasn't always exciting.

He knelt down next to her, eyes looking out into space as he said flippantly, "You don't like me very much. Glad to know the feeling is mutual. I'd hate disdain that is one-sided. It seems like such a waste."

"I take it yer gonna be chatty for th' both of us, then?"

"Someone needs to fill the space."

Sunay's ears flattened, and she grumbled, "Joy..."

~ ~ ~ ~ ~

Socrato had remained true to his promise, as he led her through a narrative tour of Kartage for the entire trip. By the time they actually reached their destination, Sunay wasn't sure if she or Negri was going to strangle the mage first.

"The Southeast District interestingly enough, was the first," Socrato said, "and what is now the Center Square only came into being about ten years ago when the latest addition to the Outer Keep was opened to the public. You can even see remnants of the old wall as they become cornerstones for the buildings. Ah, Negri, stop here! The lady and I will continue the rest of the way on foot."

This part of the world was indeed much neglected. The tributary of the Great Trade Line had not seen maintenance for a good many years judging from the churned up stone riddled with thin coastal grasses. Negri had no problem whatsoever with not pushing her horses further down the rough terrain, pulling the wagon to a stop and allowing Socrato and Sunay to disembark.

Immediately upon the door opening, Sunay smelled people, a large gathering of them, the collective scent catching her nose almost due south, carried by the spring winds off the ocean.

We're here. Sunay declared. *And I can smell a lotta people still on the beach.*

That's good, honestly. We had only managed to locate one boat. We were worried that the other had slipped away before we could chase it down. If you're smelling a group, it's possible the other boat hasn't left yet. Keep me notified.

Aye aye.

"Judging from the intense look in your eyes, and your silence, I suspect we're in time, and your kin are formulating a plan?" Socrato asked.

"Uh huh. Let's go." Sunay moved south, through the tall grasses that flanked the crumbled trade line. The weeds broke at the edge of the rocky coastline projected on Socrato's map, only the coast was marked with a series of three open air tents, surrounded by brigands defined by tattered clothes and cutlasses, and with groups of children huddled together under the shade of the canopies.

"Friends of yours?" Socrato asked in disgust.

Sunay scoffed in reply, "Hardly. Don't insult me and mine by lumpin' us in wit' these mercenaries."

"I'll admit to being infinitely more curious in this 'Minister' fellow, but I doubt he's one of the raggedy miscreants ahead."

Sunay concurred. She doubted even desperate people would buy in so wholeheartedly to any one of the thirty men she saw standing vigil. But if he wasn't here... where was he?

"Doesn't exactly look like they're getting ready to load up any kids on any ships, now are they?" Socrato observed.

Sunay agreed, "No. Which don't make much sense."

"It does to me. This Minister knows he's sending people to die out in the Void. He's not willing to sacrifice children in such a way."

"But... why? It's not like these people got much money, I'm sure. What does this Minister gain?"

"We can contemplate that after we've secured the children," Socrato advised. "Do continue planning, I need to send a message."

What sort of plan could she come up with? There were at least thirty grown armed men defending at least a hundred children. Even if she *did* somehow manage to get the upper hand, the number of potential hostages would make sure that it didn't stay that way.

"My apologies, but I needed to send word for these poor children to be transported to Kartage," Socrato said as he appeared at Sunay's side once more. "So, any thoughts?"

"*What* thoughts?" Sunay said, gesturing towards the assembly, "It's thirty against two."

Socrato huffed, flipping open a tome and running his fingers along the pages. "Thirty isn't that many. You forget who you are with."

The smell of salty sea air rushed into Sunay's nose, followed less than a minute later by a strong wind and a heavy fog rolling over the waves. "Goodness, squalls come in off the sea so abruptly this time of year," the Dominus said as the fog became a nigh blinding blanket. "And the storm winds can get oh so very loud."

On cue, the howling and rumbling of storm clouds above resounded along the coast, though the wind speed at ground level didn't pick up much.

"That's good an' all, but that doesn't quite neutralize the fifteen to one thing," Sunay remarked, even as she was amazed by the effortless display of power on Socrato's part. Her only experience with mages had been Marco during the raid on Sacili, and he needed a focusing crystal the size of Sunay's head to pull off something equivalent to this.

"No, but *that* would." Socrato replied, pointing out to the sea, where three Aramathean warships emerged from the fog. Sunay now understood what his messages were for. "Yah. That changes things a l'il."

Socrato ordered sharply, "Use the cover to start evacuating the children. Now go."

Sunay sprinted forward, dropping to all fours to stay low to the ground, even as she wondered how she was going to be able to move that many children without *someone* noticing, fog or not. At least, until she could hear shouting ahead.

"Black hells! How the hell did the Bronzes sneak up on us?"

"Where the hell did the brats go? They're gone!"

"It was a feint! The Bronzes are to the east as well! They're running off with the kids!"

They were all illusions. The ships... the extra men... the running kids... all of it was fake.

"Marellus! Take ten and follow! The rest of you, up with me!"

The movements surprised Sunay... she expected the brigands to break upon seeing a military presence. How charismatic *was* this Minister fellow that run-of-the-mill pirates were willing to throw themselves at the Aramathean military?

She didn't have too much time to worry about it though. Since the buccaneers weren't bolting in terror, it wouldn't take long for them to discover the ruse. The first group of children panicked when Sunay burst through the fog, no doubt because she didn't look much different than the fiends that had been holding them. Fortunately, the shrieks didn't draw any attention. Socrato's illusions were *good*.

"I'm here to take ya all to safety, okay?" the foxgirl hissed. "But'cha gotta no north. There will be an old man in white up there. He'll keep ya safe. But ya all gotta git now. Go!"

The little ones complied, tentatively, though they were buoyed by their guards swinging wildly at the air, and once it became clear no one was paying attention to their flight, the escape was on. The second group of children didn't even need prompting. Once they saw the first group flee without pursuit, they made their break as well. The third group, however, remained frozen in place.

And that was because one pirate wasn't moving from his position, and in fact trying his damnedest to get the attention of his kin.

"Damn it all! It's'n illusion, ya twits!" the buccaneer screamed. "Da brats are walkin' right out tha back door! Damn it!"

He then pointed right at Sunay, and howled, "*You!*"

"Run kids!" Sunay shouted, dropping to all fours and charging. With the sole guard occupied, the children did as ordered, joining the other two groups in their sprint towards Socrato. Sunay and her foe met in a tumble, his larger frame taking the early advantage. But the foxgirl's nimbleness allowed her to shimmy out from under him and roll to her feet while drawing one of her knives at her waist.

Her opponent rolled to his side, and jumped to his feet. Before he could unsheathe his cutlass, Sunay was on the attack, and drew first blood across his left elbow and forearm. It was important that she take this man down before he got to his weapon, because the longer reach of the cutlass would quickly turn the fight against her.

He tried to push Sunay away, and the foxgirl countered by leaning right and trying an uppercut stab into her opponent's side. Instead, he smashed her with an overhead chop, catching her on the shoulder and driving her to one knee. As she spun away from a follow up blow, that gave the pirate the opportunity to draw his cutlass.

"Aww, shi..." Sunay grumbled, before having to lean away from a slash that threatened to slice her eyeballs clean through.

She sidestepped a chop, and ducked under another slash, using that leverage to try and tackle the larger pirate. It was somewhat successful, while it didn't knock him down, it did cause him to stumble, and allowed Sunay a quick slash across his abdomen before she had to retreat.

She charged again, sliding under her opponent's counter slash, then trapped his blade hand under her shoulder as he swung it back. Sunay could feel part of the blade digging into her side, but without any swinging force behind it, the cut wasn't going to be fatal. He then tried something similar as she swung her knife, but the smaller blade wasn't as easily caught. While she didn't cause a mortal wound like she had hoped, stabbing through his hand most certainly didn't feel good.

He got a burst of adrenaline based strength, ripping his hand away and shrugging off Sunay, the cutlass that had been digging in her side now drawing across and lengthening the gash almost to her breast. She howled in pain, then bit her tongue to keep from making more noise. That wasn't a trade she could make too many more times.

The pirate's rage didn't abate, and now his slashes and chops were coming faster and blindly. This was actually a good thing, because if she timed it right, there were no end of openings in his stance and defense that she could take advantage of.

She took advantage of one such opening to remove the threat of his cutlass, sidestepping a downward chop, then driving her knife into his wrist, cutting the tendons and making him lose his grip of the blade. Without that weapon, the tide of the fight turned again, as the buccaneer desperately tried to ward off Sunay's knife hand.

With two wounded hands himself, he made one last desperate lunge, and while he certainly did tackle Sunay to the ground, she had more than enough time to put her knife in the perfect place for it to split his ribs and drive into his heart. The pirate wheezed twice, his body going limp, and once that happened Sunay was able to roll him off of her.

The foxgirl rose to one knee, trying to catch her breath, staring down her opponent to make sure he was well and truly finished. He wasn't dead, and would have been alive for several more minutes if Sunay hadn't granted him mercy with a stab to his neck that severed his spinal cord.

And through it all, the rest of his kin kept fighting mirages or chasing ghost kids down the coast.

Then Sunay felt another Void-inspired chill run down her spine; she warily turned her head right, where a male figure stood not even twenty feet away, his back to her and shrouded in a full length cloak. He had *not* been there before, and Sunay had no idea where he could have come from. But whoever he was and wherever he came from, he was setting off every gut clenching, spine freezing, skin crawling sensation she had ever felt when in the presence of the Void.

"You do realize I had no intentions of harming those children?" He asked. Even though his voice should have been perfectly normal, it still grated Sunay's ears like fingernails on a chalkboard. "You killed that poor fellow for no reason."

The man's head turned south, towards the sea, though his face was still completely shrouded in some sort of magical shadow. "And it appears that my other ship was intercepted. How very unfortunate. I suppose I need to take measures to protect myself now."

His voice shifted melodic, almost like he was singing more than talking. "My friends... go out into the sea. Walk, do not swim. Show your devotion to your minister and the Coders' will."

The pirates stopped fighting, their arms dropping and releasing their weapons, like puppets with their arm strings cut. Without any argument or resistance, every single brigand she could see took deliberate strides into the waters, steadily going deeper.

"Wh... what are ya fools doin'!" Sunay shouted. "Don't do that! Ya'll drown!"

"They can't hear you," the Minister chided. "They are nothing more than props in this play. They aren't even 'Chosen.' The world will not mourn their loss."

Admiral! The Minister is here! He's a mage! Ya gotta get here quick!

Somehow, Sunay felt the man's eyes upon her, and his voice turned bemused. "No one can hear you, girl. So you are a member of the world's police, are you? Fascinating. I offer you this advice, because I like you. I would suggest resigning from your post. If you linger too long, I promise, it will be your end."

"Y... ya shut up!" Sunay retorted. She tried to stand, but the sickness squeezing her gut made the attempted movement stomach churning.

"Well, I suppose I shouldn't linger. I have so many things to do. Such a waste..." he shook his head disparagingly, then vanished before his next foot landed.

Sunay found herself alone on the beach, the sickness dispelling, and with both the *Goldbeard* approaching from the sea, and Dominus Socrato appearing from the north, looking quite perplexed.

He spied the entire stretch of beach, and asked a question that Sunay wanted to ask herself.

"What happened here?"

Sunay shook her head, as much because she didn't want to discuss anything until she could consult Ahmin as she wasn't even sure how she was going to explain it. Socrato didn't push the issue, instead turning his attention to the gash in her side as he helped her to a sitting position on her knees. "You're going to need that mended, dear. Off with your shirt, please."

The foxgirl's eyes bulged at the suggestion, and Socrato glared at her disapprovingly. "Young lady, you are bleeding heavily. Let me assure you that open wounds kill what little libido I may have nowadays. Now please... I need to see how much work I need to do."

Sunay obliged with a wary look, pulling up her shirt and holding her wrap to her chest while Socrato examined her. "Yes... deep enough to warrant a cleansing spell I think," he said. "Do stand as still as you can. This may tickle."

"Tickle" wasn't the word Sunay would have used. It felt like a handful of ants crawling around the wound, and it was everything she could do not to shudder violently and wriggle away from the unpleasant sensations. Once that subsided, it was followed by what felt like the shock of static electricity, which also caused her to wince.

"I hope your friends managed to stop the other ship," he said conversationally.

Sunay decided to find out. *We're all secure on this end. All the kids are safe. How about you?*

Ahmin answered, *The ship has been commandeered, despite some less than light resistance. We're on course for you as we speak. Should be there by evening.*

"They did," Sunay then relayed.

"Oh very good," the Dominus said in relief. "I've seen enough terrors of the Void in just my research to not wish that sort of oblivion on anyone. Too many lives have been lost to that faceless nightmare as it is."

"Why are ya studyin' the Void anyway?"

Socrato released a slow breath. "I am hoping to discover a way to stop its spread... and maybe even reverse it. It's probably a fool's errand, as Morgana likes to say often, but I have to try. If anything, it's my penance for all the hurt and damage I caused in my younger years." He patted Sunay in the side, demonstrating that the healing had worked, because it didn't cause her any pain. "There you are, young lady. All patched up."

He stood, took a deep breath, then called out to where the assembled children hovered nervously on the rocks. "Your parents and loved ones are well and coming for you. If you wish to get out of the sun, you can return to your tents." In a softer tone only meant for Sunay's ears he added, "That's what I plan to do. All this magic work tires these old bones of mine."

Socrato made for the nearest tent, dropping down into a cross-legged position with his head down. Sunay joined him at his side, beckoning the children to follow while they waited for signs of her ship.

That sign occurred as the sun approached evening, the masts of the *Goldbeard* and its sail pattern giving Sunay the energy to hop to her feet and wave even though it was doubtful even Balco with a spyglass would see her. A second ship pulled up beside it, and rowboats began ferrying people to shore, retreating back to rotate except one, bearing Admiral Ahmin who greeted Sunay with a warm relieved smile.

Adults reunited with children, aghast at the truth of what had almost transpired. Neither Ahmin nor Socrato had been able to glean much from questioning any of them, even as they queried every person they could well until evening. The answers were largely the same... lost people clinging to whatever shred of hope they could for a better life, and falling for the promises of a man who offered it.

Socrato was growing rather irritated by the lack of information being shared, but Ahmin expressly forbid discussing anything the foxgirl had seen with Socrato present.

"I'll have you know that I was instrumental in saving those children," Socrato protested.

"And I am grateful for that," Ahmin replied, though his voice didn't reflect any gratitude. "But this is Gold Pirate business."

Socrato inclined his head towards the refugees, and asked, "Are *they* Gold Pirate business as well?"

"I certainly wouldn't trust them to *you*," Ahmin said bitterly. "I already know how *you* welcome those fleeing certain death."

The Dominus stiffened as if he had been struck, and Sunay could see the pain on his face. It was clear Socrato understood the reference. "I see. Dear sir, I have made many mistakes in my life. One of the most tragic was made in my zeal to prove myself to my land and my empire, to be venerated by the Emperor as a leader of war. Instead, I killed hundreds of innocents. Thank you, sir, for reminding me of that."

Socrato turned to the mass of refugees and declared, "While I certainly don't have room in Kartage, I *will* promise you that these poor folks will find sanctuary in the First Empire. I will not fail people in need again while I have to means to aid them. Ships from the fleet should be arriving in the day to escort them to Kartage, and then... well, we shall see."

Ahmin didn't like that idea. "You think I'm going to..."

"And where will *you* escort them, I wonder?" Socrato asked skeptically. "Is there a haven you Gold Pirates have I don't know about?"

The tigerman went silent, brooding.

Sunay put a hand on Ahmin's arm, and said, "I think it'll be okay. I really do. And it's true that it ain't like we have anywhere we could take 'em all, and it'd be days before another ship in the fleet could arrive even if we did."

Ahmin growled very much like his animal namesake before he turned away abruptly and snarled, "Fine. But I'm going to be watching, Dominus... and I swear..."

"Watch as you wish if it will clear your conscience," Socrato replied, finally getting tired of the tigerman's attitude. His head then jerked upward in time with a bird's call, followed by a gray falcon with a snow white belly landing on the Dominus's outstretched arm. It had a clear tube tied to its left leg, where a rolled up white note had been tucked inside.

Sunay had heard about these messenger birds, magical creatures in that they always knew where their owner and their target was. She wished she could have one of those. It would make correspondence so much easier.

Socrato took the rolled up sheet of paper, and dismissed the falcon, who spiraled upwards and eventually out of sight. "Oh! From Torma!" he chirped, his eyes scanning the sheet, "I wonder what she has been up to... oh, how very interesting..."

He turned away from Sunay, who was unconsciously leaning in. "You have your secrets, I have mine," he grumbled. "I would also, in the spirit of cooperation, inform you that you might wish to be elsewhere as my allies arrive. I suspect they might have a bone to pick with the ship that led the raid on Sacili."

Ahmin's eyes narrowed again, not that Socrato was wrong. "Come along, Sunay. We have work to do."

The foxgirl complied, though slowing her pace and stealing glances back at Socrato, who was gathering up the refugees and introducing himself properly. She climbed into the last remaining rowboat, across from Ahmin and said, "Ya know... and yer not gonna like me sayin' this..."

"Socrato's a much different person now," Ahmin grumbled. "And if I want to be forgiving, I already know that. But I don't want to be forgiving. So let's drop it, and instead since we have the time alone, start talking about what the black hell happened over there."

Sunay gave that report, including as much detail as she could about the "Minister" that had been the source of all this. "And he reeked of the Void, did he?" Ahmin asked. "This is bothersome, to say the least. The only three mages we know of that have been doing any research into the Void are all accounted for, and there's been no indication that anyone else even has the *means* to play around with it... much less do anything with it. This is going to be something I need to relay to the other Administrators. Someone is playing with powers they shouldn't be."

If Sunay had been looking for assurances that everything was going to be okay... she didn't get it.

Ahmin dismissed her the moment they both hit the deck, telling her to go get some sleep. While that certainly was a good idea... there was a nagging something she had to deal with first.

She shut her cabin door behind her, and settled at her desk and took a piece of paper that she had been saving specifically for this purpose... writing a letter for Laron once she had figured out what to say.

Dearest Laron,

I am so very sorry it has taken so long for me to

reply. I have been horribly occupied, but that's no excuse.
I'm so sorry to hear about your family. Hopefully nothing's
happened yet, and they can get out as soon as possible.

I just had to deal with some refugees myself, and
they told us stories about how crazy it's getting up north.
Thankfully, Dominus Socrato has taken up their cause to get
them homes and a safe place to live.

She took a deep breath before she wrote her next words.

And that's actually why I'm finally writing. I'm still
not entirely certain what happened on the Gold Coast, in
Torad's estate. I can't say for certain who has the real tome,
or even if there was a real tome to begin with, nor do I have
any earthly idea what your role was in it, or if you even had
a role at all and are right now reading this and wondering
what in the hell I'm prattling on about.

But what I will say is that I trust you, and that no
matter what, I won't ever doubt you again. Be safe, Laron.
We still have a ton of promises to keep.

With Love,
Sunay

Chapter Four: Creeping Dread

"Another year older, another year wiser," Matron Miriam used to say, and it was something that she felt she agreed with. She had learned so much about her crew, little tells and details about them that helped her know what each of them really felt or thought at any given time.

Juno, for example, would twitch her right eyebrow ever so slightly when she was lying or bluffing. The left side of Bolin's lips would shift whenever he disliked an order. Gurgn's arms muscles would clench when he was angry, and his leg muscles would tense when he was happy.

After another spring and into another summer, she had finally gotten a hint of a tell about their Admiral. Whenever news was grim, his eyes would turn downward ever so slightly just before he addressed the crew. It was a tell that she saw when he stepped onto the deck, and ordered, "Bolin! Set a course at three hundred and thirty. We're sailing for Beredon to pick up some assets, then to the South Gibraltar Islands. Sunay, join me in my cabin for the briefing."

The foxgirl thought she was braced for bad news. She had been wrong.

Ahmin got straight to the point. "The Void has advanced. Towards South Gibraltar. It's reportedly a day's sail off the coast now."

Sunay's heart dropped straight through her stomach and to the floor. She couldn't speak. This was what the Gold Pirates spoke in hushed whispers about. That moment in time when the Void made the final push to devour their continent, the last refuge.

The "Endgames."

Ahmin himself looked disconcerted. "Our mission is to coordinate with two other ships that will be meeting us at the islands, the Lively and the Indomitable. You know Captain Roberts already, he's the man in charge of the Indomitable. Captain Voria is in charge of the Lively. The assets we are picking up in Beredon are investigative teams directly answering to the Administrators themselves."

"Investigative teams?"

Ahmin shook his head and said, "I'm not supposed to explain this, but... there are two levels of Administrator. Those like me, who control operations of the Gold Pirates. And a second level above even us... that we don't even know exactly what their duties are. It's believed, not confirmed, that these Administrators know exactly how the world is supposed to end, and they govern all activities in accordance to that plan. Judging from the response... this... isn't part of the plan."

Sunay eyes narrowed.

"Now, this is just heresay, so don't let your mind dive too far into all that," Ahmin warned. "But it *is* something to keep in mind. Things might be turning sideways on us, and we need to mind that. For now, we do as ordered."

"Aye aye, sir."

"Good, because you'll be in command for this mission."

Sunay blinked rapidly, and said, "Me?"

"Yes. I'm needed elsewhere, and I'm trusting you to oversee this mission. I'll be stepping off in Beredon, and I will rejoin you once you return after the mission."

The foxgirl nodded. Truth being, commanding the ship wasn't that difficult. The *Goldbeard's* crew was so solid that as a result the ship damn near ran itself outside of exceptionally bizarre and unforeseen circumstances. "Aye aye, sir. I'll try and not burn th' ship down." She then smiled playfully and added, "But I make no promises."

Ahmin shared a bitter laugh. "Your attempt to dull the gravity of the situation is noted. Be safe, Sunay."

"As safe as we can be."

The admiral sighed, and dropped down in front of his desk. "Dismissed," he said, and lowered his head down onto his hands in thought. Sunay left, and stopped just outside of Ahmin's door as she closed it. She lifted her head, sighed, and forced herself not to cry. Everyone needed to be strong, especially those in command.

~ ~ ~ ~ ~

She felt she kept her composure well as the *Goldbeard* came up to the coast of Beredon, Joffe lighting a red "candle" to signify their approach and that the investigators were to row their way over.

The teams must have been waiting for the *Goldbeard*, because Balco spotted the approaching boats within seconds of the candle's brilliant and smoky pop in the sky.

She felt she kept her face well intact as Ahmin took a seat in one of the boats that the crew was expecting to send back with nothing but the row-man. "Sunay is in charge for this mission," Ahmin declared. "I have administrative business that I need to attend to, and it apparently needs to be done in person. I trust you'll follow her order as studiously as you all follow mine."

Sunay had no doubt about that, and also knew that the crew's astonishment was more about the surprise departure rather than the foxgirl being left in command.

But just as she had learned about the tells of her crewmates, her crew had learned her little ticks as well.

Juno was the one who spoke for them as she sided up to Sunay during the trip to the Gibraltar Islands, "Okay... I *know* you ain't anxious about bein' in charge. So, what's eatin' at ya?"

"I'm fine," Sunay said dismissively, actively avoiding eye contact.

"Then look at me while ya say it," Juno replied smugly.

Sunay *did* lock eyes with the spidergirl, but only to say, "Okay, yeah... there's a lot on my mind. But it's nuthin' I can talk about, okay? At least not yet."

"Why not?"

Sunay's eyes scanned the deck, where every eye was now on her. They could all see the concern on her face. They were all like family to her at this point. She couldn't lie to them, and Ahmin didn't expressly forbid her to discuss what was going on.

The foxgirl licked her lips to moisten them, and declared, "All right... here's the deal. The Void's moved. Towards South Gibraltar."

The entire deck went deathly silent until Bolin coughed nervously. It also gave Sunay the reminder that she needed to speak again. "We all knew this day was a'comin'. That doesn't mean we don't 'ave to do our jobs anymore. We gotta believe that what we're doin' has a reason for it. The admiral is countin' on us, and we can't let 'im down."

To their credit, the crew set right back to their tasks with a grim determination. The chatter normally found on the deck was gone, and the energy had been sucked straight out of the crew, but they were still at work. It was more than most crews would be when facing their darkest fears.

~ ~ ~ ~ ~

The news didn't get much better as they passed the North Gibraltar Islands and started getting communication from the other ships. The *Lively* had been the first on the scene, and began sending messenger pigeons once the *Goldbeard* was within flight range.

Sunay read one of those messages, and groaned, "Wonderful..."

Juno popped out from the rigging above, and asked, "What's up, ma'am?"

"The Aramathean Navy's here. They're supposedly evacuatin' citizens."

"Well... that's good... ain't it?"

"Supposedly," Sunay replied grimly. "They also might recognize the ship an' start firin' on us."

Juno nodded. "I'll run the alternate colors. Tell Gurgn he and th' crew are gonna have to take over for thirty."

The spidergirl scampered back up into the rigging as Sunay called down to the row team. After the incident with Socrato, Ahmin had ordered a second set of sails with different colors for when they were in areas with a noted Aramathean naval presence. Joffe had developed some sort of mechanism that allowed for one or the other to be deployed without completely removing either, and so Juno just had to trigger those mechanism as she jumped along the masts and rolled up the originals.

The *Goldbeard's* alternate colors were a gold field with a black stylized Tiger head in mid roar. She honestly liked those more than the boring diagonal stripes... but it wasn't her ship. Wasn't her call to make. The alternate colors unfurled, the sails caught the wind, and their speed picked back up.

The North Gibraltar islands were the continent's oceanic resort, one of the few such tropical climates that remained. Older than their southern siblings, the volcanoes that formed them were older and more dormant, the few eruptions bubbling a slow moving lava that an average person literally could outrun. As a result, the northern islands were frequented by the richest and most prominent citizens from around the continent.

At least usually. As the *Goldbeard* passed Achinda, the largest island of the chain, it was a ghost town... not a soul on the beaches, the flag poles bare of any of the usual wind indicators for hang gliders or surfers. Clearly news of the advancing Void had reached them far sooner than it should have, and the tourists were getting out while the getting was good. But how was word spreading?

Further notes from the *Lively* and the *Indomitable* cast further light on the situation. "Sounds like Dominus Socrato learned about the movement of the Void 'fore we did. General Argaeus o' the Second

Army issued the order to start evacuatin' people once 'e confirmed the Void had shifted," Sunay relayed to Juno as she caught up on the news herself. She decided that was a good thing rather than worry about the implications that the Dominus was figuring out things with those tomes he had.

That was Ahmin's job to worry about.

Another two days of sailing brought them to the South Gibraltar Islands. By all accounts of scholars, the two archipelagos weren't related at all, different deep sea volcano systems giving birth to them at much different times, and only grouped together due to proximity.

The atmosphere reflected this. The southern islands were basically fiery balls of hell, with very active volcanoes that spewed plumes of smoke that could often be seen by anyone looking south from the northern islands. Vegetation was not to be found anywhere on the volcanic rock, just black charred surfaces when they weren't being painted by lava.

Sunay almost didn't want to let the investigators off the boat considering how dangerous the environment was, but orders were orders, and the investigators themselves didn't seem terribly concerned. The teams didn't even ask anyone on the crew to row them to shore, taking the oars themselves and chopping through the waves, undaunted by the rumbling of angry earth ahead.

Garth whistled, impressed by their courage. "Why can't we send *these* guys on raids?"

"Prob'ly because they ain't trained in combat," Sunay answered, "whereas we are, at least in theory. *Your* sparring chart is dismal."

Garth cringed and smiled guiltily. His right wrist still probably still sore from his last match with Sunay. Turned out wrestling with a foxgirl wasn't as easy as he thought it was. "So we just wait here, then?" he asked.

"And try and stay outta the way of the Aramatheans," Sunay confirmed.

The Aramathean Navy was here as well, combing the island for what few researchers, miners, and suppliers still remained on the islands. If they objected to the Gold Pirates investigators, they didn't act on those objections, the two parties giving each other as wide of berths as possible, the investigators going as far as to point any civilians they came across to nearby naval scouts.

Was their presence what Ahmin was sent to look into?

Socrato's foreknowledge of the Void movements could have been the realization of his fears, that the Dominus was starting to access knowledge he wasn't meant to have. Was Ahmin being sent to... deal with it? Was Ahmin taking his own initiative without approval of his superiors?

Or did this have anything to do with the mysterious "Minister" that Sunay had encountered a year before? That man had such a pervasive stench of the Void that it had rendered her immobile with nausea just being in his general vicinity. Could a *person* be manipulating the Void in such a manner? Could Ahmin be trying to hunt that man down? Had Ahmin already hunted him down and was trying to end the threat?

Sunay's brow crinkled in worry as those and other concerns all started cramming into her mind in the down time. Like Laron reporting that Daynish attackers had been nipping all spring at the border towns in the free provinces near his family's homestead in Vakulm, attacking less defended caravans and cutting off shipping lanes. It was not behavior consistent with raiding, but army tactics. It's like they were practicing for something larger... and no one Laron had talked to liked that one bit.

His mother steadfastly refused to leave, and the rest of his family followed her lead. Laron had tried with increasing desperation to make them see reason, but his mother's mind was made up. She had resigned herself to death years ago when judgment had fallen on her husband in Snake River, and figured it didn't matter if the Daynes finished the job.

Perhaps it was because she was so lost in her thoughts that she didn't realize what had happened. Perhaps it happened so quickly that she didn't have time to think about it. But there *was* something... different nearby. The wind dwindled. The sky shifted to a pallor gray. Scents and sounds felt muted. Her ears twitched nervously as it felt like the world around her was literally dying away.

Sunay could feel it, that sickeningly familiar ghostly hand clenching her gut.

"Are ya *sure* the Void is far off?" she hollered over the deck towards Bolin.

"At least a day's travel for us, said the scout ships!" was the unconcerned response. "The dire water doesn't spread *that* quick, ma'am!"

Sunay could understand why Bolin was testy. He was busy enough keeping his distance from the Aramathean Navy while staying close enough for the investigators to easily get back to the ship after they finished whatever tasks had been set out for them. So she didn't want to snap at him. But every fiber of her body was now cringing from the malaise.

She crossed the deck towards the main mast, and shouted up into the rigging in the general direction of the spidergirl. "Juno! Hop up to the crow's nest and check to the south!"

Bolin didn't like being second guessed, and his protest was immediate. "Ma'am! I'm tellin' ya! The Void isn't anywhere near us."

They were interrupted by Juno's cry a minute later. "*Dire water!* Not even a half mile off!"

The helmsman didn't *want* to believe it. "How? The Void doesn't move that fast!"

"Well, apparently it does!" Sunay shouted in retort before barking out orders to the rest of the crew. "Light the candles! Get the teams back on the ship! We're buggin' out by sundown!" In a lower grumble to herself she added, "The Admiral can suck eggs. I ain't risking everyone on board for whatever crazy claptrap he wants."

The "candles" were in truth signal flares, that burned a bright red and would be visible from the coast, signaling the rest of the *Goldbeard's* crew to return to the ship immediately. They even stood out on the daytime tropical sky, screaming with a bright crimson trail and screeching hiss before bursting with a deafening pop that made Sunay's ears ring.

"Juno, send messages to the Lively and the Indomitable, tell 'em what we're plannin', tell 'em that the Void is a *lot* closer than we thought, and *strongly* recommend they follow our lead."

The first of the boats bearing the crew arrived an hour later, understandably confused why the first mate was calling off all operations, then understanding exactly why when they learned that dire water was far closer than it should be.

Another hour after that prompted Sunay to ask, "How many left?"

"One crew on the north side of the nearest volcano. It's no doubt going to take them a while to get packed up," Garth reported.

"Well they better hurry up," Sunay growled. She then called up again to the crow's nest, demanding, "How close is it now?"

"No change, ma'am!" was the reply. "Dire water is holding steady!"

Well, *that* wasn't unusual or anything, Sunay thought with internal sarcasm. The only thing more worrisome than a rapidly advancing Void was an unpredictably advancing Void. She unclipped her spyglass from her belt, and started scanning her surroundings for any sign of the remaining boat. What she saw instead caused her stomach to drop.

"Oh no..." She moaned. A single Aramathean naval craft, distinguished by its low resting hull, small sails, and oar movement, had made the turn around the island, and was heading south out to sea, directly towards dire water. If they were going by similar information the *Goldbeard* had from before, the Aramatheans wouldn't know that the Void had moved so suddenly.

While she wasn't fond of the Southern Empire, she was less fond of watching people get swallowed up by the Void.

With a growl, she said, "Damn it," then jumped into action. "How long do you think it'll take our last team to get back?" She asked Garth.

He shrugged and estimated, "Could be another hour. They *were* supposed to go pretty high up the volcano."

"Good, then you're with me."

The deckhand was confused. "With you? Where?"

She handed over the far viewer, and let Garth take a look. "We're going to take one of the boats, and intercept the Aramatheans before they throw themselves into the Void."

"Ma'am, no offense, but even wit' two o' us, we aren't gonna to be able to row out that distance in time..."

Sunay snarled at being second guessed. "You just prep the boat. *I'll* worry 'bout getting us there. I'll be back in ten. The boat'd better be ready."

She sprinted through the aft door to the lower decks, vaulting herself around corners by the handrails, then took a sharp left at the lowest deck to Joffe's cabin. The craftsman was sprawled across his cot, still completely uninterested in the happenings above, even though he must have heard the candles lighting.

"First mate, whatcha need?" he asked, his interest piqued by Sunay's flushed and hurried appearance.

"Ya said you could make a rocket that could power a boat, right?"

Joffe's eyes twinkled. "Yah."

"Well, yer gonna get the chance. Ya got ten minutes. Get yer biggest rocket ready to go and enough rope to secure it to a rowboat."

Joffe smiled broadly. He *loved* a challenge.

Nine minutes later, he needed Sunay's help to bring the

massive rocket he had been toying with in the hold up to the deck. The damned thing was nearly as wide as the rowboat that the crew started securing it to. "This is insane, you know that?" Sunay asked Joffe as she put five knots into a rope that led from a grip on the rocket to a handhold on the rowboat.

"I'll have you know I designed this rocket specifically for this purpose." Joffe retorted indignantly.

Juno interjected, "And what purpose is that? To explode and kill everyone on board?"

"It's not going to explode!"

Sunay ended the bickering by snarling, "It better not. If we die out there, I swear to the Coders I'm gonna kill ya."

It was successful if only because Joffe and Juno stopped talking and crossed their eyes instead. It allowed Sunay to finish the knotting without distraction, then pointed at the interior of the rowboat. "Garth. Joffe. In. Now."

To his credit, Joffe showed proper confidence in his abilities, readily climbing into the boat and taking position at the stern where he could light the rocket. Garth took a cold, withering stare and another insistent point for him to concede to her order, though he took the seat farthest away from the rocket as he possibly could. Sunay took the middle bench swiftly after that, and Juno lowered them to the water with a cheery wave.

"Bon voyage!" she said cheerily. "Better you than me!"

"If I die, guess who's gonna be tha first mate?" Sunay shouted back just before the rowboat reached sea level.

Juno's smile vanished, and she then shouted, "Hey! Wanna trade places, ma'am?"

"Nope!"

Juno sighed in defeat with a muffled, "Damn it."

Joffe then shouted up towards the deck, "You might want to move the Goldbeard clear! *We're* gonna be fine, but anything behind us probably won't be!"

Sunay and Garth glared at him, prompting the craftsman to explain. "All the force and fire trail is going to be coming out behind us, and we'll be moving too fast for radiant heat to cook us."

The foxgirl didn't even get a chance to protest any further, because Joffe had already pulled the wick forward, which apparently lit some internal mechanism that caused the rocket to ignite.

Sunay had expected something much more violent, having braced herself to be shot out like the candles that had inspired this particular rocket. This was barely faster than Ahmin could row. "We ain't gonna catch that ship going this fast!" Sunay shouted.

Joffe grinned and replied, "This is just the first stage! Can't go full speed right from the start!"

"First... sta..." Sunay began, only to have the words stolen from her mouth as there was a loud pop and the boat lurched forward at twice its previous speed, and steadily increasing its velocity. Joffe had Sunay and Garth grab onto some of the ropes on both sides to help steady the rocket while the prow of the boat lifted out of the water.

Now their target was coming closer, and it was even drawing the attention of those on the ship, armored soldiers forming along the railing and pointing in their direction. The naval vessel hadn't changed course, and that was there Sunay discovered an increasingly alarming problem. That they were directly on a collision course with said navel vessel.

"Uhhhh... so... how do we slow down?" Sunay asked over the roar of the rocket behind them.

Joffe looked like her like she had grown a second head. "Slow down?"

Sunay cursed and pointed at the vessel getting ever closer, "Damn it all... how do we turn then for Coder's sake!"

Joffe finally processed the dilemma, and his eyes widened. But like all good Gold Pirates, he was quick to think on his feet and find a solution to the problems in front of him. "Sunay, pull tight on the ropes on the right side. Garth, let go of the left and do the same. Quick!"

The pair complied while Joffe turned about with a knife ready. As the boat began to list to the left due to the change in rope tension, Joffe began cutting the rocket free. However, the craftsman wasn't quite fast enough. The boat listed too far by the time he had successfully separated the rocket, and while it tumbled to the right while mercifully missing the Aramathean vessel, it sent their rowboat into a corkscrew, tumbling in a spiral and tossing all three occupants into the sea.

Sunay's ears rang as she hit the water head first, her eyes flooded with stars as she quickly tried to sort out which was was up. It was harder than a landlubber might think, having been spun about frequently before entering the water had messed with her equilibrium, and thanks to the volcanic ash in the air turned her entire surroundings a mostly uniform shade of gray.

The foxgirl exhaled sharply, and followed the bubbles that

formed up to the surface, taking a huge breath as she breached the surface. Surprisingly, she hadn't been discarded far from the boat, and even more surprising was that the rowboat had somehow managed to come to a stop upright and hadn't taken much apparent damage.

She swam to the boat to make sure, pulling herself up and testing her weight inside. There was maybe an inch of water in the bottom, but it didn't seem to be taking on more as she settled into the seat. The oars were no doubt lost to the waves, and that forced Sunay to paddle with her hands when she saw Garth treading water about forty feet away.

Sunay helped the deckhand into the boat, and he offered a lopsided smile, "Okay... that last bit was kinda fun. Let's never do it again."

"Agreed," the foxgirl said, then started scanning the sea for Joffe. Ahmin would never forgive her if she managed to lose the ship's handyman. They weren't easy to replace.

Both she and Garth jumped when the craftsman pulled himself over the port side of the rowboat. "If you want to be able to *stop* and *steer*, do say so in the initial planning phase," he grumbled just before coughing his lungs clear of any residual saltwater.

"Never thought to think that'd be sorta important?" Sunay growled. "I had minutes to think 'bout this. Ya had what... years?"

"Hold!"

That jerked the heads of all three pirates upward towards the sound of the voice, an Aramathean captain leaning over the railing of his warship with seven archers on each side, their arrows nocked and aimed downward. "If you were attempting to attack us, I'm afraid to say your plan failed!"

"We weren't tryin' to attack! We were tryin' to get yer attention!" Sunay called up angrily.

"Consider your plan successful then! I trust there was a *reason* you desired our attention?"

"Ya were all sailin' straight into tha Void!" Sunay said, pointing off to the south. "Ya'll were lucky we caught ya in time!"

The captain raised his right arm, and the archers drew back to a ready position. "The Void is still a day's journey south, woman! I suggest you find a better excuse!"

"It shifted fast!" Sunay protested, mention of the Void reminding her of the cold chill now clenching her spine from the base of her neck to her tailbone. "I'm tellin' ya, take not even five more lengths south, and ya would'n be able to be firin' those arrows yer drawin'!"

The captain was clearly weighing the option of ordering his archers to fire or if it would be worth the arrows. In that drawn out silence, another soldier sided up to the captain, and the pair exchanged words that not even Sunay's hearing could quite pick up. Something about the starboard side and disturbing.

The captain disappeared from view for a painfully long moment of time. When he returned, his face was grim. He ordered the archers to stand down, then called out, "We thank you for your warning, pirates. We would suggest you return to your ship while that appreciation lingers."

Sunay would have been smug if not for the crash of adrenaline that followed now that everyone was safe, if for the moment, as well as the Void sickness that took advantage and twisting her internal organs into knots. She curled up in the center of the boat, and neither Garth nor Joffe needed an explanation.

Further evidence of how close they were to the Void came as the Aramathean ship turned about to retreat. Garth pointed, and said, "Look at that!"

Sunay really didn't want to, but her eyes betrayed her. Several oars on the naval vessel's starboard side looked like they had been sliced clean halfway across the blade, no doubt as they had turned to confront the seemingly suicidal pirates and their rocket boat. The foxgirl groaned, then shuddered animatedly, trying with all her might not to vomit.

Joffe reached into his drenched coat pocket, and sighed. "Fortunately, I've got these flares that can light even when wet. Hope the ship can see it from here..."

She more sensed the light of Joffe's flare ignite in front of her than really saw it. All she wanted to do was curl up and hide until the Void ate her up. It was too close... too damn close.

Garth wrapped his arms around Sunay for warmth, even though he knew it wouldn't do one whit of good. The foxgirl appreciated the tactile contact, though. She felt so isolated and alone when the Void was near, the touch told her she wasn't, and *that* helped, if just a little bit.

The waves picked up and rocked the rowboat gently as the *Goldbeard* approached and displaced the water around it, and Sunay forced herself to uncoil, not wanting to show weakness around the rest of the crew. It was bad enough that Joffe and Garth saw her break down.

Ropes dropped down from the ship for them to secure the boat for lifting, which Garth and Joffe took to tying, but that plan had to be abandoned when Garth discovered that one of those tie downs had been torn from the rowboat during its chaotic tumble, while another had been loosened and came free as Joffe tried to secure it.

Juno shimmied down the hull head first, stopping just short of the water line, lifting her head to assess the damage. "Ah... I think we're gonna 'ave to write this one off. All o' ya well enough to climb the ropes?"

Garth was about to express concern for Sunay, until he could feel the foxgirl's baleful glare fall on him. "Yeah," she said, "We're a little sore an' all, but we're okay."

Joffe cut in, taking one rope and handing it to Sunay, "But the first mate hit her head in the spill, so she's going to climb first. Just in case."

No amount of glares was going to dissuade any of the pirates present, even if she was silently grateful for the courtesy. And it was a good decision too, as she found she needed Juno's assistance to pull herself up over the railing and onto the *Goldbeard's* deck. Now, she was shivering for reasons other than the Void... as even in warm Southern waters, being drenched to the bone will lower your body temperature.

And Juno knew it too. "A'ight, ma'am. Git down below and git changed before ya freeze."

Sunay no longer wanted to argue or look tough. She was chilled body and soul, and wished she could shed her skin as easily as she could shed her clothes. She staggered down to her cabin, yanked off her drenched shirt, and struggled with her pants that had decided to cling to her legs like a frightened kid.

Her underpants were less troublesome, and her chest wrap came off like it was ready to disintegrate. Once she was undressed, she found herself drawn to her hammock more than her clothes chest. She knew she shouldn't, she knew she should get dressed and get back up onto the deck... but sleep sounded so very tempting.

There was a knock on her door, and an unfamiliar voice, one of the newer deckhands whose name she couldn't remember offhand. "Ma'am, all th' investigators are back on tha boat. Juno's got us goin' back to tha mainland. She says ya can get some sleep if'n ya want."

That Juno was a smart, observant little spider. She smiled to herself, then replied, "I think I'm gonna do that. Thank you... eh..."

"Baker, ma'am. Sorry. Only been on 'bout a month, mostly

night, so ya probably hadn't met me much."

Sunay would have slapped herself if she had the energy. She had met him on two separate night watches. She should have been able to remember it, and maybe she would have if her brain and thoughts weren't so emptied out. "Baker, right... well, I'll let ya get back to yer business. Dismissed."

"Thank you ma'am. Sleep well."

Sunay doubted that much... but honestly any sleep, good or bad, would be welcome right now. She didn't even bother throwing on undergarments or even a blanket, mostly because she was asleep the instant her head dropped onto her pillow.

~ ~ ~ ~ ~

She was very, very cold. Chilled through and through.

Her mother seemed to agree. "Dear Coders, I don't remember it being so chilly this far south. We aren't going to make it to Lourdis at this rate before we freeze."

Her mother coughed twice, and shook off her daughter's concern. "I'm fine, baby. Just got a wee bit of a cold, is all."

If colds meant getting those angry red splotches and sores across her cheeks, the little girl never wanted to get a cold. Her mother hadn't been seeing well either, nearly taking the wrong road to where they wanted to go.

At least, the little girl thought that was where they wanted to go. Her mother had become obsessed with Lourdis, saying that was where they were from, which made no sense to the girl. She was from the castle, not some town way south. Where she played with V, and V's brothers tried to pull her tail.

Her mother knelt down and smiled. "I'm sorry, do give me a moment to breathe. I tire so easily nowadays."

The older woman focused on her daughter, and said, "Do you want to be with me forever?"

The girl nodded. Of course she did. Her mother was the only person she knew in this land.

Her mother held open her arms. "Then rest with me a moment, dear Sunay. I'm just so tired..."

Expecting her mother's warm embrace, she instead was jolted by an insistent shaking, though the girl figured it was because her mother was cold.

"Oh... Sunay... my dear Sunay... I will love you always my

~ ~ ~ ~ ~

"Miss Sunay? Ma'am?"

The shaking became more insistent, and that finally prompted the foxgirl to protest and demand whoever was doing it to leave her alone and let her sleep. Not that she was able to voice that protest coherently, and that sound encouraged her tormentor to continue.

"Please Miss Sunay... wake up... please wake up..."

Since sleep wasn't going to be an option, Sunay resorted to violence, swinging in the general direction of her tormentor with the back of her right hand. She was a bit surprised to see the first attempt held back by a fur blanket that she didn't remember putting on her, and her second attempt dislodged said blanket but tipped off her foe to move out of her reach.

Still sluggish, she blinked her eyes repeatedly to try and clear out the fog in her vision, the blur eventually taking shape in her cabin and a distinctly Garth-shaped figure.

"Whudd... d'ya... wan...?" the foxgirl snarled.

The deckhand was blushing furiously, and turned his head. "I'm... sorry... ma'am. But it'd been several hours... and... and... Miss Juno sent me down to check on ya. You didn't answer... so I came in. I'm so so sorry, ma'am. But you were so cold. So... I... uh... put the blanket on ya."

So that was where the blanket... oh dear.

The thought that Garth had seen her stark naked was only made worse by the fact that the blanket had been thrown back in her attempts to hit him, and that her chest was still completely exposed. With a yelp, she hastily clutched the fur up to her neck, and growled, "Well... thank ya muchly."

With Sunay's decency restored, Garth was able to look at her again, even if he was still flushed brightly with embarrassment. "Well... ya still didn't wake up and you weren't gettin' any warmer, so I was gettin' worried. I'm sorry, ma'am. I'll git goin' now."

Sunay's still rousing mind slowly put the pieces together, and she groaned at her own stupidity. Falling asleep in her condition was damn near the dumbest thing she could have done. Garth, unwittingly, might have just saved her from not waking up at all. "Dismissed. And thank ya 'gain."

"My pleas..." he began before quickly rethinking his choice of

74

words. "You're welcome, ma'am."

He retreated hastily before any more discomfort would have the potential to happen. Sunay took the return to privacy to force herself out of bed and get dressed, even though her every muscle protested the movement, and her eyes drifted back towards her very welcoming hammock.

The foxgirl resisted the urge, lifted the lid of her clothes chest, and retrieved a dry set of clothes. Dressing was simple enough, if slow, and another button near the collar of her shirt popped as she exhaled. Sunay sighed in defeat. She needed new clothes... preferably something that didn't need to be buttoned up in the front.

Gathering up her old damp clothes, she rolled them into a ball and dropped them outside the door of her cabin as she left to return to the deck. She ignored any looks from crew as she passed them, head forward and warding off any questions with a stern upraised hand.

She stumbled into the blinding morning light, the *Goldbeard* now far enough away from the South Gibraltar Islands that they were out of the blanket of smoke and ash. "How long was I out?" Sunay wondered.

Juno spun about and sighed in relief, "Oh thank the Coders yer awake! Garth was able ta wake ya up finally."

Sunay repeated her question. "How long was I asleep?"

"Only the night," Juno replied. When Sunay looked at her skeptically, the spidergirl shrugged and added, "I'm serious. The whole damn island's kinda... died... lately... I guess."

Sunay did notice that there wasn't nearly the same sort of rumbling or choppy seas that she would have expected, and that the southern islands didn't look that far off. She concurred with Juno's assessment, that the islands had lost a good portion of the "life" about them.

The foxgirl somewhat regretted calling off the investigators, especially since her gut told her the Void hadn't done any more advancing, and this was something that probably needed investigating. "The Lively and the Indomitable already bug out?" she asked.

Juno nodded. "Didn' need ta be told twice, either. Ain't faultin' ya either. Balco got a good look at the Aramathean ship that very nearly got eaten up. That's as close to tha Void as I ever wanna be, thank ya. Dunno how you kept your head together, considerin'."

"I dunno either, honestly," Sunay answered.

"Ya still look like warmed over hell, jus' sayin'. Ya gonna be okay?"

Sunay nodded slowly, the sunlight giving her a headache. "Gonna have to be, Juno. Now you should get some sleep. You've been up all night, haven't ya?"

The spidergirl nodded indifferently. "I done longer. But it prolly wouldn't hurt to konk out for a little while. By yer leave."

Sunay forced her eyes fully open, blinking furiously, then pointed towards the stairwell. "Granted. Sleep. Now."

Juno retreated, and Sunay took command of the deck. She looked back again at the volcanic islands with concern, because even considering the Void... something wasn't right back there.

Chapter Five: Diversions

Ahmin didn't need a report by the time the *Goldbeard*
retrieved him in Beredon. "I already got word from both Captain
Roberts and Voria. I even heard word passed along the Aramathean
Navy about the Fire Fox saving one of their ships from certain
destruction."

Sunay groaned in dismay. That damned name was catching
on.

"You did well, Sunay," he continued. "Considering the
unforeseen circumstances, you put priority on lives rather than
investigation. Every administrator is in agreement that you are to be
commended."

The foxgirl blushed, and rubbed the back of her head. "Well,
thank ya, I guess."

Ahmin walked past her and onto the center of the deck, taking
a slow spin around with a wistful sigh. He chuckled once and said, "I
think we've earned a bit of a break, don't you think?"

Sunay's mind began racing with the possibilities. Terrasa was
a handful of days away by horse... depending on how long the leave
was for...

Ahmin stamped out Sunay's thoughts with a guilty frown. "I
know what's on your mind, Sunay... but I hate to say you have business
to attend to. I need you to go to Kartage. There's a cart and horse
waiting for you just outside of the east wall."

"Kartage? What for?"

There was that twinkle in Ahmin's eyes, the playful one that
told Sunay he wasn't telling nearly as much as he really knew. "New
sails for the Goldbeard, special order and very expensive. About time
we changed the main colors. The old ones, even the alternates, are
getting too recognizable."

Sunay didn't pretend to hide her contempt. "An'... ya need *me*
to do this, now?"

"I just know you are required to be present."

Like hell that's all he knew. She glared, snarled, and said,
"Right..."

Ahmin's smile behind the mask never wavered. "You'll have
time to visit your old family once you get back. I promise. But I really
need you to do this for me."

Sunay gave her admiral another skeptical glare, before her

features softened in defeat. "All right. Outside the east wall, ya said?"

"Yes, ma'am."

She slumped off with her tail dragging along the street despondently. "You better not be lyin' to me," she grumbled with one final snarl. She hadn't seen Matron Miriam, Kaeli, or the bratlings since she and Ahmin visited years ago. Granted, she got and sent letters to the orphanage all the time, but it wasn't the same. And she had barely had time to get excited about that visit before Ahmin stomped it flat with some stupid errand.

Stupid errand. Stupid tigerman. Stupid everything.

The cart she was looking for was surprisingly difficult to find considering the traffic coming in and out of the city. Fortunately, she did eventually locate her escort due to a familiar face.

"Well, hey, I remember you!" a rather well-endowed blond girl remarked, waving animatedly with a flower print yellow towel to get Sunay's attention.

It took a moment for the name and face to click together in Sunay's memory. "Uhhh... Negri, right?"

"That's me! I'm taking ya to Kartage, right?"

Sunay blinked rapidly, and replied, "I suppose so."

"Well, hop on in. I can't be gone too long."

The foxgirl sat down on the bench next to the stable-hand. "I thought ya were workin' for Dominus Socrato."

"Still am. Just on leave for the time being. Which is why I can't be gone too long now."

"Ah," Sunay said. "And so they got ya workin' while supposedly on vacation too, eh?"

Negri shrugged indifferently before flicking the reins to get the horses moving. "Yep. It happens. Not like I have anywheres to go anyways. Can't go home or nothing."

"Where *is* your home?"

Negri frowned sadly. "What's left of it is in Sparia. Nicine is its name. One of the last cities in the region to be independent before the Aramatheans finally pushed everyone out about ten years ago. Doubt there's anything left of the old place at this point. My family is scattered about the Free Provinces nearby at this point. Kinda hard to keep up nowadays."

"That sucks. And ya work for an Aramathean citizen on top o' that."

Negri pried her eyes off the road long enough to give Sunay a scathing glare. "I work for the Gold Pirates. Dominus Socrato is my mission objective."

"Well, I meant that yer watchin' the man that made the entire invasion of Sparia possible, ain't ya?"

Negri's focused returned to the road. "I guess. But that's kinda like blaming the blacksmith for the sword that was used in a war, don't you think?"

Sunay smirked. "You like the old fossil, dontcha?"

"I agree with my mission lead that he's not the menace he used to be. Wouldn't say I *like* him, but I wouldn't say I *hate* him either. He was a lowly citizen that sought to be venerated, and he was hellbent on that goal. It's kinda hard for people like us to really grasp love of country like that, I guess."

The foxgirl's mind caught on something Negri said earlier. "So, our folks have *multiple* people watchin' Socrato?"

Negri nodded. "Two that I know of. Probably more. I'm not supposed to reveal my association with anyone but the mission lead, and even that is through telepathy stone, so it's possible I've never met her in person. I'm even supposed to abandon the whole yellow indicator thing except when told, like when you showed up with the Dominus and now."

"Is that what land agents normally do?"

Negri nodded again. "If we have reason to believe our objective is at least generally aware of our existence. At least, that's as I understand it. I'm pretty new to the whole thing. This has been my first and only objective."

Negri bit her lip, and said, "Ya know... while you're at Lanka's Clothiers... you could probably get some new clothes. Lanka's always doing work for unusual sizes. She does a lot of my clothes at considerable discount because of..." she dropped one hand of the reins to gesture at her chest. "This. Lanka likes chesty girls. A little too much, I think... but you won't be bursting out of your shirt anymore."

Sunay blushed at the sudden turn in the conversation. "That... would be kinda nice. I..." the foxgirl gestured at her cleavage, "Well... as you can see..."

"Yeah. Embarrassing, isn't it?"

"Always."

"And of course, young men think you're asking for a 'good time' all because you can't keep your damn shirt buttoned up without damn near suffocating yourself."

"Or can't keep it buttoned up a'tall. Yer own crew looks at ya like yer a foot shorter than ya are."

"Even the girls?"

"*Especially* the girls. Juno loves pointin' out every time I pop a button."

"Well Lanka can fix that. I don't know how much money a sailor gets, but I'll bet you can work something out."

Sunay agreed to the suggestion. "I think I'll do that. Is that where we're going specifically? Lanka's Clothiers?"

Negri confirmed, "She does a lot of stuff on the side as a trader. She has access to rare materials that you can't find much anymore, like Cantan Silk. Stuff makes for great sails, which I understand is what she has for you."

Sunay knew that's what Ahmin liked the *Goldbeard's* sails to be made of, so that part of the story checked out at least. But she couldn't shake the idea that there was more to this entire errand than just some sails.

~ ~ ~ ~ ~

A series of slight delays the moment they crossed the imperial border meant that Negri and Sunay didn't arrive at Kartage until past sundown. Initially worried that they would be denied entry into the keep until the following morning, Sunay was pleasantly surprised to see the gate open.

Negri apparently found this odd as well. She presented her papers and asked, "While I don't want to sound like I'm complaining... what's going on?"

"Lunar eclipse celebration," the Phalanx soldier inspecting the cart said. "The Dominus invites those outside the keep for the party on such days. We're going to be manning the gates all night as people in the vicinity come and go."

"I feel for ya," Sunay said.

"Someone's got to do it, right?" the soldier replied before waving them through. "They're clear. Let 'em in!"

"Much obliged, sir," Negri said in parting, flicking the reins and clicking her tongue to get the cart moving again.

They kept to smaller, less occupied side roads to avoid the mess of people in the town square. Fortunately, Negri knew enough about the city within the keep that they didn't get horribly lost. "We need to come in through the back entrance anyway. That's where we'll be loading the cart," the stable-hand explained as they took a right turn.

They stopped in front of a run-down rear of a building, with what looked like what was *supposed* to be lines of flowerbeds, though actual flowers were sparse and not in the best of condition.

"The front of the shop isn't much better," Negri noted when she saw Sunay's expression. "But that's by design by what I'm told. She has very specific customers, and doesn't like encouraging 'ruffians' and walk-in customers."

A pair of double doors at the back of the shop opened, and a tall, black haired woman emerged in a sleeveless ruby red gown that shimmered in the flickering torch lights lining the road. "Ah, I assume you are the special order I was expecting!"

Sunay hopped off the cart to meet the greeting. "And I assume yer Lanka?"

The tailor's eyes widened at the sight of Sunay. "I am. And you... you... must come with me!"

Lanka grabbed Sunay by the forearm and tugged her into the store, through the storage space, and what looked like changing rooms. The foxgirl spun around to try and face Lanka, only to be held in place. "Don't move, dear. I must get some measurements."

Sunay felt a flexible tape wrap around her waist, then the broad portion of her hips.

"Arms up, dear," Lanka ordered, then measured vertically up the foxgirl's side, hip to armpit.

The tape then circled around Sunay's chest, then soon after Lanka's hands groped the poor foxgirl, who yipped in shock.

"Magnificent. We simply *must* find clothes to show this off!" Lanka exclaimed happily.

Sunay pushed the tailor's hands away and snarled, "No. We. Mustn't!"

Lanka had already moved to taking measurements of Sunay's legs, from calf to knee, then thigh to knee. "Stand up naturally, dear," she ordered again, before measuring between her legs.

From there, Lanka had moved to Sunay's tail, running her hands along the length from base to tip.

"Oi! Hands off th' tail, lady!" she protested, her face bright red and yanking said tail out of Lanka's grasp.

"Sorry, dear. That was horribly unprofessional of me," Lanka said in apology. "Just need two or three more measurements here..."

Those were done quickly: the circumference of her tail, as well as its position relative to her hips and waist. "And done. Come back in the morning."

"But..."

"You aren't going to be leaving until morning anyway. I'm sure your driver needs her sleep."

"What about the sails?"

"I have hands to deal with that. It'll be ready for you to leave in the morning. Come back then. There's a nice festival going on. Enjoy some of it."

Lanka pushed Sunay back out the way she came, and shut both doors. Negri was already gone, in her place seven very large, very well muscled and bare chested Aramathean men moving canvas covered rolls into the back of cart, their leather trousers held by bronze belts. One of them handed her a white envelope with a key inside. "Room 212 of the Gold Standard Inn. Go to the central square, cross onto Serenity Lane, and it's the first inn on the right. Huge Avalonian building. Hard to miss."

"Uh... thank ya?" the foxgirl said, before making her leave.

She really didn't have any desire to party. She really just wanted to get out of Kartage and back to Beredon as soon as possible. She kept her head down as she kept to the perimeter of the square, never more thankful that people on this part of the continent gave chimeras little notice than she was now.

At least until an unwelcome and familiar scent caught her nose, coming from the other side of the fountain, along with a voice that she knew as well. For a brief moment, she thought that her senses were deceiving her until she remembered that Ahmin had warned her that he had been transferred to Kartage.

Now Captain Daneid. That bastard.

This was probably a very bad idea, and Sunay knew it, but her anger wasn't something that was going to listen to reason. The foxgirl weaved through the increasing traffic and climbed up the fountain, wanting the higher ground to survey the scene to determine if she even had time and opportunity to pounce.

Quickly upon reaching her perch, reason allowed her to admit there wasn't going to be room for a fight that didn't wind up hurting a lot of other people instead. The square was even *more* packed on the other side of the fountain. But that didn't mean she could walk away, because that ball of slime was currently right below her, offering wine to a slight blonde haired girl that couldn't have been any more than twelve.

"Of all o' the..." she grumbled, clenching her jaw. Was this man shaped by the Coders solely to prod her every moral sensibility?

Finally she shouted, "Oi! Cap'n! Shouldn't you be playing

with someone more your age?"

Both the girl and Daneid looked up at her, though Sunay didn't give the girl much thought. She was far too focused on the Phalanx captain.

He jumped to his feet as Sunay dropped down to confront him. "You pirate scoundrel! When did you get here?" he demanded angrily, his jaw setting firmly.

Sunay lips curled. The way that Daneid used the term was intentionally grating, lowering her to the average ruffian as an insult. Bastard. "Pirate? You can't prove nothin'. I come and go as I please, and I don't answer to you."

He repeated his question. "When did you get here?"

"When you weren't at your post. Whatcha gonna do about it? I haven't broken none of your laws. Don't plan to either. Though you could make me change my mind."

Daneid's fists clenched, and his eyes flashed in challenge. "Is that so?"

Sunay leaned forward and onto her toes to violate his personal space. "Yeah. If you're willing to explain to your men tomorrow morning how you got all scratched up, I'll fight ya right here and now. No skin off my teeth. I'd be back out roaming free by this time tomorrow."

That was probably a bluff. Something told her that Ahmin would be furious to learn she got incarcerated in Kartage fighting with a Phalanx captain when she had been trusted with a supposedly important errand for the *Goldbeard*. But Daneid didn't need to know that. As long as it got this creep anywhere other than here.

And that was when the foxgirl offered that alternative. "Otherwise, why don't you go back home and leave this little girl alone?"

As she had hoped, Daneid wasn't interested in making a scene. "One of these days, wretch, I'll see you in a dungeon, and I'll laugh," he snarled angrily, then said to the girl, "My lady, be careful with this one."

Sunay almost laughed at the thought, instead spitting at the retreating soldier. While keeping her focus on Daneid to make sure he was going to go and stay gone, she offered to the girl, "Feh! You gotta be careful with the likes of him! Aramathean men have some very loose definitions of consenting age, let me tell ya."

She took the bottle of wine, and figured she might as well remove the opportunity to get the child further inebriated. Though after a few swallows, she remembered it was Aramathean wine. How *anyone* could get drunk off this swill was a mystery to her.

Sunay looked at the bottle and frowned. It wasn't worth finishing. "Feh! Aramatheans can't make a good brew to save their lives. No bite at all." The foxgirl set it back down, and figured now was good as any of a time to make her leave. She had experienced more of this celebration than she wanted to. She spared one last concerned glance towards the little blond thing and said, "See ya girl. Watch out for the men around here."

The foxgirl hovered on the periphery long enough to see the girl be joined by another older Aramathean woman. Their interactions suggested they were friends, and freed Sunay's conscience from lingering too much longer. The foxgirl had enough partying for one night.

She realized just how tired she was by the time she stumbled into her reserved room. She quickly undressed, then slid under the thin covers. She hadn't experienced such a comfortable mattress in her life. The people of Kartage certainly knew how to live in style.

Sleep came easily, and it was a dreamless sleep at that, which considering how Sunay's dreams tended to go was a good thing as far as she was concerned.

~ ~ ~ ~ ~

Sunay had seen a collective hangover before... but she had never witnessed it on a city-wide scale. It was well past morning light by the time Sunay emerged from the inn, litter still strewn about the central square and the lamps still lit, though burning down, barely a soul on the streets except those who absolutely had to be, and even a good half of them were staggering like walking dead through the streets.

The foxgirl crossed the center square towards the rear of Lanka's Clothiers. Negri still hadn't returned as far as Sunay could tell, though the rear of the cart was now loaded with canvas rolls that would be the *Goldbeard's* new sails and strapped down with long leather segments that looped underneath the cart.

Sunay scanned the door for some kind of knocker, and failing one settled for rapping her fist against the door itself. There was a long stretch of silence to the point that she was about to knock again when the left side door opened, and Lanka stuck her head out.

"Ah! I was expecting you to come in the front," Lanka said.

"Oh well, come in, come in! I'm all done! Didn't need many alterations at all!"

The tailor again yanked Sunay through the door, and as the foxgirl asked, "Done with..." shoved a twine wrapped parcel into her hands.

"Go try it on," Lanka said happily, pointing to an open curtain in a side room. "Just pull the curtain closed and change! Once you've got it all on, I simply must see!"

Of course it was clothes. She had been warned that Lanka would do this, but was surprised that the tailor had been able to work so quickly. It at least felt more robust than the glorified string that Rola had tailored for her. Once inside the changing room with the curtain pulled she opened the parcel and gave it a good look.

It *looked* practical at first glance, though she wasn't used to dressing in layers. "Is there an under-wrap to this?" Sunay called out, not seeing one.

"Absolutely *not!*" Lanka exclaimed, astonished by the very idea. "That is not at *all* healthy or necessary!"

Sunay had tried working without a wrap. It rather stopped being viable when she turned fourteen. "But..."

"Just put it all on," the tailor insisted. "You will see."

The foxgirl undressed, then picked up a long sleeved cotton shirt that was both padded in the chest and loose over her torso, hanging down to the flare in her hips just above her tail. She then put on the trousers, with well tanned leather that fit snugly after tucking the shirt into the waistband and had a slot in the back where her tail could settle without chafing, then buckled closed just above.

She tested the freedom and movement of her tail, astonished that she felt no restriction at all. "Well... ya already won me over wit' the tail," the foxgirl said, then moved on to the corset.

Sunay had preconceptions about corsets, and found that the one that she wrapped around her waist fit next to none of them. It didn't suffocate her or constrict her or force her body into shapes that it wasn't meant to be, and the leather was sturdy and cured to be able to take some punishment. The laces were in the front, which allowed for her to handle tying it up herself, and when drawn and tied made for a snug fit that also created a firm yet comfortable fit for her chest.

"Oh Coders... this... is amazin'," Sunay muttered, awestruck by the freedom of movement and control. She finally felt like she was fully in control of her own body. Bicep wraps enhanced the fit even more, and the gloves and boots also tied closed for the best possible fit.

No more popping buttons. No more squashed breasts or maddeningly compressed thighs. This was heaven.

She emerged from the changing space, and Lanka clapped happily. "Perfect! I think you'll enjoy that outfit! That is Daynish Wolfen Leather, my dear. Very difficult to trade for and only properly tanned in a couple of cities. Take good care of it and it will take good care of you for a very long time."

Lanka retrieved more three more parcels on a nearby table, saying, "Here are extras. You may try them on for a fit if you'd like, but I am confident in my work, and if you are happy with the one you are wearing, the others will fit just as well. Feel free to leave those rags you were wearing. I'll dispose of them, likely with fire."

Sunay took the three sets and said, "I'll trust ya. But... this can't be cheap. I don't exactly have much money."

"Already paid for, and I know the credit among your peers is good."

Sunay's eyes bulged. "You..."

Lanka shushed her with a finger. "Let's not make assumptions, shall we? Now off you go. I suspect your driver is ready for you."

That was as close to a confirmation as Sunay was ever going to get, she figured, and so with a polite bow and parting, she stepped out the back doors where Negri was indeed waiting. "Wow, you look nice!" the stable-hand complimented.

"You were right," Sunay acknowledged. The foxgirl took a deep breath, and exhaled it in satisfaction when she could do so without any straining cloth getting in the way. "It was worth it."

Negri clicked her tongue and flicked the reins to put the horses into motion. Sunay, for a brief moment, forgot about being bitter about making this side trip, and had to force herself to feel guilty about that admission. But it was fleeting. Friends and family were wonderful... but well fitting clothes were the definition of bliss.

~ ~ ~ ~ ~

The return to Beredon was fairly short, Ahmin didn't even let her get on board before he spun her about and pointed down the docks. "We'll take care of all this. As promised, you have another week to yourself. I'd recommend getting to the north road. Your escorts have been waiting rather patiently."

Sunay took off in a sprint, any demands she would have made

about Ahmin's secrecy forgotten as she dropped to all fours and tore through the town. She had a strong suspicion about who her escorts were, and wasn't the slightest bit disappointed to see Rola, Law, and Laron waiting for her with broad conspiratorial grins.

"There's our favorite Fire Fox!" Rola chirped.

Sunay was too happy to be cross, hugging the wolf spirit warmly and giving similar sentiments to Law, who went stiff as a board at the contact until he confirmed a lack of jealousy from his wife. The foxgirl then plastered herself on Laron, kissing him quickly before trying to climb into the cart.

Rola stopped her as Sunay had one foot on the bench. "I think this time, I'm going to have to *insist* you take a seat in the back of the cart," Rola said with an impish grin.

Sunay understood why, as Laron was already leaning back into the cart bed, and the foxgirl figuring out why when she circled around herself. "We're delivering down comforters to Matron Miriam's orphanage," the apprentice said. "There's some rainbow pomegranates next to my head that Kaeli wanted, but the comforters are the big thing."

Sunay dropped down next to him, where he rolled onto his side and circled his arms around her waist. "I haven't been to the orphanage yet."

"They've been worried about ya," Sunay said.

"I know, but it didn't feel right just dropping in. It's not like they didn't know I was okay or anything. I only wanted to be with you when I made my return."

Sunay was already in full relaxation, closing her eyes, her arms under her head, his breath on her cheek, though she sensed his gaze was focused somewhere else. "Ya can stop starin' at my breasts anytime."

"Noted."

If her breathing slowed, and the rise and fall of her chest more pronounced, Sunay would swear up and down it was coincidence. "Ya can see right down my shirt, can't ya?" she said flatly.

"Yes. I like the outfit, by the way."

"I'm sure ya do. It was expensive as all hell, I'd wager. Doubt my admiral's gonna be happy wit' that bill. But 'ey, he sent me. His fault."

His arms around her waist tightened, and he kissed her neck. Sunay playfully swatted him. "Down boy. At least... for now."

Laron rolled onto his back, though he kept his right hand

around her. "Very well... I suppose it would be awful inappropriate to get too frisky, especially on goods meant for the orphanage."

"They can be cleaned!" Rola offered helpfully.

"If only your mind could be so easily," Law added with a grumble.

Sunay wriggled into the down filled blankets, getting real comfortable for what she expected would be a potentially bumpy ride, both in the road and in her company.

~ ~ ~ ~ ~

She would be wrong, as outside of a handful of playful spats between Rola and Law, there wasn't much drama at all on the road to Terrasa. It was arriving at the orphanage when things started to get rowdy.

It was sometimes hard to grasp that it had been about seven years since her time in the run down orphanage outside of Navarre, and nearly three since her last visit. That fact came crashing in her face at the sight of a teenage Megan slamming through the door happily.

She was damn near as tall as Sunay now, and probably twice as strong as the doggirl lifted the foxgirl right off the ground with her hug. "Sunay! You're back!"

The doggirl then saw Laron, and pounced again, tackling the merchant's apprentice to the ground. "And about time *you* showed your face!"

Laron tried to laugh away the accusation. "I'm amazed you *remember* my face considering how rarely it appeared."

Megan sniffed in Sunay's direction, eyes narrowing. "I don't see a ring on her finger, mister."

Laron said in his defense, "I offered earrings. A very valuable family heirloom at that. She's wearing one right now."

Megan locked eyes with Sunay, and said skeptically, "Is this true?"

"I suppose so," the foxgirl replied, gently cupping the earring in her hand, rather self conscious by the thought that she had exposed such a valuable piece of jewelry to open sea air for years.

"I'll give her the other one and have a formal ceremony when we're both ready to settle down," Laron finished. "But that's going to be some time yet."

"Well hurry it up!" Megan ordered. "She ain't going to stay young and give you lots of babies forever!"

Sunay flushed bright red, but only because she guiltily had similar thoughts herself, even if they weren't horribly fair. It's not like *she* was ready for a husband and a room full of bratlings yet, either.

"I'll worry about the litter when there's a safe place to have them," Laron explained rather firmly. "It's a work in progress."

Megan huffed, and climbed off of Laron, retreating back towards the orphanage. "Well, the Matron will want to see the both of you, I'm sure. If for any reason than to cuff you both upside the head for being away for so long."

Laron helped himself off the ground, rolling his neck, saying more to himself, "Clearly. That girl was barely up to my chest the last time I saw her."

Sunay put a hand on his back, and led him towards the front door. "Well, let's get the rest of 'em outta the way. 'Cause I bet Megan ain't kiddin'."

Miriam was waiting right across the threshold, arms crossed and a judging expression, looking every bit as cross as Megan implied. "I was wondering what all the racket was about. About time you drug yourself back here."

Sunay felt like a scolded child again, and didn't like it. "Hey! Believe it or not, it's not easy getting extended shore leave!"

Miriam dismissed Sunay, and pointed at Laron. "Not you. Him. I know for a fact he has been in Terrasa twice a year."

The foxgirl could never figure out how Laron was able to stand up to Miriam without the slightest hint of intimidation. "You knew I was well. I didn't think it would be proper to return without Miss Sunay as an escort. I seem to recall that being one of *your* rules, Matron."

Miriam was undaunted. "You remember incorrectly, nor would those rules apply once we were no longer under threat of the torch, and you know it."

If Sunay didn't know any better, she'd have thought Miriam and Laron *enjoyed* the sharp tongued tit-for-tat. "It's dangerous to assume rules have changed without an invitation that they have. Since you are aware of my twice-annual visits, it seems odd that you didn't reach out yourself."

The annoyance in Miriam's voice grew despite the curl of her lips in a resigned smile. "You are learning *far* too well how to mimic that wolfgirl's clever tongue," she said, finally giving both him and Sunay welcome embraces. "Let's get you inside and something to drink in your hands before said wolf finishes giving Kaeli whatever she has now and drinks our entire pantry dry."

Miriam led them into the main room, sitting as she herself poured out a light red wine. Rather than do the rounds to greet everyone, this allowed for the rounds to come to them, happily sharing stories and greetings, or introductions to the larger number of unfamiliar faces, including many non-chimeric children.

"The number of chimeras without homes here in Terrasa are dwindling," Miriam explained when Sunay voiced the observation, "but there are children of all kinds throughout the province that find themselves without family or homes, especially lately. It was decided three years ago that this orphanage would be open to all who need a bed, full bellies, and a roof to keep them warm and dry."

"I'm sure such a 'sacrifice' also has some political capital for neighboring city-states who are having population influxes from refugees of their own," Laron noted.

"Perhaps, but that's not something I concern myself with," Miriam retorted testily, her eyes narrowing at Laron for the implication that she was acting in any way outside of politically neutral. She shifted the topic, asking Laron, "Speaking of people up north, how is your family doing? I assume they've relocated somewhere with all the uncertainty?"

Sunay showed concern to her paramour as he instantly looked downcast. After three long, steadying breaths, the merchant's apprentice went into surprising detail considering all the matters of his family, including his mother's apparent desire to die at the hands of the Daynish army that seemed to be forming.

Miriam absorbed that news solemnly. "Sometimes, that is what people get reduced to after too many heartbreaks in such a short time, especially for those who had wealth and privilege and lose it all very quickly. I am sorry to hear that, especially since her chosen way won't be merciful nor a slow withering away. The Daynes kill violently and quickly."

She gulped nervously, her fingers absent-mindedly playing with the rim of her wineglass. "I was but a young sister in the church when the last Daynish Campaigns happened. Such tragedy that was felt for decades even after the conflict ceased. The resources and money and men that Avalon threw at the menace paved the path for the violent revolution that usurped the crown. I dread the thought that such days are coming again, especially if they are organized in the way you claim."

Sunay offered comfort, leaning between their chairs and

putting her arms around Laron's neck. She had heard his story before, but it still hurt to know how it hurt him. She remembered all to well her own dread about the fate of the people in this very orphanage, and she could only hope and pray that Laron would have similar relief in time.

Kaeli skipped into the main room, and with deceptive speed dashed to Laron and kissed him on both cheeks. "You are a true *darling!* So much so that I'll forgive you for not visiting sooner!" she straightened, spun about, then skipped back towards the kitchen, singing sweetly about, "sugar cookies with pomegranate jam."

All three occupants looked at each other in confusion, until Rola appeared with the explanation. "I told her the sack of rainbow pomegranates was Laron's idea," the wolf spirit said, approaching the locked pantry where Miriam kept her collection of spirits, wines, and liquors. "Figured it would take the edge off his absence."

Expert fingers popped the lock open, retrieved a tall glass and a bottle of Timin amber whiskey, poured a fourth of the bottle into the glass, locked the pantry again, then left the glass on the bar in front of the pantry as she slumped into one of the empty chairs near the fireplace with the bottle.

"Rola," Miriam said tersely in introduction.

"Miriam," Rola chirped back happily before taking a long pull on the bottle.

The matron took the battle she felt she had a chance at winning. "I hope you weren't planning on leaving that glass out where any child could take it."

Rola pointed lazily towards the hall to the kitchen as Law stepped through. "There you are, matron; the comforters you requested. If I may be so bold as to ask for a drink?"

Miriam sighed and gestured to the pantry bar, and said, "I do believe your wife has already prepared that for you."

Law's eyes brightened and he worked around the perimeter of the room to take the glass. "Wonderful!" he said in satisfaction, then sided up to Miriam, reaching into his left breast pocket. "And before I forget..."

He emerged with a small brown velvet sack that jingled with what Sunay figured were some extremely valuable coins. Miriam exhaled slowly in reluctance even as her eyes betrayed her interest. "You *do* understand that you are under no obligation to give me or my orphanage money with your every visit?"

Law answered, "Of course we do. But we give it anyway."

91

Miriam held out her hand to accept the donation, and said with genuine gratitude, "Thank you."

"It is our pleasure, I assure you."

Law took a seat across the fireplace from his wife. "Our normal road is already being disrupted with the latest developments in the north," he said after taking a long sip. "Daynish scouts have been seen crossing the Dead Lands, which is *not* something they are generally willing to do. It's got everyone in the Northern Free Provinces all worked up. Avalon has been steadily building reinforcements at their northernmost settlements. It looks bad."

Miriam sighed. "You've been saying that every year for the last three."

"I know. And *that's* what worries me most of all."

Sunay didn't follow the logic. "Wait... yer worried there *haven't* been any attacks?"

Law gave her a stern glare. "The Daynish actions have been premeditated. This isn't the behavior of independent raiding parties. This is coordinated. They are assessing the strength of their neighbors. They're turning up at strategically important locations."

Rola agreed with a nod. "The Daynes are enough of a threat as a mess of loose tribes fighting themselves as much as everyone around them. A united force could throw the entire continent upside down, especially with the Winter Walkers gaining more and more sway as more and more of the spirits of the wilds are killed."

Rola and Sunay shared a brief glance. Sunay could see the fear in the wolf spirit's eyes, the first time Sunay could remember Rola displaying such an emotion. It made the foxgirl's blood run cold... this was something deathly serious. "Is there anythin' we can do?" she asked.

Rola shook her head, and replied, "You have your duties. If there's any way the fleet can be of help, Law or I will be sure to let you know." She clapped once, and declared, "Now... let's move on to happier subjects, shall we? For example, Miriam dear, tell us more about Stevens!"

"Who?" Sunay asked.

Miriam glared at Rola angrily. "A refugee from the north who doesn't seem to understand the sisterhood's vows of celibacy. And the wolfgirl here knows that."

Rola scoffed in distaste. "Celibacy. Such a ridiculous 'virtue.' Probably the worst of the lot, really. Depressing how humans create an entire set of morals to deny experiencing everything the world has to offer, then call it a virtue. Bah!"

"Okay... *different* different subject." Sunay interjected with a raised voice. She turned to Laron with a sweet smile, and asked, "Tell us about your efforts to secure a plot of land."

Laron shrugged. "I'm starting to think of *where* I want to settle down. I want it to be somewhere in the Free Provinces, along the southern coast, but with all the uncertainty and refugees, it makes even *finding* a good location, much less making a claim extremely difficult."

He frowned, then added with more hope, "But there's chatter going on in Southern Avalon. There is talk of the entire Versilles province declaring itself independent, growing increasingly angry at the heavy taxation by the Parliament as they gear up for the Daynish threat. Depending on how that susses itself out... if it declares itself a Free Province, the area around Lourdis would be amazing for trade... for a family..."

He offered Sunay a sideways glance and warm smile, patting her on the knee. "But we'll see how that all shapes up. Still want to save up a bit more money yet."

Kaeli entered the room, with some pomegranate lemonade and appetizers, little pastry rolls wrapped around sausages. With the vittles occupying mouths, talk became more sparse, then abandoned completely as dinner was announced.

Miriam offered lodging after dinner, and she warily stared down Laron when he declined, saying he already had reserved a room elsewhere. She became even more displeased when Sunay offered to escort him, and promised she'd be back in the morning.

And her blood pressure *really* shot up when Megan called out to the retreating pair, "Are you gonna sex her up or what?"

Sunay stopped and turned long enough to see Matron Miriam drag the doggirl back into the orphanage by one of the girl's ears, the foxgirl laughing as she jogged back to Laron's side.

He smirked once they were out of earshot of the scolding matron. "You did that on purpose to get the ol' matron's dander up, didn't you?"

Sunay looped her arm through his elbow, and pressed herself up close. "Only partially." She saw his questioning look and added, "You've... had to deal with so much... with your mom... the rest of your family... Law and Rola are scared about the Daynes... a whole buncha stuff that's not happy."

Her fingers danced along his forearm, and she blushed, dropping her head. Biting her lower lip nervously, she added, "I want to... give ya somethin'... somethin' to look forward to... somethin' that puts a smile on yer face for once. And considerin' that at this point, it's not a matter of *if* we up an' get married but *when*... I... uhhhh..."

Laron stopped her, kissed her soundly, and asked with a lopsided grin, "Are you sure?"

Sunay only nodded, and leaned her head into his shoulder until they reached the front door of the inn. From there, Laron checked in and led her up the stairs, then through the door, hanging a "Do Not Disturb" sign on the knob as he closed it behind them.

~ ~ ~ ~ ~

There was this idea that true love made everything amazing... that your first experience was this magical thing where you knew exactly what to do... somehow... that you let your instincts take over and that the entire act would sort itself out.

That idea was... inaccurate at best.

Sunay's first sexual experience had been clumsy, awkward, and painful... but not in the expected way. She suspected she was going to learn she had a nasty bruise on her forearm when it smacked against the bed frame, and Laron would likely have a nice bit of color on his abdomen where she kneed him. Not to mention that she drew *blood* across his back several times. She didn't want to know what other damage she did over the course of the night.

But if Laron was in any pain, he didn't seem to mind too much. She could feel his breath on her neck as he spooned firmly against her back, his right arm looped under her shoulder, and his left over her waist. Her tail lay over his hip and curled into the small of his back.

At least *this* part of the whole debacle felt comfortable, if boring. She still didn't want to move, though... not wanting to wake him when he finally looked the closest to at peace since they were still bright eyed kids drinking lemonade and talking about running away together.

The foxgirl felt her love's breathing shift, followed by his arms tightening, and his voice mumbling groggily, "Morning, my dear. Have you been awake long?"

"Nah," she replied, while internally adding, *only an hour or so.*

"We probably should get about our business," he said reluctantly, even though he didn't exactly make any move to go about said business.

"Yeah... I gotta get back to my ship... I guess."

Laron nuzzled then nipped at the back of her neck, asking suggestively, "Think they'd be disappointed if you ran an hour later?"

Sunay smiled, and teased, "*Someone* has a bit of an inflated sense of his prowess."

He moved swiftly, rolling on top of her and pulling her arms over her head. She could have rather easily slipped out of the hold, but instead pretended to be helpless. "Oh? Gonna try to prove me wrong now?"

He released his hold, kissing her, and then saying earnestly, "Thank you. For everything."

It didn't exactly take an hour... they were quickly getting better with practice...

~ ~ ~ ~ ~

Rola spent near the entirety of the return to Beredon talking about Sunay and Laron's affections. It got to the point where even Laron finally had enough.

"Madam Rola... could you *please?*"

The apprentice rarely, if ever, spoke out of turn when Rola was rambling. That he did now earnestly surprised the wolf spirit. Her eyes widened in surprise, and she tried to recover. "Well, it's like I'm watching my favorite child grow up before my eyes!"

"I understand that," Laron said with a measured voice that leaked annoyance, "but at this point, I think I am well aware as to what I have done. As is Law and probably the entire trade line at this point."

Sunay actually felt bad for Rola as the wolf spirit visibly slumped in defeat. The foxgirl understood why Rola was rambling. It kept her from thinking about more troubling things, this sort of teasing was her distraction from the gravity of the impending extermination of her kin.

She poken Laron on the arm, and said gently, "Now, love, ya know Rola don't mean nothin' by it all."

"No, he's right," Rola replied, suitably chided. "We should part ways more amiably anyway. Still no guesses as to what your Admiral is planning?"

Sunay shook her head. "Honestly haven't spent much time thinkin' about it. I ain't gonna guess right no matter what, and ain't no

95

point in tryin'."

The merchant trio *insisted* on taking Sunay straight to the docks, which got all her suspicions tingling that the only person who didn't know what this surprise was about was *her*. The cart pulled right onto the boardwalk, and damn looked like it was going to go straight up the gangplank until it turned ten feet short and came to a stop.

All three smiled broadly at Sunay, and she glared at them as she jumped out of the back of the cart. Ahmin was waiting at the end of the gangplank, and led her up to the deck. She could see his lips turned upward even with his damned mask.

At this point, the foxgirl was just annoyed. "Alright. Out wit' it. What'd ya do?"

Ahmin cupped his hand around his mouth, and shouted, "Let 'em go, Juno!"

A second later, the sails started unfurling from the from the front to the back... and nothing like Sunay was anticipating. She was expecting some variant of black or gold... instead she saw a dark burnt orange, marked with a white stylized fox complete with a fluffy tail curled in a rising arc.

"What the fresh hell is this now, Admiral?" Sunay asked, turning to Ahmin in accusation.

Finally, the tigerman let Sunay in on the big secret. "The Goldbeard needed new sails for its new Captain."

"Say wha?" Sunay screeched. "What's happenin' to *you?*"

Ahmin chest heaved and he said, "I'm being... reassigned. I'm needed for a mission on land for an indeterminate period, and it wasn't right to leave for Coders know how long and just have you as the acting Captain. I insisted to my fellow Administrators that if they were going to use me, then you needed an official, permanent promotion."

"And ya didn't think to consult with *me* about any of this?"

Ahmin chuckled. "Are you going to say no?"

Sunay frowned. "Now, I didn't say *that*..."

"I felt confident enough in your reply that this one time I decided it would be more fun to see the look on your face," Ahmin explained in apology. "I know that I normally make a habit of keeping you as informed as I am able. I hope you don't think ill of me."

The foxgirl slapped him on the shoulder. "I can't possibly think any less of ya than I already do."

Ahmin clapped her on the back, and caused her to stagger. "That's my girl! Now, follow me to your new cabin. There are many things I need to tell you before we part ways and you take full command."

Before she could do that, Laron hugged her happily from behind. "Congratulations, love!"

Rola tugged him on the sleeve of his shirt. "Now boy, let the girl get her bearings. We have things of our own to do."

"I'll catch you again!" Laron said in parting, smiling broadly. "Try and write more, will you?"

Sunay smiled and waved in silent confirmation before jogging towards the stairs to catch up to the Admiral. He was already in his cabin by the time she hit the third below deck, and she skipped inside just before he closed the door and locked it shut.

He crossed his cabin to the curious steel cabinet she had seen oh so many times during her time on board, and said, "Really... the only thing you have to learn about is this. Come here, I'll need your hand."

Sunay complied, taking Ahmin's side in front of the cabinet. He placed his hand on the door, and it left a glowing red imprint of his hand. He motioned to that imprint and ordered, "Place your hand right there."

The foxgirl did as instructed, watching Ahmin's red hand-print turn into her smaller, white one that flashed three times before vanishing as if it had never been there. "And now the cabinet is set to you, and only you," Ahmin declared.

He handed her the key to the lock, and added, "To anyone else, it will appear as a regular old steel box. To you, it is where you will get any and all pertinent materials for whatever missions you are assigned to by the new Admiral of the Fleet. Normally, you'll get a little... feeling... in your head when you've got new orders, but why don't you try it now?"

Sunay regarded the key in her hand, a remarkably simple thing made of silver with two square teeth. It didn't go into the lock particularly smoothly, requiring a considerable amount of pressure to get the teeth to fit into the notches within the lock, but the lock itself popped free smoothly and allowed for Sunay to flip open the doors.

Sure enough, the depth to the cabinet was far greater than what its position on the wall would suggest, followed by that nauseating tingle of the Void that made her initially recoil. Ahmin noted this reaction, then looked to the cabinet. "Yes... I had forgot about that. I am sorry, I had become so used to it that I no longer give it any thought."

"It's okay." Sunay mumbled swiftly, forcing herself to get right up to the cabinet. Inside was what looked to be a small mirror, standing on a base. As far as she could tell, it was the only object there, and so Sunay took it out, and held the base in both hands before taking it to table and setting it down.

"Ah, so Roberts wants to speak with you personally," Ahmin said. "Normally, I just send letters so that the various captains can get to the matter on their own time."

The mirror stopped reflecting Sunay's image, and replaced it with what she now guessed was *Admiral* Roberts aboard the *Indomitable*. "Good day to ya... Captain."

Sunay offered a half grin, and replied, "And to you... Admiral."

"I take you got everything I sent you?" Ahmin asked over Sunay's shoulder.

Roberts nodded. "If I need anything else, I'm sure the Higher Administrators can supply it."

Sunay looked around the cabin and then said, "Surprised ya didn't want the Goldbeard to run the operations as Admiral."

Roberts scoffed. "I wouldn' want dat floatin' fortress. Too visible, too much work switchin' around crews. Ya can keep that lumberin' monstrosity, and I wish ya the best of luck wit' it. Fer now, Captain, maintain yer current orders. I'm sure I'll have new ones for ya once I've sorted everythin' out. Good luck to you as well, Admi...nistrator Ahmin."

"I suppose that's my cue to get on task," Ahmin replied. He clapped Sunay on the shoulder. "I think you'll do just fine, Sunay. You've got a good crew that respects you enough to help me near around the clock to get this whole surprise ready. They'll serve you well."

"Ah, I know that already," the foxgirl growled playfully as the mirror shifted back to her reflection, and she put it back into the cabinet, then shut and locked the cabinet again. "But we're still gonna miss ya."

The tigerman nodded. "Hopefully, I won't be *too* far. I'll miss all of you, too."

She surprised him by hopping across the cabin and hugging him fiercely. "There's so many things that I wanna say, but I don't think I can make the words right." There were tears running down her cheeks, and staining his vest as she tried. "Ya been everythin' to me. Ya were my hero, my leader, my inspiration..."

Ahmin laughed nervously. "Well, you're doing good so far." He gently pushed her away, and opened the door. "I will do everything

I can to keep in touch. What I'm going to be doing will no doubt have an impact on the entire Gold Pirate operations, fleet included."

Sunay fell in stride alongside him. "And why ya can't say nuthin' about it?"

"Of course," Ahmin grumbled in distaste, "I'm going to be on land now, which means I'm not allowed to say anything about anything."

They shared a bitter chuckle, then emerged back onto the deck. Gurgn and the rowing crew began singing the same song they did when Jacques departed, though Ahmin desperately tried to wave them off. "You all be good for Sunay. I'll know if you give her grief!"

In the back of her mind, Sunay felt that tingle that Ahmin warned her about pertaining new orders, but she figured the new Admiral Roberts could wait a few minutes. There were heartfelt partings, especially between Juno and Ahmin. It hadn't really dawned on her how this would affect the spidergirl... but Ahmin was damn near the closest thing Juno had to a father. It would no doubt be something that would tug at her for a good long time, no matter *how* much she respected Sunay.

Well, the foxgirl figured to give Juno something that wouldn't give the spidergirl time to think about it much.

When Juno sauntered over to Sunay's side, she said saucily, "So... was *that* golden haired cutie from earlier the Laron who you were so hung up about? Lucky girl, you."

Sunay wasn't quite expecting *that* line, and any guilt she might have had for what she was about to say went out the window. "Ya know how ya hated the idea of gettin' more responsibility?"

Juno sighed in resignation. She knew what was coming. "Yep."

"Well, now ya ain't got no choice. Move yer stuff into the first mate's cabin pronto."

"I knew it." The spidergirl reluctantly trudged to the stairs with her shoulders slumped in defeat. Meanwhile, the tingle of incoming orders resounded again, and Sunay figured she needed to answer it sometime. "Gurgn, get yer team back down below. We're gonna be movin' out soon. Garth, make sure the sails are secure until Juno gets back topside. I'll be back shortly."

She jogged back down to her new cabin, pausing to look up at the unnaturally high ceiling. While she rather liked it, she also knew that space on a ship was precious, and that the massive head space she had could be put to better use. She'd have to consult a shipwright the next time they were in Grand Aramathea or any other larger port.

The foxgirl opened the cabinet again, and found the same mirror as before. Curious as to why Admiral Roberts wanted to speak to her in person again, she set the base down on the table once more and waited for the face in the glass to shift.

"What 'ave ya been doin'? Where is Ahmin?" Roberts demanded angrily.

"Sending him off, ya prat!" Sunay retorted angrily, torqued that the new Admiral would be getting high on power already. "He's good and gone now. Why'd ya need him?"

Roberts reigned in his anger, to his credit. "Damn it..."

"Why? What's wrong?"

"I got in touch with da Administrators," Roberts explained, "Ahmin... ne'er cleared *any* of dis wit' dem."

"Say *wha?*" the foxgirl yelped.

"There's no mission he's on. No one ordered him anywhere, much less to leave his post. He's completely dropped out of detection, Captain. Former Admiral Ahmin... has gone rogue."

Sunay's heart dropped straight through her chest and into her stomach. Had *that* been the *real* reason for all the secrecy about her promotion? But... why?

As Sunay's thoughts ran through her mind, Roberts continued, "I 'ave no reason to suspect ya of aiding 'is flight, if'n only 'cause I know ya were as unaware about all this as I was. I'm gonna trust that ya aren't helping him now, and sending ya and the Goldbeard back to Northern Avalon."

"What for?" Sunay asked.

"Apparently, dere's reason ta believe dat Ahmin is going north, and considerin' Northern Avalon is former stompin' grounds of 'is, he might 'ave friends and allies dere willing ta 'ide him. You'll be coordinatin' wit' land agents along da coast. Our primary mission right now, above all else, is ta find Ahmin and bring him 'fore the Administrators fer judgment."

Sunay's heart was heavy trying to understand this betrayal and what it meant. This was such a complete shift in mood from not even ten minutes ago that the foxgirl suspected her head would still be spinning a month from now. Had every sentiment the last two weeks been a lie? The last *year?* Since the *beginning?* Why show his hand *now?*

There was one way to find out, she supposed. "Aye aye, Admiral. We'll depart immediately."

Chapter Six: The Battle at Tortuga

Finding someone who didn't want to be found was difficult, apparently even when that person looked like a damned tiger. The *Goldbeard* had sailed up and down the coast of Avalon, north *and* south, for the better part of three months, coordinating with agents on land, searching suspicious ships, and being such a general pest that the Avalon Navy had finally been mobilized to curb Gold Pirate activities along their coastline.

At least, for the three months before The Daynish Campaigns officially started up again. At which point every available ship and able-bodied human being within the Republic turned to their northern border. But instead of their job being easier since the Navy was no longer actively harrying them... it was harder because of all the chaos within the country.

Land agents couldn't secure contacts, there were so many people streaming from the north at the last minute that the focus was on making sure families were still together and there were was food and blankets and other essentials for merely living in poverty.

Sunay and the *Goldbeard* actually tried to offer as much aid as could be spared. Sunay remembered living in just barely above squalor, with a makeshift roof over her head and a pile of straw to sleep on. So she made sure whatever space was available in the hold was filled with supplies from the south that she carried north with every sweep the *Goldbeard* made on their search.

They had just emptied out their stock of food, clothes, and blankets at Winter's Cape. Juno dropped the sails to full, and the *Goldbeard* caught the current going northward.

"Well should be at the current battle line by the week," Juno said as she dropped down to the deck. Despite her promotion to first mate, the spidergirl insisted on manning the sails because she claimed no one else could do it right. "Balco has orders to watch out for the blockade, because Coders know how it's shifted."

They weren't going that far north, as Admiral Roberts wanted to avoid any potential naval battles, but with how the battle lines shifted during the last Daynish Campaigns, where the navy set their line could shift with the tides.

"Good," Sunay acknowledged. Juno could damn well be a captain with how well she managed the ship. At times, it felt like Sunay barely did anything. Of course, it seemed whenever she thought that, something happened that demonstrated things that only Sunay had the authority or means to accomplish.

Like now, when she felt that very familiar tug of impending orders in the back of her mind. She wondered if Ahmin had been as micromanaging as Roberts was. With a resigned sigh, she said, "Watch the deck... I'll be right back."

Juno didn't need to ask, merely waving Sunay down below decks. "Tell Roberts I said 'ello."

Sunay chuckled, and chided herself for being so exasperated. It honestly wasn't like Roberts was doing a bad job, nor was he nearly as much of a nag as she liked to claim. He just... wasn't Ahmin, and that was horribly unfair for a good many reasons.

Most notably, he hadn't abandoned his post for Coders knows whatever reason.

Having talked herself down, she felt she could approach whatever orders Roberts had for her and her crew, but she was surprised to have all that effort wasted. Admiral Roberts wasn't the face that appeared through the looking glass.

It was Law.

The merchant had given no indication whatsoever that he even *knew* about this method of communication, much less had the means to *access* it. "Law... what in the...?"

Law looked frantic yet worn down. She could see the dark circles under his eyes and the worry that still was in them. "I know this is very peculiar, but Rola insisted I contact you because she couldn't trust anyone else."

"Okay... okay..." Sunay said soothingly. "Let's start from the beginnin', can we?"

Law took a deep breath, and while it didn't approve his appearance any, his voice leveled off. "Right. It began when Rola, Laron, and I made one last appeal to Laron's family in Valkalm. We knew we were cutting it close... but... but..."

"Law. Breathe."

"They came out of nowhere. I was watching, and *I* can't figure out how Rola beat them back. But she was hurt... one of the Daynish blades had a poison, and it's killing her. Laron and I have been stabilizing her condition as well as we can, but she's fading... slowly. I think I know where I can find help, but we need someone to get us through the blockade."

"Where are ya now?"

"Tortuga. Domina Morgana has granted us sanctuary, but

nothing else. The keep is nigh entirely surrounded by Daynes, and that damn blockade isn't letting any ship south."

Sunay's chest inflated with a deep breath. Sunay suspected Admiral Roberts had a much colder relationship with Domina Morgana than Ahmin did, and as a result felt no compulsion to aid Tortuga, either in terms of supplies or manpower, and why he expressly forbade any ships of the fleet to cross the blockade line. "Ya realize yer askin' me to defy a direct order, right?"

The desperation appeared in Law's voice again. "Please, Sunay... Rola won't let me approach anyone else on this matter. I really shouldn't discuss it, as it's not my place, but you have to trust me on this."

Sunay sighed heavily. There really wasn't any doubt what she was going to do here, even if it meant it was going to cause no small amount of drama with Admiral Roberts. "Alright. We'll make for Tortuga straight away. Keep Rola in as good of condition as you can in the meantime. And if you can, smack that Domina upside one and say it was from Admiral Ahmin. That might stir her to do more than be a miserly little creep."

Sunay trudged up the steps from the third deck to topside. Normally, a trip to Tortuga from here would only be about a week with the winds and the current, but getting around that blockade would make the trip much farther.

Unless...

She grabbed Garth by the collar as she emerged onto the main deck and asked, "Joffe up here or is he in his playroom?"

The deckhand pointed to the fore of the ship, and said, "He was up near the prow earlier, and I didn't see him leave."

"Excellent," the foxgirl said, then shouted, "*Joffe!*"

His much quieter response of, "Yes, ma'am?" drifted to her from the fore.

"Git yer ass over here! Juno, you too!"

The spidergirl dropped down from the rigging above about fifteen seconds before the craftsman appeared around the main mast. "Juno, how fast do you think we could go if we got into the current and full sail? Think we could outrun the Avalon Navy?"

Juno scoffed at the question. "Of course. Those boats ain't got nuthin' on us. Why?"

"We've been ordered to Tortuga," Sunay replied simply, leaving it implied that the orders came from someone authorized to do so, rather than a land based agent from the Free Provinces.

"Well, I doubt they'd give much chase if we broke the line... but how d'ya suppose to break the line? Last I heard, the navy was damn near lined up stem to stern."

"*That's* where you come in, Joffe," Sunay said, patting the engineer on the shoulder. "Whaddya think? Think there's a way to make those big candles you like into a weapon?"

This time, Sunay *liked* seeing that grin spread across his cheeks. "Oh... *can* I..."

~ ~ ~ ~ ~

Joffe's solution was put to the test two days later, as the ships of the Avalon Navy came into sight.

It was actually rather awe inspiring to see such a display of military might... large galleons as far as the eye could see in all directions lined up with barely enough between for each ship to maneuver if they needed to move. Smaller frigates and schooners zipped along both sides of the line to intercept smaller vessels that tried to slip through the gaps, but those were of no concern for a ship the *Goldbeard's* size.

"Alright, Joffe..." Sunay grumbled. "I hope this works, or this is gonna be one *real* short rescue mission."

"No one is going to be in them this time. Stopping and steering are hardly required," Joffe reasoned. "The timing is going to be crucial though. We want to be pushing through as the boats ahead have fallen apart but before the Avalonians have regained their wits and moved to close the line."

Sunay stepped back in deference to man who theoretically knew what he was doing. "Well, I'll let ya handle that, then."

Joffe called out, "Juno... are you ready with rocket number one?"

From over the railing, the spidergirl shouted, "Aye aye! Just lemme know when ta pull!"

The craftsman put his spyglass to his right eye, assessing their course. "Balco! Keep our heading steady!"

"Aye aye!" the helmsman replied. If he was the least bit nervous about proceeding at full speed towards the Avalon Navy, he wasn't showing it.

At this point, the Avalonians acknowledged the *Goldbeard's* presence and approach. Several of the smaller ships began to tail and come alongside the galleon, and Sunay heard a declaration from over the rail, "Unidentified craft, by the order of the Avalon Parliament, no ships are allowed past this point. Turn about now or drop sails and prepare to be boarded!"

Sunay lightly tapped Joffe on the shoulder and said, "Carry on. I'll handle this part."

She approached the railing to see a distressingly young Avalonian man in a formal officer's uniform at the railing of his frigate, a smooth face and coal black hair unweathered by the sea. He was new to his role, the poor guy.

"You are approaching a formal blockade, if you do *not* cease your course, you *will* crash into our ships. Do *not* think you're going to bluff us into moving!" he called up once he saw the foxgirl appear.

"We ain't bluffin'!" Sunay shouted down. "Ya seem like a good kid, so I'm only gonna warn ya once. Git outta the way or we'll make ya!"

Truth was, Sunay wasn't going to give them the option. They didn't have time for that even *if* the naval vessels were going to be so inclined. She just wanted to feel like she was doing *something* in regards to this whole insane scheme.

Then she heard Joffe shout, "Fire first rocket!" and the fun began.

There was the telltale hissing of one of Joffe's large candles, then the whoosh of the main stage ignition. The craftsman didn't waste time admiring his work, giving further orders. "Bolin! Adjust heading eight degrees starboard! Garth, get the second rocket lowered!"

Sunay *was* able to admire the coming carnage however, watching the rocket propelled rowboat skipping across the water, the path cleared of the smaller boats that had reacted to the *Goldbeard's* approach. Halfway to the target, Joffe ordered, "Fire second rocket! Garth, make sure rocket three is lowered in case we need it!"

It wouldn't be. Sunay's eyes widened as the first rocket reached its target, the fore of the rowboat colliding with the large galleon in its path a mere blink before the head of the rocket exploded with a towering plume of fire that nigh entirely engulfed the ship, tossing shrapnel so high that Sunay had to crane her neck to see a chunk of the target's main mast launch straight upward before crashing back down onto the rapidly crumbling vessel.

The waves created by the catastrophe even caused the *Goldbeard* to lurch. The smaller ships around it struggled just to remain upright, and several smaller schooners capsized. The waves *also* caused the second rocket to skip off the water's surface, but not enough off course that it didn't hit it target. It crashed into the second galleon mid-decks, slamming through the hull before detonating near dead center of the ship.

The location sent shrapnel flying in long arcs that caused Sunay alarm. "Heads up! Debris incoming!"

Fortunately, the larger pieces fell short, and what littered the *Goldbeard's* deck were smaller fragments and splinters that couldn't do much harm except to the unwary. Had the sails not been of very sturdy and high quality silk, Juno might have needed to make a few patches, but that would have been the extent of the damage.

"Straighten us out and make for the gap, Bolin!" Sunay ordered. "Let's see how many of them are stupid enough to try and follow us!"

That answer was predictably none, especially considering the fact that there was at *least* one more of those rocket boats hanging right off the edge of the *Goldbeard* and potentially aimed at any pursuers. Sunay's crew quite easily sailed through the wreckage without even needing to slow down on their way to Tortuga.

~ ~ ~ ~ ~

The Tower of Tortuga seemed to have lost its luster, though that was likely due to heavily overcast skies that were blotting out even the afternoon sun. But it wasn't until after she had rowed out to the docks and met Law that she got a full grasp of the situation within the keep.

The streets were packed to near capacity with refugees, makeshift tents strewn about and often blocking anything beyond two people wide from progress. "Domina Morgana has allowed in any seeking refuge, but she's done absolutely *nothing* to help people who come inside," Law explained. "The citizenry has done what they can, but I swear there's nearly three hundred thousand people here in a space that probably is best suited for a tenth that number."

The two had to fall into single file to get through the next choke point, and Sunay had to force herself not to look too closely at the tragic conditions all around. Because she knew if she did, every shred of compassion would take her mind elsewhere than where it needed to be. There was little she or her crew could do for these people... only the end of this war could do that.

They finally were able to push through the refugees, and onto the tower grounds, which were perhaps distressingly clear of people.

107

"You came at the perfect time... I don't know how much longer this keep is going to hold," Law said grimly, nodding to the guards that let him and Sunay pass into the tower itself.

"Whatya mean? Tortuga runnin' out of supplies?" the foxgirl asked in concern.

"It is, but *that's* not the dire concern. The Daynes have already attacked twice. This most recent assault actually breached the outer walls in two places. If the Daynes attack again, I don't know how the defenders will push them back."

"And Morgana hasn't even done anything about *that?*"

Law shook his head, grabbing the railing of the stairs that led upward further into the tower. "She hasn't gone below the seventh floor in the last month or so, by the account of the servants. Most of time she's out on the top floor balcony looking out to the east. After the latest line of appeals, she raised the stairwell."

The second floor of Morgana's tower was expectedly luxurious, rich dark wood walls and what looked like red velvet carpeting with rooms aligned all around the circle. It wasn't hard to figure out which room Rola was in. Laron was standing right outside the appropriate door, and nearly crushed Sunay in a hug once he saw her.

Sunay comforted him as well as she could. Just from implication, she knew that his family had most assuredly been massacred, and Rola had been grievously injured before being stuck here where it looked like the entire damn keep could be killed off any damned day.

"You need to see Rola," he said while his face remained buried in her shoulder. "You really do."

He released the foxgirl reluctantly, then stepped aside so that Sunay could again follow Law, this time into what apparently was one of the servant's rooms. The room was "plain" in regards to the rest of the tower, though from Sunay's perspective, anything with a bed and carpet and sturdy furnishings should hardly be classified as "plain."

Rola herself was in the bed, with the blanket rolled up to her neck. The wolf spirit would never be considered dark skinned to begin with, but this was a sickly pale tone even for her, veins of a sickly gray visibly running across her cheeks. She turned her head weakly in Sunay's direction, and said, "I see Law was able to use my connection after all. I figured I'd let him try because I didn't think the messaging system would authorize it."

"How do you have access to the system anyway?" Sunay

asked.

"Rola is the administrator for the Western Free Provinces," Law admitted, "though she goes well out of her way to prevent people from knowing that."

"I suspect the attack on Valkalm was intended for me, in retrospect," Rola said. "We had gotten word that Laron's family had finally changed their mind, but they hadn't."

"Why would the Daynes want ya?"

Rola coughed. "I'm not entirely certain it's the Daynes as much as the Winter Walkers. The Daynes at this point..." another bout of coughing and hacking interrupted her momentarily. "Anyway, I'm made out of sturdier stuff than they thought."

"There is a medic in Winter's Cape that specializes in poisons, a kindly old woman that Rola and I worked with once before," Law said. "How fast could you get us there?"

Rola finally pulled one arm out from under the covers, and settled it on Law's hand. Sunay felt a little embarrassed to watch the scene. Despite all of the grumbling and bickering the two displayed public, if the foxgirl had any doubt of the affection Law had for his wife, it would have been dashed seeing the desperation and dismay he had as he looked down on the bedridden wolf spirit.

"I am sorry that he drug you out this way, but what is wrong with me isn't something that can be fixed," Rola said to Sunay, though her eyes remain fixed on Law. "This is no poison like anything that has existed before. This is tainted with the Void."

Sunay had felt that queasy feeling in her stomach consistent with the Void, but had assumed it was the same lingering presence that she had felt the *last* time she had been in Morgana's tower. "But why?" the foxgirl asked. "Why target you?"

Rola shook her head weakly, "I only have guesses at this point, nothing concrete, and I certainly don't want to cast aspersions on anyone based on wild guesses."

"There was an administrative gathering after learning about the Void's advance on South Gibraltar three years ago," Law said, his jaw clenching. "Rola declined to attend because she finds those meetings dreadfully boring. But this... something was odd about it. Your former admiral was deeply disturbed by something that happened during it, but he went dark before he could consult Rola about it."

Rola chided her husband. "You're worrying the poor girl over things that don't concern her."

"Well, it concerns me now!" Sunay snarled. "I blew up two

Avalon ships to get here! I'll be damned if I ain't goin' back empty handed!"

The wolf spirit smiled wanly. "I have been truly lucky to have such wonderful friends."

"Now don't ya dare keep talkin' like yer gonna die here!"

Rola's ears perked, and she said, "Oh, I think we're *all* going to die here soon enough, my little fire fox."

Sunay heard it soon after... the screams of people dying and the bone-chilling thud of stone tumbling to the ground. An officer screaming out orders to abandon the outer wall and focus on the tower grounds and inner circle. The refugees were to retreat to the dockside, apparently to make them easier to defend.

Or easier to massacre.

"Won't be long now," Rola said.

"Like hell it will," Sunay growled, stomping back out into the central room and looking up at the closed off stairwell above.

"Hey you up there!" the foxgirl bellowed angrily, the volume causing Laron to wince painfully. "I know ya can hear me! So you open up that damn floor and you get yer ass down here!"

The Domina's response wasn't total obedience. The ceiling parted, and the stairwell rotated downward, but Morgana didn't follow it down. Sunay didn't waste time waiting, stomping up the steps angrily the moment the circular stairs locked into position.

The foxgirl was regretting that decision by the fifteenth floor. Why the hell do mages build their damn towers so damn high? Fortunately, the walls parted into an open aired observation deck two more flights higher, and Sunay emerged to see Morgana's back, the Domina standing near motionless out on an extended balcony off the east side.

"Good day, Miss Fire Fox," Morgana said amiably.

The foxgirl had to fight the urge to shudder. Morgana's creepiness wasn't going to be a factor here. No one could afford it right now. "So, this is how its gonna be? Stand up here and watch yer whole keep get razed to the ground?"

"Not much point to fighting," the Domina said simply.

"Why do you say that? No point? Every single person in this keep is gonna die!"

"It might be a mercy knowing what I know now."

Sunay grit her teeth, trying to block out the sounds of screaming and dying drifting up from the ground level. "And what do you know?"

110

Morgana finally turned. "That there is no escape from the Void. There is no redemption. This continent, what remains of this greater world, is a mere thin curtain draped over the Void. I knew this because I drew back this curtain many years ago. The Code that Dominus Socrato thinks will save us is merely the other side of that coin. There is no pushing back the Void. It's not advancing. It's already everywhere. And when the time comes, it will all end."

"Oh, and that's gonna be tomorrow, is it?" Sunay scoffed. "You make it sound like the Void eatin' everythin' up is some shocking story. Hell, I already know that. Every single Gold Pirate already knows that. But we're out there every day doin' what we can to keep this damn world going. Because every day that the Void doesn't swallow the continent up is a good day."

The foxgirl strode to the balcony, and with a bravery that she hoped to the Coders she looked more than felt, drew up face to face with the tall sorceress. Berating a woman of Morgana's power no doubt fell in the realm of extremely bad ideas, but it was a gamble Sunay was willing to take. "Now, yer gonna get your ass down there, and you're gonna fight for your keep like I know damn well you can."

She took and released a deep breath, and said, "Oh very well. I already defied that dark voice once. Might as well do it again."

Sunay didn't know or care what the Domina was prattling on about. She also decided not to make an issue of Morgana's negligence only to be swayed into action so easily. The most important thing was that Morgana was acting *now*. The rest could be punched out of her later if need be.

Morgana stepped around Sunay, back down the stairwell, the foxgirl giving chase as the Domina didn't exactly seem to be in much hurry. Sunay ground her teeth at the slow pace while fighting the rising sickness in her stomach. She wondered why until she saw a black circle appear in the floor where the stairwell would normally be. The foxgirl bravely fought through the coming surge of sickness until Morgana crossed the line and it vanished as she crossed it.

Morgana herself hadn't shifted either, and Sunay wondered what the hell had happened until she saw that the Domina was now holding a suspiciously familiar black book, this one with white trim and with an emblem of a triangle with an eye in the middle, along with a small red book tucked into her sash, and a brown leather satchel slung across her shoulder.

The foxgirl had to fight back another dry heave as *another* black circle appeared on the next floor down that brought them straight to the ground floor of Morgana's tower. Morgana flashed a teasing smile as she glanced back at the foxgirl and said, "You look a little green, my dear."

"Hush. You did all that on purpose, didn't ya?"

Morgana was unrepentant. "Of course I did. Your sensitivity to the Void wasn't exactly subtle. Now... you may continue to follow if you wish."

She didn't wait for Sunay to decide, taking purposeful strides towards the exit to her keep, coming five strides away before the door was forcefully kicked inward by a remarkably large Dayne even by their standards. He didn't get one step further as Morgana flicked her right wrist and quite literally flayed the flesh straight from his bones, said bone crumbling into a pearly dust and carried away by a gust of wind.

Two more were charging as Morgana crossed the threshold, and they were both similarly dispatched, as if peeled layer by layer until there was nothing left. The Domina surveyed the scene and the carnage, and frowned. Distastefully, she said, "Appears I need to clean up more than I should. What were my police *doing*?"

Sunay again bit her tongue. The Domina *was* out of touch with the world around her even in the best of situations by all accounts.

"This will not do at all," Morgana continued as if she were complaining about an inconvenience. Touching the white-covered tome, the Domina raised her head with her eyes closed.

Which was then followed by the most ferocious gale Sunay had ever experienced, even worse than the most massive typhoons she had encountered on the south seas. Yet the foxgirl remained rooted in place despite this, watching as entire parties of Daynes were rather forcibly ejected over or *through* Tortuga's outer wall.

Morgana followed as if she were on a casual stroll, her every step somehow finding a path in the rubble so that she didn't break her stride. The Daynes had assembled into ranks by the time the Domina crossed the nearest gap in the outer wall. Sunay didn't quite have the same courage, stopping *at* the wall and peering around the side. Had the foxgirl not known better, she would have thought it a bit curious to see an entire army in a standoff with a single, slight woman with nothing but a few books as weapons.

"I do believe I told you and your kin you were not welcome here twenty-nine years ago," Morgana declared. Even though it didn't seem like she was shouting, her voice no doubt carried all the way to the back of the ranks.

The Daynish response was... well... nothing. No bragging, no loud, boisterous yelling, no violent charge, completely running against any perceived behavior she had heard about the northern people.

Morgana didn't seem terribly concerned by this lack of a response. "I see. You are already gone. Not that I was going to have much guilt anyway, but this will be even less weight on my conscience. At least I don't have to make sure to spare one of you to send a message."

The Domina then reached around her back to the red-bound book, though didn't actually take it. Apparently, just the contact was enough for her to do what she wanted to do next.

Sunay had heard Ahmin talk about the day that the skies of Tortuga cried fire and ice. Even his spectacular telling didn't come close to what happened. First came the ice, hailstones bigger than Sunay's head crashing down on the army, shattering Daynish shields and bones. Even as the army fell in wide swaths, they refused to break, a tenacity that Sunay would not have figured even Daynes would possess.

Then came the fire.

There was a tremendous, earth shaking roar from above, then a flash of bright light as something streaked impossibly fast from above, smashing into the ground.

It looked like the world itself was being reborn in fire, a shockwave that ripped the already charred earth, casting boulders of molten rock beyond what Sunay could see. Somehow, everything behind Morgana was spared the cataclysm while everything in front of her turned to ash and lava. Anything that survived the first wave most assuredly didn't survive the second.

And yet... something did.

The flames bent around the solitary figure, a loose conglomerate of pieces held together by sinew of ghostly purple energy. A head, flecked with long blue white hair and beard rotated then bent back in something that resembled an upright position, its eyes flashing with the same dark power.

If Morgana was surprised by this development, she didn't show it. Her face remained impassive, her voice flippant. "Well, that's quite fascinating. I assume you are one of the Winter Walkers that I keep hearing about in whispers from the Daynelands?"

Just like the Daynes it commanded, the inhuman creature didn't speak, at least not in any words that Sunay could hear. Morgana, on the other hand, tilted her head in amusement. "Dispelled my magic,

113

you say?" she asked, opening her satchel and looking into it. She touched one of the books inside, and confirmed, "So you have. Quite fascinating. I can see why you'd think that I'd be in great peril."

Then Morgana finally retrieved her black book from where she had tucked it away, and all the whimsy in her voice vanished, replaced with cold anger. She snarled, "Fortunately, I have more magic than my own."

Compared to what she had seen before, the magic of the Administrator's Tome wasn't visually astonishing, but the effect was just as impressive, if not more so. The Winter Walker warped, twisted on itself, eventually vanishing into a single point that flashed brilliant white before leaving nothing.

A single page dropped from Morgana's tome, spinning about on a phantom wind before disintegrating. She slapped the book shut, and grumbled under her breath so discreetly that not even Sunay's ears could pick up what the Domina had said. Morgana passed Sunay on the way back to her tower, and said, "Since I've already had to waste a page, might as well waste another. Your wolf spirit friend is on the second floor, is she not?"

Sunay nodded, and said, "Uh... huh."

The Domina replied reluctantly, "Finding friendly administrators is extremely rare, especially now that your former Admiral has decided to abscond. I suppose now that Tortuga will stand for another day, I shouldn't be letting people die in my tower."

Sunay had moved from wanting to tell the Domina off for her abrasiveness to punching the woman. But along with biting her tongue, she stilled her fist. It wasn't worth making enemies, especially of someone so powerful that the foxgirl could be... erased with but a thought.

Morgana knew exactly where she was going, nudging a catatonic Laron out of the doorway. The young man was looking up, then down repeatedly, boggling even further when he saw Sunay emerge from the floor below. "How did...? I would have seen..."

Sunay put an arm around his waist, and replied soothingly, "The ways of mages are best not to think about. I assure you."

Morgana assessed Rola's condition, and clicked her tongue. "I'd expect someone of your importance would be more careful."

Even in her current state, Rola had a retort. "And I'd expect someone of your position to act sooner in defense of her land and people."

The Domina was *not* used to being talked back to, that much was clear. Morgana visibly bristled, and then replied, "Well, better late than never, especially for your sake."

Morgana once again opened the Administrator's Tome in her possession, and finding the page she wanted, cast something that was just as unimpressive at first glance as when she dispatched the Winter Walker. Yet the results were once again undeniable. The color near instantly returned to Rola's cheeks, the unnatural black veins vanished, and the wolf spirit's eyes lit up with amazement that quickly turned to suspicion.

She rejected Law's assistance, rising up on her own power and pushing the blanket off before spinning her legs so that she was sitting on the edge of the bed. "That's not power you should have, mage," Rola said darkly as another page fell from Morgana's book, and tumbled about before disintegrating.

The Domina was unrepentant in her reply. "And aren't you lucky that I do?"

"Clever how you dispose of the evidence of its use, at that."

"Indeed."

Morgana spun about on her heels. "Now, I suspect our little Fire Fox wants to berate me, and I will *not* tolerate such a display in the presence of others. So, if you will excuse me, I wish you to leave my tower immediately now that you and yours are in no need of my services or refuge."

The Domina flipped a finger, and said, "Come, dear Captain."

Sunay suddenly didn't have the desire to do or say anything to Morgana, but at the same time figured that Morgana no doubt had something to say to *her*. So the foxgirl complied, taking three flights of stairs up into what Morgana felt was relative solitude.

It was her study, the entire floor from wall to wall circled with books, littered with tables and desks in various states of disarray, a surprising state for a woman that Sunay would have pegged as keeping everything as neat and ordered as possible.

"I am in the process of moving everything I had from the floor above to here, do excuse the mess."

Sunay cringed. Ahmin had asserted this woman couldn't read minds, yet the foxgirl was repeatedly getting indicators that Ahmin was full of it.

Morgana smiled playfully. "Your former admiral is correct. I can't read minds, but I can read faces and bodies quite well. You've wanted to know what compelled me to finally come to the aid of those under my tower."

Sunay nodded slowly. "Yeah... was kinda curious what finally changed yer mind. I have a hard time believin' it was my little rant up at the top of yer tower."

Morgana's eyes dropped, and she laughed bitterly. "It was... in fact. You sounded so much... like him."

"Like who?"

"The last true king, Richard. Not that wastrel that somehow called him father. How such an incredible man birthed such a miserable wretch is beyond me. He talked like that, about honor and courage and living each day to the fullest because you won't know if it will be your last. And he actually believed that drivel."

Sunay snarled, "I ain't in a mood for stories right now, woman."

Morgana shook her head. "But what made him special was that for a short time, he made *me* believe it too. He gave me the strength to defy the chosen voice in my head. I'm sure you've heard your voice speak to you on occasion."

Sunay could, though the instance was one where it had been the right choice to follow. "What did it want you to do?"

"Cast what remained of the world into the Void," she said bitterly. turning back to the east. "I defied that voice, out of my love for a man I could never have. Now, it seems to have found a new avatar."

Rola's voice echoed up from the floor below. "Well, that's most interesting."

The wolf spirit soon followed, and Morgana did not even pretend to hide her distaste. "I do believe you were instructed to *leave*."

Sunay had never seen Rola in possession of an Administrator's Tome, nor where the wolf spirit would have hidden the large black book with a green wolf emblem that floated above her right hand. "Now now... I may not be a mage, but I can promise you I can use *my* book a lot more effectively than you can use *yours*."

"Didn't seem to help you much while you were poisoned," Morgana noted coldly.

Rola nodded, conceding the point. "While I was corrupted, I couldn't access it, that is true. But I am not now, am I?"

"Do you wish this one back then?"

"Oh no," Rola answered. "I think it's right where it can do the most good. I merely came up to inform you that there shouldn't be any more Daynish forces knocking down your walls."

Morgana's voice didn't sound the least bit curious, but her words did. "And why is that?"

"The other Winter Walkers were slain in Hrothstead."

That caught the Domina's interest. "By who?"

"An adventuring party lead by the mage Pirogoeth."

Morgana's eyebrows rose. "Pirogoeth, you say?"

Sunay's eyes danced back and forth between the two. "Who's dat?" the foxgirl finally asked.

"A journeyman, formerly the apprentice of Dominus Socrato," Morgana explained. "I had not thought much of her, to be blunt, but perhaps I will need to... reassess my opinion of her worth." The Domina then nodded to Rola, and said, "Thank you for the information. Hopefully that will mean this damn blockade will come to an end."

"That *is* the hope," Rola said. "Well, I suppose I shouldn't dawdle and stretch your hospitality even thinner."

The wolf spirit turned to leave, and took one step down before she abruptly stopped, then turned her upper half about. "Oh! There was *one* more thing I was supposed to *demand* from you. Something that you *had* to divulge."

Morgana's eyes narrowed. "And what is that, may I ask?"

"You had an apprentice... one that caused an 'incident', as I am told. I need to know what happened."

Morgana openly snarled, and declared, "My apprentice can't be the one responsible for this."

Sunay's eyes again darted between the two women. How did Rola know about the incident? The only person that Morgana had revealed that information to as far, as Sunay was aware, had been her and Ahmin.

Did Rola know where Ahmin was?

"That wasn't what I asked," the wolf spirit said sweetly.

There was a long pregnant pause, and Sunay swore she could hear Morgana's teeth grinding. "Very well. If you *must* remain and you *must* know trivial matters, then come with me."

She stood, and summoned the stairs upward while saying, "I would warn our dear Fire Fox. I suspect what you are about to witness will make you horribly ill."

The foxgirl's stomach clenched more in anticipation of what was to come than the presence of the Void she was already feeling. "Do I have to come, then?"

"Yes," Rola answered.

"Damn it all," Sunay grumbled under her breath as she fell in

117

step behind the Domina and the wolf spirit.

Morgana hadn't been lying. The next floor above was clearly the heart of the Void presence within the tower, and Sunay honestly wondered how she had missed it on her way up to confront the Domina earlier. Much like the floor below, it was a single room, but this one looked like it had been hit by a hurricane. Shattered glass from flasks and bottles, torn linen, cloth, and paper strewn everywhere, shattered furniture, and an inky violet haze floating in the air. The only thing that still looked intact was a brown, wooden altar with candles burning along the edge with a purple flame.

Each breath felt like a little death, and Sunay as a result breathed in as little as possible. Her skin felt like a million maggots were crawling all over her, and her tail looked more like a dusting wand with how every tail was standing on end.

"I reinforced the stairwell, but the rest would require more power than I am willing to expend at this time," Morgana explained. "Be careful, as the veil that is our world is paper thin here. Try not to touch anything."

Sunay retched, and fought the urge to fall to her knees. "I wouldn't be touching the *floor* if gravity didn't demand it."

Morgana chuckled softly, though her voice regained its terseness. "As you might be aware already, Madam Administrator, I and each of my peers have been exploring different means to try and save this world from the inevitable. Dominus Socrato has been trying to stall or reverse its advance. Dominus Augustus has been trying to infuse beings with the Void in the hopes that they can live within it.

"I on the other hand devoted my energies into trying to rebuild the world through the Void, creating another sanctuary as this one collapses. I knew that beings *can* survive transfer through the Void for short times, as the portals my colleagues and I created can attest... but I have not had much success with anything longer than that.

"My apprentice, Mohraine, had become tainted by the dark voice within the Void, and by the time I realized that fact he had already dominated many of my servants, and tried to kill me, using the controlled pool of Void that I had conjured to try and rip apart the veil of the world entirely. But he underestimated the knowledge I had gleaned of the black tome I carry, and I used it to offer myself protections against his treachery. From there, I dealt with him, and have been planning to use him for experiments to try and further my research."

At that point, Morgana gestured with her fingers towards the altar that Sunay had seen earlier. "Go. See the body of my apprentice."

Rola and Sunay approached the altar, which actually proved to be a casket. Sunay saw what was inside, and finally couldn't hold it back, vomiting bile onto the floor.

Morgana ignored the foxgirl's mess, and said simply, "I can only imagine it would be hard to serve the Void without a head."

Rola hummed thoughtfully. "Quite a remarkably clean decapitation."

"I gave him what he wanted," Morgana replied. "To see the Void. And saw it he did, for the fraction of a second before it consumed him from the neck up."

"Well, that doesn't answer any questions then, does it?" Rola said in a pout. "Come along, little fire fox. I suppose there's nothing more to be gleaned here."

Rola more drug Sunay back down the stairs than anything, and it wasn't until that they were down to the second floor where Law and Laron were waiting that the foxgirl even felt steady on her own legs.

It was also at that point, with all the adrenaline and Void sickness starting to wane that she was reminded of the buzzing in her head that she had been ignoring about three times a day over the past week. "Damn it," she grumbled. "Admiral Roberts is probably thinkin' to declare *me* gone rogue. I didn't exactly obey his orders comin' here in the first place, ya see."

Rola grinned playfully. "Why don't you let *me* talk to him?"

~ ~ ~ ~ ~

Rola meant exactly that, following Sunay into the Captain's Cabin of the *Goldbeard*, taking the mirror from Sunay's hands, and putting it on the desk. The wolf girl sat down in the chair and leaned back smugly.

Roberts's face appeared, twisted in rage, and he bellowed, "*Captain Sunay! I'm of halffa mind ta scrap yer commission and sink yer entire damn bo...*"

Rola's grin broadened. "Greetings, Admiral."

Now Roberts was aghast. "And who in da black hells are *you*?"

"My name is Rola. I'm the Administrator of the Western Free Provinces. Feel free to authenticate me. I'll wait."

The admiral huffed, and his eyes turned down and to his left. "Best believe I will..." it wasn't long after that his face fell and he looked back in resigned defeat. "What can I do fer ya today, ma'am?"

"I am under the impression that you are about to reprimand Captain Sunay here rather harshly, and I am afraid to say I can't have that."

"We 'ad orders to *not* run the Avalonian blockade, ma'am," Roberts protested. "The captain not only did dat, she damned *blew up* two Avalon Navy ships in th' process."

Sunay grimaced and shrugged nervously as Rola turned to the foxgirl and raised an eyebrow. "That's rather... impressive," the wolf spirit continued as she turned back to Roberts, "and I'm afraid the reason for that is mine. I was the one who insisted upon her to make it to Tortuga as soon as possible. So, feel free to take up those orders with *me*. I do apologize for borrowing your captain without your approval, but I was in dire straights and didn't have time to navigate fleet bureaucracy."

Roberts backed down. "I... I understand, ma'am. Now, wit' the reprimand stalled, I *do* 'ave orders fer the girl. Can I give 'em?"

Rola nodded graciously, and rose with a parting, "Thank you for your understanding. Captain, the seat is yours."

Sunay complied, addressing Roberts with a nod, "Admiral."

"Captain, th' fleet 'as been havin' problems in Reaht. Dere navy is expandin' and gettin' more aggressive. We lost three ships in ambushes, and we need a large ship in da region to help coordinate and mebbe dissuade th' Reahtans from gettin' even bolder. I suspect yer reputation of bein' a capital ship killa will reach Reaht even before you do."

Sunay asked, "So I'm off the hunt for Ahmin, then?"

Roberts exhaled deeply. "We're *all* off the hunt for Ahmin. If he's doin' anythin' now it's all in th' mainland. The administrators 'ave told us to resume normal activities. And dat's gonna be yer normal activity for the time bein'. Don't dally around, will ya? Roberts out."

Sunay put the mirror back in the cabinet and locked it. Rola's hand was on her chin in thought by the time the foxgirl had turned around, the wolf spirit stating grimly, "They want you as far away from me as they can."

Sunay blinked rapidly. "Wait, ya think I was just given bogus orders?"

Rola shrugged, though didn't change her posture. "I doubt it, I'm sure that Reaht is giving our ships all sorts of trouble. Tales of their rapid expansion into the Eastern Free Provinces even have reached *my* ears. But I *also* believe it's a convenient excuse to get you away from me."

"Why do you say that?"

Rola turned the desk chair around, and sat again. "To be honest, that's more Ahmin's suspicions bubbling up than mine," the wolf spirit said. "He's been on edge ever since that last full Administration meeting."

"So you *are* in contact with Ahmin!"

Rola shook her head. "No. In fact, he expressly said he *wouldn't* keep in contact with me after our last meeting so that I *couldn't* be tied to him or his actions."

"So what exactly... happened?"

"It was during an emergency meeting about the Void movement at South Gibraltar. I never go to those silly things, because they rarely ever involve me, and the few times they do, I'm ignored anyway. Ahmin, on the other hand, was convinced some 'Minister' was involved in the whole of it, and suspected Morgana's apprentice was the likely culprit."

Sunay remembered "The Minister", and that memory *still* gave her chills. It wouldn't surprise her at all that the man was the one responsible.

Rola meanwhile continued, "He contacted me after that meeting, saying that 'he had gotten to our leaders.' I assume he meant that 'Minister' character. His recommendation to me was that he couldn't guarantee just how far the corruption has become, and that the only ship he could guarantee was 'clean' was you and yours. I hadn't thought much of it... but recent events are suggesting I should take this matter more seriously."

"So, what should *I* do then?" Sunay asked.

"Go to Reaht. However, I *do* ask *one* more favor of you."

The foxgirl replied, "What's that?"

"Could you take Law, Laron and I to Lourdis?" Rola asked. "Rumor has it that the mayors of the cities in Versilles are about to reach an agreement to declare their independence, and become a Free Province. That's something I have a vested interest in."

Rola then flashed a suggestive grin as she added, "However, we're going to need special lodging. Simply throwing us in the barracks isn't going to do at all. I'm sure your first mate would be cooperative and allow Law and me to use her cabin, but poor Laron will need some place to lay his head. I'm sure *you* can think of something, can't you?"

Sunay grinned in response, and replied, "Ya know... I think I know just the place for him..."

Chapter Seven: Tales of a Past's Future

"There are many things the mayors of Versilles have to think about before they officially declare independence," Laron explained to Sunay as the flags of Lourdis, a blue swan on a white field, started to become visible from the *Goldbeard's* deck. "While the bulk of the wealth *is* here, the bulk of the population and military might is in the north. And while the Avalon Army and Navy *again* took a beating at the hands of the Daynes, it would be a gamble on Versilles's part that Avalon wouldn't be particularly willing or able to engage in another military conflict so quickly."

"Hunh," Sunay replied with a grunt. She really didn't care much about any of this, in all honesty. She had put this entire part of the world behind her more than a decade ago, and hadn't really given it much thought in the time since. Whatever happened to this province was none of her concern. By this point next year, she'd be completely on the other side of the continent anyway.

He hugged her around the shoulders, and said, "This is a bittersweet thing for you, isn't it?"

"More bitter than sweet."

"You've never been back in this province since you left, haven't you?"

"Sure I have!" Sunay protested. "The Goldbeard's sailed these waters many times!"

"But always to sail by. Never to stop."

Sunay's ears flattened, and that unspoken gesture was more confirmation than any word she could have said.

"Maybe we should," Laron said. "Rola and Law are going to spend no amount of time getting the feel of the land, and that will leave us time to go back to our old stomping grounds."

Sunay wasn't terribly excited with the idea. "Feh. I've got a mission to attend to, and Admiral Roberts would likely have mah head if I wasted any more time."

Laron finally laid down his trump card. "*I* haven't been back to Navarre either, you know. I'd like for you to be with me when I do."

"Damn it..." Sunay grumbled, defeated. "I guess Robert's ain't gonna be *too* upset by another small delay."

"We'll rent some horses in Lourdis!" Laron chirped. "We won't even be gone two days, I promise!"

"Yeah... yeah..." the foxgirl said dismissively, gesturing him forward. "Let's get this over with."

~ ~ ~ ~ ~

For a land that was still officially a province of Avalon, the feel Sunay got while on the road was of a land that had moved on from the Republican yoke. She and Laron passed all of two Republican Police on the road between Lourdis and Navarre, and neither even gave Sunay much more than a second look before moving on.

That's not to say that the road was unprotected, as the bulk of the patrol duties were being done by the cities themselves. The majority bore the insignia of Lourdis, but Laron identified Navarre's coat of arms as they got closer to their old homeland.

"Why don't you consider a plot of land in Navarre if the whole province is gonna be free?" Sunay asked as Laron started seeing landmarks along the road he remembered.

"Navarre isn't a port town, even though it is close to the coast. I want a plot near a major trade route, that's where the money is if you want to be a settled merchant," Laron explained, like it was the most obvious thing in the world. "If a merchant is going to be in one place, they need to be able to move volume. If I were to *really* start getting money, I could see myself buying a little weekend getaway out here, but that's not something I'm considering right at this moment."

Sunay couldn't fight the urge to look towards the south, and the treeline off in the distance that was the forest where Miriam's old orphanage once stood. She was certain it was long gone by now, if not from Cavalier Norman's rampage than simply by the passing of time.

"Would you like to go that way?" Laron asked.

The foxgirl shook her head. "There's nothing for me there. Let's just do what you want to do, okay?"

Laron nodded, and clicked his tongue while flicking the reins to increase his horse's trot. Sunay followed suit and the pair continued their trek to the town of Navarre.

The town was both familiar but different, even to Sunay who had visited it all of twice in her life. The streets were the same, the buildings she passed were all ones she remembered, or at least hadn't changed so significantly that it struck as peculiar in her memory.

But Laron, however, could see the differences, not so much in the streets and the buildings, but in the people.

A single, old man sat at a bench in front of one of the town's taverns, a person that Laron felt compelled to address.

124

"Horace!" he shouted, raising his hand in greeting and pulling his horse to a stop.

The man on the bench looked up, squinted, then his entire face lit up. "Laron? Is that you, my boy? Hah! I had you pegged for dead the moment that Cavalier from Snake River round you and your family up and shipped you off north!"

"To be fair, *I* pegged me and my family for dead," Laron acknowledged. "But we got lucky."

"Seeing your face around here makes me think there's a lot more than talk going on about breaking away from the Republic. You *and* the fox lady here." His eyes squinted, and he asked Sunay, "Ain't you the girl that Laron was parading about town all those years ago?"

Sunay nodded. "Yeah, that was me."

"Never would have guessed you had such a big bushy tail. Man, chimeras trotting around in the broad daylight with exiled noble sons... time's sure are changing. Speaking of nobles, where is the rest of your family, Laron?"

Laron frowned, and he said, "We were lucky to avoid the axe of Avalon... not so lucky to avoid the Daynish hordes coming down."

Horace's face fell. "Marcia and the whole lot of them?"

Laron nodded sadly. "I was the only one who left before the barbarians brought their thunder down."

"Aww... I'm sorry, my boy. No one your age should suffer that much loss. Makes my troubles seem trifling, it does."

"Now, there is no trifling when it comes to the troubles men and women of this region face," Laron said reassuringly. Though the merchant's apprentice got a hint when he asked, "What's Henry up to lately?"

"That's part of my troubles, Laron my boy," Horace said. "Henry... passed away last year."

Laron was astonished, "Come on now, he wasn't *that* old to be passing on!"

"Not normally. But when you're relegated to the mine, and you have breathing problems to begin with..."

"Wait... the mine? *What* mine?"

Horace jerked a thumb behind him, and spat. "Half day north. Burrowed down and under the mountains, I'd wager."

Laron's eyebrows furrowed. "But *why?* Prospectors have frequently been through those mountains, and never found anything better than pig iron."

"Yeah, but when you're an empire desperate for whatever

metal you can get your hands on to fuel your war machine, you take what you can get. You'd think with news that the Daynes have been pushed back, that Avalon wouldn't need that damned mine anymore, but no one's come back yet."

"And Henry was sent down there?" Laron gasped. "Why?"

"Any able bodied man was either sent out that way or drafted into the military about three years ago. They'd get joined by anyone arrested for committing a crime. Like in Henry's case, public drunkenness," Horace answered, his lower lip trembling as he relayed the information. "We were both drinking... right here... when that Cavalier, Norman's the name... accused us of being drunk in public. Now we hadn't even had one ale each at this point, but then Henry gets this crazy idea to claim both beers are his and that I was just keeping him company."

Horace wept openly, and cried, "I should have said something... I shouldn't have just let them take him..."

"And then ya *both* would be dead in those mines, and I think Henry knew that," Sunay finally interjected.

Laron's eyes misted over, and he asked, "Have you heard anything about Donovan?"

Sunay blinked rapidly, trying to remember why that name sounded familiar before it clicked into place. Donovan, the captain of the family guard, and Laron's half-brother.

"He accepted the draft, and he went to the front lines, as far as I am aware. He hasn't returned, and I haven't heard any news of him."

Laron's spirits dropped, and he slumped forward in the reins. "The front lines of battle were killing fields, on *both* sides. No news is not good news in this case."

Sunay's teeth began to grind. Cavalier Norman, the Dog of the Republic, a name that still stirred anger whenever she heard it. Ahmin had spared the louse all those years ago, and this was how that bastard used that opportunity. How many more lives was he going to ruin before he was stopped?

She quickly decided that answer was none. Because she was going to end this herself today.

"Do you have any idea where this Cavalier is now?" Sunay growled, and Laron eyed her warily in concern.

Horace shrugged. "He could be anywhere at any time. He has to have his hand in everything, and where he goes to throw his weight around might as well be random."

"Sunay... what are you thinking?" Laron asked warningly, but hadn't even managed to finish the question before Sunay had flicked the reins of her horse and kicked the mare's flanks to set it into a gallop. She charged past the central square, and towards the mayor's castle, though she turned a hard left just outside of town, trying to remember where the damn escape tunnel into the castle was. She remembered it was on the south side, and if you didn't know it was there it was very easily missed.

That delay allowed Laron to catch up to her. "Love... what are you doing?"

"Tryin' to get inside. There's a tunnel 'round here, and I just have to remember where. Once in there, I can squeeze the mayor on where to find that bastard Cavalier."

"You aren't... are you...?"

Sunay jumped off her horse to get a closer look from ground level. She looked up grimly at Laron, and pointed at her horses reins. "Watch 'er for me, will ya?"

"Sunay!"

The foxgirl snarled with clenched teeth, "That man razed the only home on land I ever 'ad, even if people like 'im was what made that home a livin' hell when 'e wasn't sendin' 'normal' people to their deaths for helpin' us chimeras. Now he's sending old men to die in mines, and young men to die on battlefields. Someone's gotta say 'enough', and it's lookin' like that someone needs to be me. Ya can do me a favor by tellin' me where the mayor's office would be in that castle."

"It's been ten years, Sunay! Who's saying that the mayor kept the same rooms as my father?"

Sunay glared at him. "It's as good of a place to start as any. Now are ya gonna help or not?"

Laron looked up to the sky, and if Sunay didn't already know he wasn't particularly a religious man she'd have thought he was offering a silent prayer to the heavens. "My father had his office on the ground floor, center room of the main castle. It's hard to miss... if you see an oval room, you're there."

"Thank you," Sunay said, then returned to her search for the hidden tunnel that would give her access past the main walls. She could distinctly remember it looked like an animal den nestled between two hills... but with the rolling land outside of Navarre before it surrendered to the coastline, that was a lot of prospective spots, especially where there were *three* animal dens nestled in the hills, one of which contained a rather agitated gray fox with two kits that did not

127

particularly appreciate Sunay's intrusion.

The fourth time proved to be the charm, and her instincts meshed with her memory that this was the spot. "Alright, stay here... but not *too* close. Just in case someone from the Republican Police start sniffin' around."

"What?" Laron asked in exasperation.

"Just... just act casual," she said in parting and disappeared into the cave, shimmying down the ladder and moving as quickly as she could. It felt smaller than she remembered, although that no doubt had more to do with her being bigger. But it ran exactly as she had hoped, and she could hear the sounds of the castle above her head soon enough. The tunnel ended with a wooden ladder that if she remembered rightly emerged into a storeroom in the south wing.

At least, until she found she couldn't move the panel that would allow her entry. Another push opened the way a crack and she saw what the problem was. No doubt when the castle had switched hands, the new owners had no idea about the underground tunnels, and someone had shoved a crate over the panel that allowed access.

"For the love of..." the foxgirl grunted, trying to dig into the wooden crate with her nails and push it aside inch by inch. She was *not* going to give up and go *all* the way back because of some stupid *box*. It was slow, it was tedious, and she suspected it was going to leave her with some bloody fingers, but her efforts *were* working.

Then the box shifted entirely, and the panel was pulled up by hands other than her own and thrown aside. The foxgirl craned her neck back to see a slight, black-haired servant girl holding a broom over her head with both hands, looking down with the same look of confusion etched on Sunay's face.

"Here I was expecting to find a mouse or two or three," the girl said with a whimper. "I'm not sure if *this* is better or worse. Why... why are you digging into the castle?"

"Ain't digging. Already been dug," Sunay answered, then decided to try a little white lie. "Listen, this is gonna seem a little crazy..."

The girl said, "Already does."

"But I'm part of an... underground movement."

"That much was clear."

"Not *literally*... well, okay... literally in this case. But we have reason to believe that Republican Police are lookin' to kill the mayor. I think they suspect that he'd vote in favor of independence for the province or somethin'."

The girl's eyes widened, and she said, "Oh no!"

"Listen, I just need ya to trust me on this. I need to know where he is."

She nodded vigorously, and said, "Come with me! I'll take you to him! I'm Emily. I just started working here, so I can't say I can help with who the killer might be."

Sunay emerged into the storeroom, and the girl said, "Come on! Hurry!"

"Ain't gonna try and cover up *these*, eh?" Sunay asked, pointing to her ears and tail.

Emily disregarded the concern. "No one cares about chimeras anymore. If anything, it's the easiest way to tell who is a Republican sympathizer. Come on!"

This girl wasn't terribly bright, leading an absolute stranger to the mayor, and she felt rather guilty taking advantage of her, but for once luck was on her side, and she didn't want to ruin it. Further luck came as Emily wasn't lying about Sunay's presence setting off alarm. Everyone in the halls gave Sunay a wide berth, but not a single one called for Republican guards or police.

They had crossed into the hall that joined the south tower from the main castle, and were abruptly stopped by a woman in a long black gown and a silver circlet settled on her forehead. "Emily, what are you doing here?"

"Madam Natalie!" She exclaimed before turning her head to Sunay. "Madam Natalie is in charge of the serving staff in the castle." Emily then whirled back to the madam and said, "This lady here has found out about a plot to kill the mayor, and I'm taking her to warn him!"

Natalie's eyebrows rose. "Oh, really? Perhaps you should be getting back to your tasks? *I'll* handle this from here."

Emily nodded, and skipped away back down the hall. Sunay didn't like this much at all, the hairs of her tail raising nervously. Somehow, she doubted this madam would be as easily convinced as the servant girl who had just left.

"Come along then, girl. Though why a chimera would be interested in warning the mayor of anything is beyond me," Natalie ordered, spinning about and starting back down the hall.

"Ya okay?" Sunay asked, as she noted Natalie moving with a pronounced limp in her left leg.

"I'm not sure how, but my knee was sore when I woke up this morning. I will do my best to pick up the pace."

Sunay shrugged. "Don't hurt yerself more on my account. Take yer time."

The pair emerged into the central building of the castle, and Sunay would have had to have been blind and deaf to not notice the disturbing lack of activity in the halls they were navigating through. "No guards? No servants? Nothing?"

"Hmm..." Natalie hummed, "I had thought that our plans had been hidden quite well."

"Eh?"

The madam's tone turned sinister. "Oh, I know *quite* well that there is an assassin in the halls." Then Natalie spun about, throwing aside the slit in the skirt of her gown in order to draw the short sword that had been the cause of her limp. "I was the one who let him in!"

Of all the luck, winding up in the middle of an actual assassination attempt while trying to play off a fake one.

Sunay had been able to draw one knife at her belt, and sidestep Natalie's first attack, but slammed her back into the wall in the process. That was going to be problematic. While Sunay had plenty of practice fighting against opponents with larger and longer weapons, the narrow confines of the hall neutralized much of her advantage.

The foxgirl skipped away from a slash, then lunged, trying to catch Natalie's blade at the hilt and twist it out of her grasp. But the madam showed no lack of skill herself, stepping back, twirling the sword into a backhand grip and stabbing downward, drawing a long gash across Sunay's vest and splitting the cloth of her shirt at the bust.

Snarling, Sunay scrambled away, ripped a torch out of the wall, and threw it at her advancing attacker. While Natalie parried the torch itself away, the spraying embers caught the edges of her gown and seared her eyes. Sunay took that opening to charge, then stab upward.

Self preservation saved Natalie, as she was expecting an attack, but Sunay was still able to draw a deep wound in Natalie's right armpit, the sudden pain and severing of sinew causing Natalie to drop her sword and her advantage.

"Honorless *bitch!*" Natalie howled, throwing herself at Sunay and tackling the foxgirl to the ground, the pair slamming into the walls as they rolled and grappled back and forth.

"*Vixen!*" Sunay shouted back, rearing back and punching Natalie in the jaw. "At least get the insult right!"

At some point in the scuffle, Natalie had wrenched Sunay's dagger out of her hand, and stabbed the foxgirl in the left shoulder.

Sunay's silk shirt kept the blade's serrated back from tearing into her flesh, and her shoulder blade prevented it from going more than a fraction of an inch at best, but it still hurt and still was going to produce a generous amount of blood.

In response, the foxgirl went into a rage, snapping her foe's wrist with a vicious counterclockwise twist, then grabbed the woman by the collar of her gown and slammed the back of her head against the stone floor. She was about to do it again when an arm wrapped around her waist, another grabbed her by the shoulder, then threw her with so much force against the wall that it shook the nearby torch holder and sent stars through her eyes.

"Let me kill the... *vixen*," she heard Natalie grumble.

It was a man's voice that responded. "No. You will not, because I have no doubt you started this."

"She was going to warn the mayor..."

"Which would have been for naught even if he was in his office, as he'd have been long dead before either of you got here. You *could* have just turned her away at the main door, you know."

Sunay's vision began to clear as the man knelt down in front of her. She *knew* that face, though the scar that ran from the top of his left cheek all the way down to the chin was new... and from the recognition in the man's chocolate brown eyes and dark furrowing eyebrows, he knew hers as well.

Natalie was also recovering, and protested, "I *didn't* let her in. That simple-minded fool Emily brought her in from the south tower. How the vixen got in from there I couldn't tell you."

That information seemed to be the bit that convinced the man of her identity. "Oh, I know how..." he said thoughtfully. "And I also know if you kill her that my half-brother will be very sad. And I really don't want to upset him... the poor man has lost enough already."

And now Sunay had the name to connect to the face. Donovan.

"Now why, may I ask, are you trying to warn that scum of the province that someone is out to kill him, eh?" Donovan said as he helped Sunay to his feet.

"I wasn't tryin' honestly," Sunay answered. "That was just how I convinced the girl Emily to let me pass. I had no idea at all ya were *really* tryin' to kill 'im. I was tryin' to find out where Cavalier Norman was so that I could kill *him*."

"Well, you're both in luck and out of it," Donovan said, "because since the mayor isn't in his office, and now I know exactly where *both* of them are. They are together, heading towards Lourdis along with a regiment of the Republican Police to arrest everyone preparing to vote on the issue of independence. The other mayors foolishly invited Mayor Bigsby, either unaware or forgetting that Bigsby was personally set in that station by Cavalier Norman after the Pontaine family was arrested and sent to Snake River."

"So he and Norman are headin' for Lourdis right now to arrest and/or murder the whole lot of the mayors for treason," Sunay deduced.

"More of the latter than the former, I'm sure. The Dog of the Republic has never met a capital punishment he didn't like to liberally use. Which means we have little time to get to Lourdis and warn them about what's coming. I highly doubt the Republican convoy is going to be going at a full gallop, so we still have a window if we hurry."

He turned to Natalie, and ordered the madam, "Natalie, you stay here."

The madam asked in astonishment, "Why?"

"Because I need you to mobilize the resistance militia here in Navarre, and start them on the road to Lourdis," Donovan said. "Sunay and I will part ways at the West River Junction, and I'll head north to Greynoble to rouse the militia there while Sunay spreads word to Lourdis. With any luck, we'll be able to trap the Dog of the Republic on all sides."

"Did you just think that up on the spot?" Sunay wondered as Donovan spun about to leave out the main door.

"Fighting on the front lines of the Daynish Campaigns teaches you to think fast," he said. "If you didn't, you wound up with you and your entire regiment dead."

"Is that how you survived that hell, then?"

Donovan shook his head. "Fortunately for me, I was identified as having 'excellent leadership skills', and the Avalon Army never put their officers in too many positions where there lives were at risk. At least, until an ambush led to my regiment being chased into the Winding Snake Rapids.

"The few of us that survived decided we had quite enough of this war, and went our separate ways. I only returned to Navarre about a week ago, where members of the resistance here brought me up to speed. What about you, what brings the infamous 'Fire Fox' back to her old stomping grounds?"

Sunay whimpered in dismay. "Coders, you know about that name *too*?"

Donovan chuckled. "I suspect everyone in Avalon does at this point. There was a wanted poster in Lover's Cove a couple weeks ago posted by the Avalon Navy. Apparently you... managed to *blow up* two of their ships of the line?"

Sunay huffed. "They were in my way."

"Remind me to never get in your way," Donovan deadpanned as he pushed open the main gates.

Sunay gestured south. "Laron's waitin' outside the tunnel with my horse. I don't wanna just leave him there."

"I need to collect my horse anyway. I'll catch up."

Being on horseback allowed him to do just that before Sunay had even reached Laron's position, lounging with a book about a hundred yards from the tunnel entrance. The merchant's apprentice was torn between relief for Donovan and concern for Sunay until she waved him off. "Won't even need stitches I bet. I've had worse, believe it or not."

Donovan also waved off his brother's questions. "There will be plenty of time for catching up, but right now we are on a tight schedule. We need to get to the West River Junction as fast as possible, then the two of you will head to Lourdis and ask for the head of the militia there to warn him that the Republican Police are coming."

Laron nodded in confirmation, then turned to Sunay. "Love, would you happen to remember much about the hunting trails south of the old orphanage?"

Sunay looked at him warily. "I wasn't supposed to go that far south, remember?"

"So, that's a yes, then?"

The foxgirl groaned. "Yeah, I know 'em for the most part. Why?"

"Because those hunting trails cut straight through the forest and come out pretty much right *at* West River Junction. It'd cut... Coders... several hours of travel out of the trip."

Donovan was *all* for that idea. "Then lead on, Fire Fox. Time is of the essence."

"*Don't* call me that." Sunay stressed as she climbed onto the back of her horse.

Laron chuckled. "It's a fine name, fitting for a true scourge of the seas."

"If I find out you helped Rola come up with that..." she threatened, drawing a slash motion across her neck for emphasis.

The young man smirked. "You'll never find out."

The foxgirl glowered, but said nothing further, taking the lead off the beaten path and towards the forest which she grew up in. The paths weren't wide, with weeds encroaching in all directions, but they were enough for horses to pass through single-file.

She tried to ignore the burned out section of forest they passed halfway through the trail, until Donovan made it impossible to ignore. "One of Norman's little raiding parties forgot to take the wind into account when they set the chimera orphanage on fire. It took an inhuman effort from civilians and police three days to fight the blaze. We're lucky it didn't take the whole forest and everything in it."

Sunay kept her head forward, even as her teeth ground against each other. One way or another, Norman was going to pay for all his crimes. In a way, she wanted this plan to fail so that she'd be able to take matters into her own hands, then felt horribly guilty for such a terribly selfish thought. She tried to banish all ideas of personal revenge out of her mind, focusing on the bigger goal that had been laid out in front of her. It shouldn't *matter* how the Cavalier got taken down, and this way helped set an entire province free.

She repeated that to herself until they emerged from the woods, and it helped to some extent. Donovan received the luck he was hoping for when he asked the militiamen posted at the junction if Navarre's caravan had passed yet and was told they hadn't.

"Then I'm off to Greynoble. Hopefully, I can rouse enough support that we can ride fast and be in time before all hell breaks loose." He said to the pair, "You need to do the same with Lourdis. If they aren't ready, all of this is for naught regardless of what other support has been mustered. Any of the militia there will work in a pinch, but try to find Captain Stark. He's the one that can muster the guard in full the fastest."

"Captain Stark, got it," Sunay confirmed. "Be careful out there."

"There's a time for caution, and a time for action. This is the latter."

Donovan took the north fork, pressing his horse into a speed that could *not* have been healthy for the animal. Sunay and Laron didn't go *quite* that fast, wanting to preserve the poor things as much as they could while keeping a pace well beyond what a large convoy would be taking.

They reached Lourdis roughly an hour after nightfall, which made stirring the militia difficult. The night watch wasn't particularly inclined to let people in after dark to begin with, much less visitors trying to get access to a militia captain who was no doubt retired for the night.

It took Rola, emerging into the torch light at the wall entrance to finally get the matter in hand.

"Is something the matter, sirs?" She asked the two guards sweetly.

"Nothing to concern yourself with, ma'am. Move along, please."

"I'll have you know the man is my apprentice, and I've been waiting for him to return from Navarre," Rola informed, brandishing an envelope that she held out to the nearest militiaman. "These are my registration papers if you doubt me."

The guard did so, pulling out a handful of folded parchment sheets and holding them up to the light to give them a read. "And what about the woman?" he asked.

"My apprentice's fiance. He tells me he's very interested in purchasing land here for him and his wife to be."

"They're saying that a convoy from Navarre bearing Republican troops are on their way."

Rola was adamant, her voice drifting towards stern. "Well, then there is a convoy of Republican troops on their way, and you should inform the militia captain immediately."

"Ma'am, if we roused our captain every single time there was a claimed threat to our city-state..."

"As I understand, it is a militia captain's *duty* to respond to any threat, real or imagined," Rola chided. "If you think he will be angry being roused in the middle of the night, imagine how angry he will be if Republican forces march through in the morning and execute the congress of mayors that have assembled here."

The other guard bit his lip, and shrugged. "She's got a point, William."

Testily, William snapped, "Then *you* go wake Captain Stark up. It can be on your head. As for you two..." he said, gesturing back to Sunay and Laron, "get in here before I change my mind. You can wait just off the road for the Captain and you can tell him what you supposedly saw."

Captain Stark did arrive, his uniform disheveled and with his long black hair uncombed and the stubble on his chin untrimmed, looking like a man either drunk, woken up in the middle of the night, or both. But that demeanor shifted immediately the moment Sunay relayed the information from Navarre. Instantly, the look on his face sobered, and he was at full alertness. "The mayors invited Bigsby?

135

That lackey of the Republic? Damn it all... they might as well have walked themselves in chains straight into Caravel. I want every man and woman armed and ready by the time that convoy arrives. We only need to hold the line long enough for assistance from other towns to support us."

Rola poked Laron in the shoulder, and said, "The two of you should probably get some sleep. I think you'll want to be nice and rested when our friends from the Republic arrive."

~ ~ ~ ~ ~

It was a fitful sleep for Sunay, and by extension Laron, though he didn't take Sunay to task for it. She was out the door of the inn by the first crack of light in the windows, perched on the roof of a nearby building from Lourdis's west entrance so she could get a good vantage point of the coming scene.

It was also a position that allowed her to eavesdrop, as voices from below drifted up to her ears.

"Scouts report that Mayor Bigsby's caravan is an hour away," one of the lieutenants told Captain Stark.

"Any signs of Republican Police?" the captain asked.

"Not officially sir, but one of our scouts confirms that she's seen several of his 'guards' wearing Republican colors last week."

Captain Stark nodded. "Understood. What about Cavalier Norman?"

"Wasn't seen, but the mayor's carriage was completely covered and the windows shaded. We suspect if he's with the convoy, he's in there with the mayor."

"And what about reinforcements?"

"The Navarre Militia is not even thirty minutes behind the mayor's convoy. Greynoble is still two hours out at the earliest. Captain Donovan has them coming from the north road, in case the mayor's supporters try to escape that way."

"Good. Keep the men ready, I want a line two deep just outside the gate when the Mayor of Navarre arrives."

Laron arrived from their inn to the east, looking around and calling out Sunay's name. She didn't respond, not wanting to give away her position and possibly get sent away by Captain Stark. Her suspicions were right, as Laron was almost immediately sent back away from the gate and told to keep his distance in case things got bloody.

"There's something a wee bit off about all this, don't you

think?" Rola whispered in Sunay's ear, almost scaring the foxgirl completely off the roof.

Sunay held on with clenched fingertips on the ledge, then whipped her head back with a snarl, "You mean like your neck the next time you do that?"

The wolf spirit smiled cheekily. "My... colleague in Avalon finally deigned it worthy to give me access to the Gold Pirate assets in this region. There are some troubling things I discovered."

"Like what?"

"Did you see Mayor Bigsby at all during your time in Pontaine Castle?"

Sunay blinked. "No. Why?"

"Did you look in the oval office?"

"Never even went in. Why? Can you just get to the point already?"

Rola took a deep breath. "Agents found Mayor Bigsby dead. Killed by multiple stab wounds, along with the knife and a set of bloody clothes."

Sunay blinked. "Then... wait... are you saying Donovan *did* kill him already?"

"It looks that way."

"Then... who is in the convoy?"

"By all accounts, it indeed bears Cavalier Norman. *That* part of what Donovan is saying appears to be completely true, with the exception of the Mayor of Navarre being present. There's no doubt going to be quite the bloody battle at the western gates."

"And Donovan would know that," Sunay said, hand on her chin in thought. "So then why did Donovan leave to get additional forces that won't be in time to see action?"

"And this is where it gets a little stranger. The story Laron told me about Donovan doesn't exactly match up with what agents within Avalon relayed to me."

"What do you mean?"

"Donovan was never promoted to officer. He was *going* to be in time, I am told, but he deserted soon after the first skirmishes of the Daynish Campaigns. He likely found your wanted poster because *his* wanted poster was right next to it."

Sunay was putting together the "what" was happening easily enough. Cavalier Norman and his forces were about to get caught in a pincer attack, while Donovan and his forces from Greynoble were going to be able to take advantage of a barely defended north side and a militia already strained from an earlier fight.

It was the "why" this was happening that was eluding her, which was distressingly commonplace at this point. "Ya'd think after roughly ten years in the Gold Pirates that I'd be used to nonsense triple-crosses whenever I get involved on land."

"It never gets boring, at least," Rola replied.

"So, why are ya tellin' me this?"

"Because while I can handle a ragtag group of militiamen without much trouble, I'd like to think there is a chance that you and Laron could talk his half-brother down. A small one, perhaps, depending on what is motivating him, but a chance nonetheless. My question is, are you willing to set aside revenge for that chance? Do you need to see Cavalier Norman get his comeuppance with your own eyes, or happen with your own hands?"

Sunay growled to herself. She knew what she was going to choose, even if she didn't like it. "Damnit all... let's go."

She met Laron and Law at the north gate, and they didn't have to ride out very far to meet the southbound militia from Greynoble, which were also *very* ahead of schedule. Intentionally so, gauging from the chatter Sunay could pick up as the four got closer. Cavalier Norman's police had just arrived, and Donovan was waiting for the trap to snap shut before they moved in.

"Gee, and here we had been told you were several hours out," Sunay shouted, catching the attention of the entire militia, with Donovan at its head.

"I would strongly recommend that you didn't see us here, Fire Fox." Donovan warned.

Laron wasn't going to let the matter rest. "What are you doing? What is your plan?"

"My plan is to kill every single last person within that assembly."

"But... why? Do you *want* Avalon to continue to control this province?"

Donovan scoffed. "Cavalier Norman and his little Republican Police are about to be sandwiched between two angry militias. He'll be lucky to survive long enough to be executed."

"And what chance do you think a leaderless province will have once the Avalon Army marches over the mountains and the Navy sails in from the sea?" Sunay retorted. "Whether you like it or not, a massacre of these mayors is a guarantee that any independence will be short lived at best."

"And do you think these mayors are *any* better? Those descendants and lapdogs of the old nobility?" Donovan shouted. "We're trading one heartless, greedy hand for another! Those... *criminals* sent men like me, like the men behind me, out into battle with fragile blades made from worthless pig iron... thousands of us died due to those inferior arms, and why? Because it was *cheap* to make and the weak metal was easy to mine! They threw us to our deaths, for lower damned *taxes!*"

"Donovan, there's no good metal in those mines to begin with," Laron protested. "It wasn't a matter of digging deeper. It's not there, and Avalon was desperate for *anything*."

"And there were other options than sending us to war with crummy equipment. But those... professional thieves chose *money* over *human lives*. They had been hoarding Reahtan steel for *years* to supply Royalist sympathizers! I'll take our chances without them against Avalon." He pointed to the southwest. "This is your last warning. If you four are still in my way by the time word comes to me that the Republic forces are being routed... I *will* mow you all down."

Rola began loosening the collar of her blouse, but Laron held up a warning hand, and begged, "Please, Madam Rola... let me handle this."

"Donovan, you're a smart man," Laron began. "I know you are. You wouldn't have gotten this far if you weren't. So I find it hard to believe that you don't see how *stupid* what you're planning to do is. You're effectively making two enemies where you only need to be making one. You think the mayors don't have supporters? You think they'll just fall in line with you after you butcher their leaders? I know you're angry, and I honestly don't doubt that everything you're saying is the unvarnished truth. But this is *not* a fight you have to have *today*."

Donovan had gone silent, his lips drawn into a line. Laron could see reason starting to war with rage, and the men behind him were muttering quietly amongst themselves as well. Rola's hands dropped away from her collar, starting to break into a small smile.

"Donovan... no..." Laron said, then corrected himself, "as much as you hate me calling you 'brother', I am going to. Our family, all of them, is gone. Our mother was killed... our brothers and sisters... all of them massacred by the Daynes in the Free Provinces. You and I are all that's left."

Laron stepped forward, and added, "If you insist on moving forward with this mad scheme, there will only be one of us, and I know you won't believe this, but it *won't* be you. *Please*, brother... let this fight rest for another day. Let's focus on one enemy at a time."

The two men were approached by a scout, who informed Donovan, "Captain, the militia from Navarre has arrived. Cavalier Norman's men are fighting hard, but they won't last long. If we are to move, it has to be now."

The tension in Donovan's frame was evident, his every muscle twitching like a plucked string, his fists clenching so tight Sunay was worried he draw blood. Finally, after thirty seconds that felt more like minutes, the militia captain's hands unclenched, and he said with a fiery glare directed at Laron, "Men... stand down. My little 'brother' is right. This is a fight for another day."

He finally broke eye contact, and turned his head to look over his shoulder. "Lieutenant Briggs, take half the men and help our kin mop up. Report to Captain Stark and let him coordinate for the time being. The rest of you, follow me and we'll secure the grounds around the assembly hall."

Donovan initially walked past Laron, until the younger brother fell in stride alongside him. Sunay, Rola and Law soon joined the pair, and Sunay with all the tension easing felt comfortable enough to ask, "So... wait... the two of ya share the same *mother*?"

"Yes," Laron explained. "In the spirit of total honestly, our mother was the one who most likely enjoyed the bulk of the affairs among my parents. My grandmother put the curse on *both* of them as a result."

"Ya think I'd stop assumin' by now..."

Laron draped his left arm over her shoulders. "Now now, my father was *hardly* a slouch went it came to extramarital relations. He was *certainly* not blameless. Consider it a primer on old Avalonian nobility... everyone sleeping with everyone else, then feigning indignity over it all."

Rola, meanwhile, had taken interest in Donovan, who while seeing Laron's wisdom, was still visibly brooding. "I won't ask if you're all right, because I know you're not. But you will be. For what it's worth, not many are going to shed a tear for Bigsby's death."

"I knew as much."

"You'll regret doing it though."

"You regret every life you take... I still see the faces of the seven Daynes I killed in the Campaigns."

"Here's hoping there won't have to be more faces in your nightmares."

The militia captain nodded and agreed morosely, "Here's

hoping."

"Call it a hunch, but I think you'll find Versilles the Free Province will be a little brighter for everyone."

"You sound so confident of that," he grumbled.

"Let's just say I have a hunch. And a good merchant's hunch is rarely wrong,"

~ ~ ~ ~ ~

Donovan's mood had brightened by the time evening rolled around, though not much. The events of the last two days were going to weigh heavily on him, that much was clear. But whether that was from regret that he didn't do more, or shame for what he *had* done, was anyone's guess... perhaps even to him.

They had been sharing a keg of hard apple cider that Rola "just happened" to have on her cart when Captain Stark approached the small gathering.

"Ah, Mister Stark!" Rola cheered, raising a wooden mug in salute. "Would you care to join us?"

"I suppose *one* won't hurt," he said, and Rola quickly filled a mug for him to enjoy. Stark took a pull, then informed those present as to the course of events. "I can confirm that Cavalier Norman was killed in the fighting. We offered him the opportunity to surrender, but that old bastard just wouldn't have it. Arrogant and unyielding to the end that one."

"Too bad I couldn't have gotten my shots in," Sunay grumbled, "but the bastard is dead and done, and that's what matters, I guess."

"Yeah, I can see why you'd have liked that," Stark said. "Hopefully, life for chimeras will be for the better in the Free Province of Versilles, but there's a lot of religious sentiment to overcome still."

"So, the mayors did indeed vote to declare independence?" Rola asked.

That got the captain to chuckle between sips. "You want to know the irony about all of it? Until Cavalier Norman showed up with his little gang of Republican Police... the mayors were actually in favor of staying part of Avalon."

Law laughed. "Seriously?"

"Seventeen to twelve in favor of staying, until word of the Republican attack reached their ears, then it flipped to a unanimous vote. In attempting to make sure that this province stayed under the thumb of Avalon, Cavalier Norman instead was the catalyst for the province's independence."

Sunay smirked. "Ya know what? That's a fittin' legacy for the ass. The man's stubborn devotion to the Republic in every way actually being part of the reason it's fallin' apart."

"I'll send a messenger to our friends in Greynoble, along with thanking them for mustering on such short notice," Donovan said.

"We're likely going to need our various city militias to be centralized in these coming months. I highly doubt Avalon is going to take this sitting down."

"Hmmm."

"We're going to need a general."

Donovan gave Stark a very narrow glare.

"The militia already respect you. I mean, you got three cities to damn near drop everything in response to a Republican threat. You've got a great strategic head on your shoulders. I'm calling the captains of the militias in the province to an assembly next month, and with the mayors' decision, I suspect we can get all of them on board. Greynoble, Navarre and Lourdis are behind you already."

Rola smiled broadly. "And I have some very reliable contacts that could supply your forces with Reahtan steel, not the flimsy piggy iron found here. I'd bet they'd be more than willing to supply a provincial army over Royalist supporters."

Donovan finished his mug, and looked up warily. "If you can actually get the majority of the militias on board... I'll think about it."

"Don't think too long, Avalon won't wait."

Donovan dropped his head. "I don't doubt it."

Stark finished his mug, and took his leave. Laron patted Donovan on the shoulders, and said, "We're here for you."

"Well... ya'll are," Sunay corrected, finishing her second mug. "*I* on the other hand have orders and judgin' from the buzzin' in my head, Admiral Roberts ain't too pleased that I've been takin' so long gettin' to it. By the time ya'll are muckin' about in another war, I'm gonna be way on the other side of the continent."

Rola smiled with saccharine sweetness and said, "I'd tell you to enjoy Reaht, but I'm not sure it's possible for the Reahtans to enjoy anything. Dreadfully serious and aggressive lot, I'm told."

"Yeah... lookin' forward to it," the foxgirl replied, standing up and giving her partings before heading back to the *Goldbeard*.

Juno was waiting for her at the end of the gangplank, handing the duty roster to the foxgirl almost immediately. "Was beginnin' ta think ya'd run off an' eloped with your boy," Juno groused. "I've been

142

givin' the crew some short shifts ashore, but they're all aboard right now. We can shove off on your order."

As the spidergirl was about to leave, she snapped her fingers. "Oh right," she amended, "Joffe's been dinkin' about on the third deck, movin' stuff 'round an' bein' a general nuisance. He said he wanted ta finish it 'fore ya came back, so could ya find out what it's all 'bout so that'll he'll put the bunks back where dey belong?"

Sunay's eyes narrowed in confusion as she did just that, confirming that Juno hadn't been exaggerating. Joffe had moved two of the bunks off to the side, disassembling the frames and leaning them and the padding up against the wall. In its place was a long thick, iron tube that tapered slightly narrower at the end and sticking out of one of the portholes that Joffe had widened.

"What in the *hell?*" She demanded.

Joffe was startled initially by his captain's appearance, but it was quickly replaced by a cocky grin. "We're going to want to clear out some more room. I have nine more of these coming from the blacksmith."

"And why would we need more of those... uh... what the hell *is* that, anyway?"

The craftsman's grin only broadened. "*This,* ma'am, is the future of warfare."

From outside the ship, a booming shout interrupted whatever Joffe was going to explain. "*Ahmin! You cowardly snake! Get out here!*"

Sunay remembered that voice. "The future is gonna have to wait. Looks like we got a past to deal with first."

The foxgirl emerged above decks just as Horal, son of whoever, pushed his way on board. He was damn lucky Juno didn't bite him and end the matter right then and there. Then again, he had the look of a man who had nothing to lose, so he might have even known that already.

"I've been chasing this damn ship since Tortuga," Horal snarled, the veins on his forehead bulging.

"Kinda surprised yer still alive," Sunay remarked coldly. "Last I heard, the Daynes all dropped dead."

Horal's face flushed red. "I didn't listen to those damned Winter Walkers. The only thing I've ever wanted, all I'll ever want, is *my* ship."

"Ain't yer ship, and it never was. Get that in yer skull."

"You *will* send that coward of a tigerman out here. I *will* scrum with him, and I *will* win *my* ship back!"

Sunay's fists clenched. "Ahmin ain't here any more. He's gone, and this is *my* ship now. Ya wanna scrum? Yer gonna have to take it up with me."

The Dayne laughed bitterly. "You think you can hold your own with *me*? Very well then, whorish woman. You will be easy prey. Do you know how to scrum?"

"Not hard to figure out, from what I'm told," the foxgirl replied. "No rules. Do whatever."

Horal amended, "No weapons. No outside interference."

"Fine by me. Yer the one that'd need both."

If there was any official beginning to the scrum, it came unannounced. Horal charged like an angry bull, and while Sunay was nimble, the Dayne was *much* faster on his feet than she expected. While it wasn't flush contact, the two collided at the shoulder, reminding Sunay that she had been *stabbed* in that same shoulder two days before. The pain flared through her body, causing her to lose her balance, spinning to the deck and landing hard.

Horal might have been able to press that advantage, if he hadn't been anticipating a clean tackle. Instead, the impact at his shoulder was enough to make him stumble, lose his own footing, and crash head first into the *Goldbeard's* main mast. The crash split his forehead open and caused blood to flow liberally down his face, and he only was able to clear his vision by the time Sunay picked herself up, rolling her shoulder to try and work out the pain.

"Might not want to do that again for *both* our sakes," Sunay quipped crossly.

Horal again went on the attack, and Sunay was perfectly fine with the Dayne being the aggressor. Her agility didn't lend to overpowering her opponent, but it *did* lend itself to countering the openings he was giving with his attacks. Those windows were small, as Horal was rather quick himself, but they were there. A scratch across a forearm, a kick to the thigh... while they did little on first appearances, the cumulative effect would become a factor over time.

It was all a matter of avoiding that one punch power Horal demonstrated as he dazed Sunay with a glancing blow to the side of her head. A second punch would have broken her nose along with the rest of her face if instinct and that she was already stumbling hadn't put her out of harm's way. As she fell, she swept her right leg, tripping Horal and sending him crashing face first onto the deck, reopening the wound on his forehead that had just been starting to slow.

"Is this how Daynes normally settled their disputes?" Sunay grumbled as the foxgirl tried to get the damn world to stop spinning for five damn minutes.

Horal at the same time had picked himself off the deck, and again wiped blood out of his face. "Just the ones that need blood spilled!"

"Well, yer doin' plenty of *that*," the foxgirl quipped, and it was one jab too many.

This time, Horal's tackle hit flush, slamming Sunay into the deck with his weight falling on her and forcing the wind from her lungs. She twisted out of a punch that would have hit her in the face, but instead struck her in the shoulder and caused her to scream in pain.

At that point, Horal noticed the bandage and the faint seep of blood through her shirt.

Horal jumped to his feet, his left hand clenched like a vice on her right bicep. "Oh, does *this* hurt, little girl?" the Dayne taunted, yanking on her arm and twisting her shoulder blade. That earned him another scream of pain, and encouraged Horal to spin in a circle twice before throwing Sunay into the main mast so that her shoulder crashed into the dense wood.

She shook her head to clear her vision, seeing the concern on the members of her crew within sight, but had little time to console them before Horal had clenched both hands around her neck, and lifted her off the ground, attempting to choke the life out of his victim.

But without securing her arms, it gave the foxgirl an opening for a counterattack. Sunay gouged her fingers deep into Horal's left arm, tearing straight towards the wrists, causing deep lacerations that would have even caused the stoutest of Dayne warriors to give pause at the damage.

But Horal was not even the average Dayne. His response was to lean forward, bite into Sunay's right ear, and rip half of it off with a swift torque of his head.

Surprisingly, it didn't hurt nearly as much as Sunay would have thought, no doubt due to the adrenaline rushing through her veins. Her response was along the lines of an eye for an ear, giving another malicious rake, straight across his left eye. She could *feel* the change in texture as she cut into the eyeball, and then slashed again going for the right eye, but Horal leaned backwards and instead got a split lip for the trouble.

That finally got Horal to release her, and they both staggered apart momentarily to asses the damage to themselves.

"Ya want this to be a fight to the death, eh?" Sunay bellowed in rage. "Well... I can do that, ya bastard!"

Half blind meant that Horal was lacking some vital depth perception, and his counter swing missing in front of Sunay by nearly a foot. It also probably didn't help matters that Sunay ducked into his blind side and took another slash across his flank. While his shirt dampened the blow, it still left five angry red lines that started seeping more blood.

The foxgirl knew that none of this, while painful, would kill any time soon. But the attacks themselves weren't the point. Sunay's mind was churning at full speed, trying to herd the massive Dayne into just the right spot. He wasn't cooperative in the slightest, but her target area was extremely large, and he didn't pose too much of a threat anymore, so she could bide her time for when it was right.

A haymaker from Horal caught nothing but air. "Stand still and fight me, wench!" he howled in frustration.

Sunay would have laughed if she hadn't been breathing heavily. She wasn't exactly bouncing around. He wouldn't have been able to hit the main mast at this point, and *that* was *immobile*.

The foxgirl then got the opening she was looking for a pair of exchanges later, digging in her fingernails across Horal's right eye. Now with the Dayne wholly blinded, she offered him one chance to leave with his life intact.

"Give up now?"

His response was a blind swing in what he thought was Sunay's general direction. Let no one say Horal was not determined.

Ahmin would have probably had someone on his crew knock the Dayne out and leave him on shore to try and recover. Sunay was not Ahmin, and Sunay was frankly tired of this nonsense. She was going to end it today.

It was little effort to herd her opponent right to where she wanted, right up against the railing. And while Horal was much larger than her, the railing was a good fulcrum to send him over and into the sea with a double kick right to the chest.

Horal splashed almost comically, face down in full belly-flop. He righted himself quickly, treading water, and trying to get a hold on the *Goldbeard's* hull, though the lacquered boards didn't give him any grip to attempt a climb. "You think you won?" He shouted.

Sunay looked down, where Horal's thrashing was mixing his blood with the water, and the telltale dorsal fins of what would be his executioner. "Yeah, actually I do!"

"I'll hunt you to the ends of the earth, wench! As long as I draw breath, I *will* have what's mine!"

Sunay grit her teeth. She had *almost* felt sorry for the fool and was going to have Juno grant him mercy. "Yeah... that's the problem, ain't it? Because you ain't gonna be breathin' much longer. See... if ya sailed the southern seas enough, and ya clearly haven't, ya'd know about *sharks*."

"What?"

"They *love* the smell of blood in the water... an' ya've been bleedin' quite a bit."

"Do you think you'll scare..."

His boast was cut off as the Dayne was abruptly drug under the water, and the blood pool turned larger and more crimson. The foxgirl walked away from the railing, not too keen on watching a man get mauled to death by diamond sharks.

"If he somehow survives this," she grumbled to Juno, "the next time... just bite 'im."

Juno saluted. "Shoulda just let me do it this time!"

"Yeah, yeah..." she snarled, before shouting out her orders. "Garth, get the anchor up! Gurgn, get the crew rowin'! Bolin, once we're clear, turn us to a hundred 'n ten! Juno, full sail! We got time to make up, and Reaht's a waitin'! I gotta get myself cleaned up."

Garth offered her a rather threadbare towel, but it was good as any to slow the bleeding on her mangled ear long enough to get to the medic on the second deck.

Chapter Eight: Smoke on the Water, Fire in the Sky

Sunay was supposed to meet the other captains in the port town of Roma, which became a dicey proposition when Reaht conquered the city-state formerly in the Free Provinces between the eastern empire and Grand Aramathea two weeks prior. So the meeting was diverted to Morganstown, the Buccaneer Heaven, far to the southeast, situated on a small isolated island probably a mile wide if using a very generous measure and a low tide.

At one time many, many decades ago, Morganstown was the birthplace of the Gold Pirates and served as their base of operations. But as the organization expanded and grew, the small tropical island became ill-suited to manage the entirety of the activities and the administration needed to manage it.

The Reahtan portion of the fleet now used it as a hideout well away from where any civilian or military ship would travel, and decided the best way to manage their space was to build up. Wood and hemp brought in from the mainland resulted in what amounted to an overgrown play fort, seven "floors" made piecemeal around the few trees that dotted the island, connected by rope bridges and zip lines, and covering nearly the entirety of the available land.

A sharply declining shelf allowed for even a ship the size of the *Goldbeard* to get close enough to dock, and where a small welcoming party was waiting for Sunay as she stepped off the gangplank, and onto the boardwalk that led to the island proper.

"Captain Sunay?" the head of the procession asked, a dirty gray haired man with green eyes and a face weathered from age and splotched with angry red marks across the side of his face. "Madam Claus, I'm gonna be escortin' ya to the meetin' room. Come along quick-like."

"Aye aye," the foxgirl answered before calling back to her ship. "Juno! I don't expect to be long! Keep her ready to sail!"

She followed Claus underneath the second floor of the structure, and up a rope ladder to the second level before turning right. The boards creaked under her feet, and she spared a look down to see no small degree of rot and decay from the sea air. She looked back up, and wasn't any more assured by the look of the supports or the ropework used to lash the floors to them.

"So... when... are you all planning on upgrading here?" Sunay asked nervously.

Claus waved off her concern. "The wood is stained Reahtan Cypress. It doesn't look pretty, but it's held strong for as long as I can remember, and shows no signs of breaking down yet."

Clearly, Claus and Sunay had *very* different definitions of "no signs," and she didn't feel any better about it as she went up a zig-zagged ramp up to the third floor, and another rope ladder to the fourth. All the more reason to get off this rickety disaster as soon as possible.

The meeting room was notable only in that there was a three-foot wide hole in the roof, with pieces of decayed wood still occasionally dropping down to the circular table below it, with the four representatives of the Eastern Fleet sitting in a semi-circle

"Good thing it doesn't look like rain." Sunay replied sarcastically.

"We do apologize for the poor accommodations, but with the Reahtan expansion, we make do with what we have," one of them, the lionman chimera that Sunay had heard of in passing said, introducing himself. "Leonas, captain of the Legible."

"Fittin' name," Sunay quipped, accepting his hand in greeting. "Ain't many pirates speak so cleanly."

Leonas got a laugh from that, and one by one, the other captains gave their greetings.

A redhead with a gold bandana and almost equally red eyes was next. "Bonny, of th' Gold Fortune."

Next was a man, with long loop earrings almost entirely hidden by his shoulder length hair, and a long scar that had closed his left eye shut. "Rackham, cap'n of th' Vengeance."

Another woman, with bright green hair that pretty much made every other feature about her slip Sunay's mind save for the accent that seemed to draw out vowels unnaturally long. "Rosaria, captain of the Ispania."

"Charmed," Sunay replied, dropping to the seat that appeared to make her the head of the table. "All right, let's make this quick. Now, I'm told ya folks have lost three ships already?"

The other captains understood the incredulous tone of Sunay's voice. Gold Pirate ships, despite whatever the appearances, were the finest constructed ships in the whole continent, using techniques and engineering that civilian and imperial ship builders hadn't even dreamed up, much less made reality. The Imperial Aramathea had made some strides due to the mind of Dominus Socrato, but a fledgling navy like Reaht's shouldn't be able to hold a candle to anything sailing under the Gold Pirates banner.

"Yes, and I know what you're thinking," Leonas explained. "Reaht doesn't seem to have any insight into our movements or the knowledge of our ships."

"Then how the *hell* are they sinkin' us?" Sunay demanded.

"Numbers," Rackham answered. "Sheer numbers. Dey build ships by th' dozens in dere shipyards at Reaht 'Arbor, flimsy things that're a minor miracle ta sail anywheres. But when yer crankin' dem out by da dozens, ya can swarm anythin' ya see."

"Reaht don't care about losses," Bonny added. "They don't care if'n two of twenty ships return. They jus' throw out twenty more for th' next attack. As it stands, their navy counts four hundred ships, and they probably built twice that."

"Use those numbers, board their target, burn it down once everyone's dead and killed, repeat as necessary," Rosaria finished. "That's the Reahtan way, victory at all costs."

"So, yer all sayin' we have to find a way to curb the number of ships that are being produced," Sunay concluded.

Leonas nodded in agreement. "I suppose so, but how exactly are we going to do that? As we've mentioned, they're swarming the eastern seas. We couldn't even *get* to Reaht Harbor if we wanted to."

Sunay grinned. "You leave *that* to me." The foxgirl had an idea developing, and it was crazy enough that it just might work. "Is there any other pressing business that needs tendin' to?"

The other four captains slowly shook their heads, and so Sunay stood up. "Then we'll consider this meetin' adjourned for now. I need all the information we have on Reaht Harbor and the ships they're buildin'. Get me contact information with agents on land if we need it. And don't wander off, I might be needin' ya and yer crews."

Sunay didn't want to commit to anything until she spoke with Joffe, and got his assessment on whether or not the idea she had percolating was even plausible, but it seemed to make sense in her head. The rest of her scheme started winding around that idea while she returned to her ship, and down to the third deck where Joffe was polishing his "cannons."

"Joffe, you know anythin' about Reaht Harbor?" the foxgirl asked.

"Like pretty much any other shipyard, from what I know. Nothing particularly unique or special about it. Why do you ask?"

"So, a lot of wood and other stuff that can burn."

"Certainly. It's a shipyard, after all."

"Is there any way we can make these cannons fire burning pitch?"

Joffe closed his eyes, deep in thought. "Well, not *pitch*... far too tacky and would muck up the cannon barrels. But there's a couple things I could whip up that would be able to set wood ablaze. Thinking of torching the whole place? How are we going to get close enough?"

Sunay's grin reappeared. "That's what's I'm figurin' out right now. Get to workin' on the burnin'. I'll get to work on the plannin'."

She needed to go back to her cabin to actually do that planning. The information she had asked for arrived quickly, her head buzzing from an incoming contact almost the instant she had closed her cabin door behind her. Her experience with land agents in other regions were not always positive, but these people seemed to be on point.

What was awaiting her was a bevy of information pertaining to Reaht Harbor, maps with significant buildings marked in red. Another map with water depths useful to plot the *Goldbeard's* course. Another one marking Reahtan Navy patrol patterns. A stack of papers with weather predictions for the next three months. Detailed dossiers on important leaders overseeing the harbor along with how they would muster defenses for an attack.

And one small handwritten note. "Hope this helps," Sunay recited with a smirk. "Yeah, I think it does." She wrote a short thank you note in response, and slipped it into the cabinet before getting to work. The beauty of her scheme was that outside of the *Goldbeard*, the Reahtan Navy was going to supply the ships for this attack...

But she *was* going to need some volunteers.

And Joffe. He had a much better head for a lot of this numbers stuff.

~ ~ ~ ~ ~

Any concerns that the information Sunay had gotten was inaccurate was dispelled as Bolin reported ten Reahtan ships approaching from the north; right on schedule, right on the path they were supposed to be patrolling. This was what Sunay *wanted*.

The *Goldbeard* was an oddity among pirate ships, that she knew, far more suited for large merchant goods or as a traditional warship rather than the quick, nimble, strike and retreat frigates and sloops common among pirate ships. If it came to a fight, the Reahtans would find her ship to be a *lot* harder to take down.

But that was for later. Right now, she didn't want a fight at all.

Sunay had alternate colors run, borrowed from another one of the ships in the Reahtan fleet because they had the colors she needed... or at least reasonably close. Granted the background field was cream, rather than white, and *no* Avalonian city-state had a bear as a mascot, she was rather confident that the Reahtans sailing in the Navy didn't exactly have a razor sharp knowledge of Avalon or the impending Free Province of Versilles.

Sunay had her crew dressed up in their finest, Juno leading the more... rugged... members of her crew and the volunteers from other ships tucked away down in the cargo hold. The *Goldbeard*, for the time being, was playing the part of a merchant vessel, with the hope that it would get the Reahtans close enough to spring the trap shut after it was too late.

The worry was whether the Reahtans would actually stop and inspect this unknown ship, or if they would just attack first and ask questions later. The eastern empire had gained notoriety for their overzealous aggression.

But at least they didn't attack what looked to be a merchant ship on sight. Two pulled up, one to each side of the *Goldbeard*, and Sunay heard a shout from below, "By the authority of the Emperor himself, we demand we be allowed on board for inspection!"

Sunay forced herself to look bothered as she leaned over the railing. Damn, the Reahtan ships *were* small and cheaply constructed. They were more like sailboats than anything fit for deep sea navigation. Two decks, one above and one below water, a single mast and sail, and four rowers on the top deck, which was half of the eight man crew.

"Seriously?" the foxgirl snarled. "Damnitall, fine. Hurry up, then! We gotta get this stuff to Reaht Harbor! Joffe, toss 'em a ladder! Garth, drop anchor!"

The pair complied, Joffe unrolling a rope ladder over the side of the deck, then ran over to the other side to lower another ladder for the crew of the second boat. The Reahtans climbed up onto the *Goldbeard's* deck, one by one, dressed in chain mail and half plate armor, completely unsuitable for sailing on the open seas.

"Coders, what happens to the likes of ya if ya fall overboard?" Sunay wondered out loud.

"We drown," the head of the first ship declared. He was a stout man, his very tight build clearly evident despite his armor, even though he was also remarkably short. Sunay never considered herself particularly tall, but this was a fellow she could look right in the eye.

"If we can't swim, we are weak, unfit to serve our God Emperor. Now, who are you and what is your business in these waters?"

"I'm Sunay, captain of the Blue Bear, and this is my first, Joffe," Sunay said. "We're deliverin' cypress wood from Lourdis to Reaht Harbor. That's what we were told, that you folks are lookin' for wood. We're lookin' for arms to aid in our war of independence. The mayors of Versilles figured we could get a trade goin'."

"All trade treaties are signed by the Emperor or his Council. You've come a long way for nothing."

"Well then steer us towards Reaht and we'll talk. I ain't comin' halfway across the world to come back with the wood I left with."

"Reaht is landlocked. You'd have to go through..."

"Reaht Harbor, I know. So why dontcha stop hasslin' us and let us do our job?"

She found herself looking at the business end of a gladius, well maintained as the polish on the sword was near blinding in the sun. "I would strongly suggest you stop that tongue of yours, especially since *I* am the one who will decide if you get to do your job, or instead find a watery grave."

The foxgirl held her breath, then reluctantly conceded, "Fine. What d'ya need me or my crew to do?"

"First and foremost, we will need to inspect your cargo."

Perfect.

Sunay made a show of gesturing to the stairs. "Third deck. Help yerself."

The Reahtan captain did so with a silent nod, motioning for eight of the crew between the two ships to follow him while the rest stayed above decks. From this point on, timing was fairly crucial. If the next step happened too quickly, then the current crew wouldn't be disabled in time... but if it took too long, then even these clowns would know something was up.

Down below decks, Juno and the volunteers would hopefully be dispatching of the investigators quietly, and with any luck in time for...

"Legionnaire Spartus! Pirates! Coming in from the southeast!"

Right on time.

The Legionnaire still on the deck immediately shouted, "Divert our ships to intercept! Sink that vessel no matter the cost!" He then turned to Sunay, and ordered, "You and your ship will not move from this spot until Legionnaire Veritas has authorized you to

153

continue."

Sunay snapped a lazy salute and said, "Yessir. Go get 'em."

Legionnaire Spartus didn't wait for his colleagues, exactly as the dossier on him suggested he would. Sunay had to fight back a grin. His crew was in their boat waiting for the rest below decks as the other ships in their patrol broke off formation to face the "pirate" ship approaching.

In truth, the ship that was coming was one that the pirate fleets had been ready to burn down and let sink to the bottom of the sea. It was one they could afford to lose as the crew abandoned ship off the aft side. She had chosen the best swimmers among the fleet for this part of the plan... swimming *underneath* their ship and coming up to ambush the unsuspecting Reahtans.

At this point, Juno and the row team emerged, dressed in the clothes of the inspectors down below. Had anyone from the Reahtans been paying closer attention, they'd have realized some of their men abruptly had horribly fitting armor. But instead, by the time they realized that the "inspectors" weren't their men, they were getting tossed overboard.

"Well, time to prove yer worth to yer 'God Emperor'," Sunay sneered down at the Reahtan soldiers desperately trying to tread water or fight out of their armor. "Meanwhile, I think we'll be on our way."

"You won't... get away... with this..." Spartus sputtered between gasps of air.

She looked out towards the southeast, where a single candle burst with green sparks, the signal that their end of the mission had been a success. "Actually, I think I will," the foxgirl replied, then gave a little finger wave and smile to the legionnaire. "Ta ta!"

Sunay no longer gave the Reahtans any further thought, mostly because she knew that drowning was a pretty miserable way to go. She instead focused on her future orders. "Garth! Pull up the anchor! Let's swing back and meet up with the rest of the gang. I wanna make sure we're all on the same page for the next phase!"

~ ~ ~ ~ ~

To the men working the docks at Reaht Harbor, it no doubt wouldn't have seemed terribly out of the ordinary at first... a procession of their naval vessels escorting a merchant galleon towards the harbor. Their first signs that something was amiss would have been as the front formation didn't start to slow or trim their sails. It would have gotten *really* curious when the crew of the lead vessels abandoned ship and were gathered up by the second line. If they were smart, they would have started running as the ships crashed into the dockside.

And they most certainly started running when those ships exploded into tall plumes of fire upon crashing.

The impact as the ships hit had been enough to set off the candles that Joffe had prepared and crammed in the lower deck. They served two purposes, decimating the docks and making it difficult for ships to launch in defense, and letting off distracting colors and sounds while the *Goldbeard* swung broadside to the harbor. Hatches swung down, and the cannons rolled into position.

"Joffe! Fire on our first target when ya got a solution!" Sunay bellowed into the mouthpiece leading to below decks, using his word for the calculations he used to determine the correct amount of powder, cannon angle, and wind conditions.

He had made most of those calculations already during the initial planning, but was currently down below decks with a spyglass to make any last-minute corrections based on current conditions. He apparently didn't need many for the first salvo, aimed at the lumber housing on the north side of the harbor.

The *Goldbeard* shuddered as the ten cast iron weapons discharged, the lacquered balls igniting from the black powder used to propel them... sending what looked like ten large fireballs into the storage building, the tell tale signs of smoke rising followed by fingers of fire. The flames would find plenty of tinder in there.

Sunay barked, "Bring us about to one hundred and seventy five, Bolin! Easy on the sails, Juno! Let's give Joffe and our gunners a good look at the target!"

Balco then cried out from the crow's nest, "Reahtan ships! Comin' in from th' north, ma'am!"

"That's what the diversion crews are for!" Sunay shouted up. "They'll deal with it! Keep us on course, Bolin!"

Said diversionary crews were using the remainder of the Reahtan ships they had appropriated, and turned to intercept the reinforcements. While there was little doubt the Reahtan military were fierce fighters, they had been successful against the Gold Pirates in the past through sheer numbers, and fighting on ships was something they had little experience in.

The pirate crews rammed ships together, creating blocks and slowing progress, jumping from ship to ship. The Reahtan military was used to being the aggressors in combat, and fighting defensively put them off balance. By the time they were able to rally together as a unit, their numbers had thinned to the point that the momentum had turned against them. The first wave of the counterattack had been successfully stalled.

That didn't mean that the pirates had won just yet - there was no doubt more reinforcements were coming - but it *did* mean the *Goldbeard* would have the time it needed to complete its tasks. The second round of flaming cannonballs found its mark in the pitch stores, which almost immediately went up with a billowing black smoke and flames that danced to the top of the tallest buildings in the harbor. Rivers of flaming tar spilled out into the streets, spreading the flames and cutting off people trying to escape the carnage.

For a brief moment, Sunay's heart bubbled with horror at the sight of workers being surrounded by flames and smoke, but forced her emotions aside. She could have nightmares about melting skin and horrified screams later. Now was time to focus.

"One hundred and sixty, Bolin! Juno, let down the sails! Garth, light the candle to tell the other crews to bugger out! We're only gonna get one shot at this, so let's make it count!"

Their target was the command center for Reaht Harbor. It was by far the most difficult shot, lying the farthest away from the docks, and composed of stone rather than wood. It was also the least essential of the sites Sunay had targeted, as taking pot shots at the harbor's leaders wasn't nearly as important as crippling their operations. But it was still a shot worth taking.

It was hard to see the building in question through the increasing smoke and fire billowing up in front of it. But that didn't seem to dissuade Joffe, because the *Goldbeard* shook once more and the streaks of flaming iron shot out with screaming speed towards their target. Sunay could hear the sound of iron striking stone, the cracking of mortar and the scraping of supports bending from the multiple impacts.

Then mind-numbing disbelief as the entire thing went up in a towering plume of flame that turned damn near the whole sky red.

The heat from the detonation was so intense that Sunay could feel it even from her position as a cool summer's day became sweltering almost in an instant. The pillar of fire billowed out, bathing almost the entire harbor in a rain of fire, and making it a moot point for anyone still trapped in the city.

Sunay knew this was beyond anything ordinary when even Joffe was awestruck. She could hear him bellow unassisted from the third deck, "What in the blazing hells was *that*?"

She wished she had an answer to that question too.

Juno descended from the main mast, clinging upside down as her jaw dropped open. For once, the spidergirl was at a loss for words. The smells soon followed, burning wood and human flesh, soon overpowered by something Sunay had no description for. It was akin to hot peppers burned in plastic, a wholly unnatural scent for anyone on the *Goldbeard*, and thoroughly disconcerting.

For a brief moment, Sunay considered turning into the harbor and trying to help anyone who might have survived the cataclysm. But a second explosion followed the first, raining even more liquid fire and starting to sizzle the waters just off the ruined docks, convincing her that the best course of action was to get clear of the entire damn harbor just in case there was more hellfire waiting to erupt from the ruined command center.

~ ~ ~ ~ ~

Partial answers came on the return to Morganstown, as she got a chance to sit down and talk directly to the Reahtan administrator. He was certainly a handsome and regal looking man from what she could tell, which quickly came as no surprise when he introduced himself.

"Greetings, Captain. I am Prince Antony of the Reahtan Empire, and the Gold Pirate Administrator to the Great Empire."

The *prince* of Reaht? Talk about having friends in high places. "Well, that explains the incredible depth of information I had available to me," Sunay said.

"Not as in-depth as it needed to be," Antony corrected. "Which was why I wished to speak in person. I wished to apologize for the horrible oversight that led you to being blamed for the deaths of many of my people. After this meeting, I will resign my position for the dishonor imposed upon you."

Sunay waved him off and said, "Feh! Yer the first good land administrator I've met." She then hastily amended, "Well... the second, I suppose. I don't want ya leaving over *my* reputation, got it?"

Antony offered a slight laugh. "I will take it under advisement."

Despite his calm demeanor, she could sense in his voice that his reasons likely had little to do with the deaths being blamed on her. This was tearing him up inside, the deaths of *his* people because of something *he* apparently missed was weighing heavily on him, despite his willingness to aid the Gold Pirates efforts.

The foxgirl tried to turn the conversation to a different topic. "So, do we have *any* idea what in the Coders happened?"

"As far as our agents have been able to discern, Governor Tablis was secretly moving alchemical materials through Reaht Harbor on behest of Dominus Augustus on the Isle of Donne."

"Why so covertly? Isn't Donne part of the empire?"

"Yes... and no," Antony explained. "Reaht governs the isle rather than controls it, and Augustus's tower is effectively its own nation. It was an agreement that he and the Legionnaire Tavaris reached when the Empire first came to his island twenty years ago. Augustus was not interested in defending his keep; he merely desired that his studies and research would not be interrupted. The Legionnaire was wary of throwing his men at a tremendously powerful mage, a prudence that my people have been ignoring lately, I might add."

"And so anythin' being sent to the Dominus would be considered foreign trade, which I'm sure requires paperwork and money that no one was particularly keen on spendin'?" Sunay wondered, even as she doubted that would be the primary reason.

Antony confirmed as much. "That may have been an added benefit, I suppose, but I suspect the real reason is that Reaht does not support arcane arts outside of a very few instances. We are distrustful of mages as a general rule, and only those who submit properly to the Emperor and have attained *years* of loyalty are allowed to even *begin* to study those arts. The sort of materials that Dominus Augustus was supposedly seeking could have gotten anyone caught handling it executed."

"That seems a bit extreme."

"Indeed, especially since the Dominus normally would have been able to secure other means to attain those goods. But these would seem to be relics found only in Reaht. Our agents in the field are exploring every lead to determine what those relics were. Would you like me to keep you updated?"

Sunay shook her head. "Nah, unless ya think it is somehow pertinent to the fleet. I've learned not to stick mah nose too deep in land business."

The pair shared a knowing laugh, and afterwards Sunay couldn't help but turn the conversation back to where it started. "So, how did a prince come to be in our fold anyway?"

"I love my land. I love my people. I think our mindless aggression and expansion will doom us sooner than it will save us. My father and brothers seek nothing but more lands to control and more people to conquer. They feel that strength is the only law, and that they have the strength. They do not realize that if not for the efforts of the Gold Pirates, the Aramatheans would have made us pay for our advances ten fold already."

"Yer talkin' about the death ray on Sacili," Sunay assumed.

Antony nodded. "That was the most prominent. I wish to add my thanks for being the catalyst to stop that. But there are *many* ways that the First Empire could choke the life out of Reaht if not for our organization. Our operatives kept the trade lines open when Imperial Aramathea wanted to slam all those doors eastward shut. They keep Aramathea's Second Army from pushing into the Free Provinces to engage our forces where, despite my father's bluster, we would be outnumbered, under-equipped, and not as seasoned in large scale combat."

Sunay hummed in thought. "Never woulda guessed."

"The Aramatheans have ages of experience over us. Fighting and conquering city-states to the north and west in the Free Provinces is hardly suitable experience for the highly disciplined Phalanx that would be waiting to crush us. We may be their equal soon, but not yet. I think it is fair exchange that I aid Gold Pirate efforts as they have helped us immensely."

"Even as we now turn on yer people?"

Antony took and released a deep, slow breath. "It has been hard to balance the two as of late, yes. But again, your efforts in Reaht Harbor were indirectly to our benefit. Our navy is not *nearly* prepared to take on any significant power, and I have little doubt that was going to be our next step. Crippling our fleet now may very well be what we need to survive in the long run. Do you wish to continue with your plans as intended?"

Sunay nodded. "I do. Stopping the production of new ships is all well and good, but there's still hundreds of ships still active, and we need to deal with that as well."

"Then I will spread the information to the proper ears. I would anticipate my people's counterattack within two weeks."

"We'll be ready."

Well... maybe. There was the entire part of telling the other captains about the next phase of her plan.

~ ~ ~ ~ ~

To be fair, she didn't expect them to take it well. And when the pirates had reassembled in Morganstown and she revealed the next stage of her plan, the other captains met her expectations.

"You want to do *what*?" Leonas demanded, his cheeks puffing in rage. "This is *our* home!"

"Oh, come off it!" Sunay retorted dismissively. "This place is a shithole. It's the rat's den ya crawl into because yer too scared to do yer job! I ain't gonna let ya do it anymore."

"We're bothered ya did'n tell us about dis until now, ya see?" Bonny said. She wasn't as visibly upset as the others, but Sunay could tell that she wasn't pleased either.

"Yeah, because I knew ya'll wouldn't like it," the foxgirl answered. "It's the perfect place to spring this trap, and let's be honest, we don't *need* this place anymore. And we sure as *hell* won't need it once we've broken the Reahtan Navy's backs."

Rackham grumbled, "Dat's easy fer ya ta say, it's *our* men dat're stickin' dere necks out 'ere."

"Yeah, and I lost two of mah own crew in the battle at the harbor!" Sunay snarled in irritation, referring to members of her rowing team that had volunteered to lead diversionary teams. Foley and Mick both willingly sacrificed their own lives charging the second wave of reinforcements to allow the other teams time to flee the scene. "Don't you *dare* be accusin' me of usin' ya'll as shields! I'll slice yer throat out right here and now!"

Rackham moved to stand. "Izzat right? Let's see ya try little girl..."

He was pushed right back down into his seat by Rosaria and Bonny. "You ain't seein' nothin', Rack," Bonny chided. "Yer barely on one good leg as it is."

"Fact is, I'm trying to let ya volunteer as a courtesy," Sunay continued. "I've been sent here to get this mess straightened up, and that's what I'm gonna do, with or without yer approval. Believe me, I'll make this an order if I have to. But I'd like to think we're all smart enough to know that the way things 'ave been can't stand, and we gotta do somethin' big."

Her fellow captains looked uncertainly at each other, but at the same time knew the foxgirl was right. Leonas offered, "I think we're more enamored by the *idea* that Morganstown still stands than actually supporting its presence. This is a significant symbol you're asking us to give up... but we shouldn't be about symbols."

Rosaria nodded in agreement readily, though of all the

captains, she seemed to be the one who had offered the least objections to begin with. "If you feel confident in this scheme, then I will support it. It's not like we've had any better ideas."

Bonny stared down Rackham, and the grizzled stubble-chinned captain finally relented with a scowl. "Ah, do whateva ya want, li'l girl. Yer gonna do it anyways."

"I plan to," Sunay replied coldly, "Most of the work is already done, really. We jus' need to give it the proper push."

"What do you need us to do then?" Rosaria asked.

"Just get the word out to the rest of the fleet. I need 'em all here."

Rackham huffed, "Ain't gonna let the four o'us in on dis plan, den?"

The foxgirl smiled broadly. "Not yet, I ain't. I wantcha all to be just as surprised as the Reahtans."

~ ~ ~ ~ ~

The first warning of approaching Reahtan ships came four days later, via the *Swaying Leaf,* a schooner that served as a scouting ship for Morganstown. Its broad sails in relation to its smaller size allowed it speed for that purpose, to the point that it had reached harbor to deliver news hours before visual confirmation from lookouts on the island could be made.

Sunay's grin returned upon hearing the news, and she sprinted off down the rickety fifth floor, grabbed a zip line that crossed the central courtyard down to the second, then straight jumped down almost on top of Joffe. The craftsman jolted and nearly dropped the pipe he had been puffing from, then panicked as he quickly reacted to catch it, finally huffing in relief when he was successful.

"Coders' mercy, captain, *don't do that!*" He protested while he tried to slow his breathing. "You just about set this whole thing ablaze long before you wanted to!"

"Whatcha so nervous about?" She asked.

"Because no one has *ever* tried heavier than air smoke in this sort of quantity," Joffe replied testily. "I can't promise you it will work the way you are hoping. And if that smoke doesn't settle like you want..."

At that point, their ace in the hole made his presence known. "I can make the smoke settle if needed, Joffe," the mage Marco said confidently, stepping into the courtyard once he realized he could offer something to the discussion. "My worry is if the wind shifts on us. Having a focusing crystal could have helped a bunch."

Joffe boggled. "Wait... *he's* here?"

"Been on the Legible's crew for the last year, in fact. The fleet had been hoping that I could fool the Reahtans into attacking illusions, but I couldn't get them to fall for it."

"That's something for another time, Marco," Sunay hissed in warning. "One that we can explore once we have the breathin' room to do it."

"So why don't we just have him conjure an illusion of the smoke?"

Marco sighed in annoyance. "As I had *just* said, the Reahtans haven't been falling for my magic. This one would be especially difficult as there'd be no reason for them to believe that smoke was hovering on the water. Illusion is just as much the target fooling themselves as it is the illusionist fooling the target. But what I *can* do is make sure that the smoke you create doesn't evaporate into the air. It won't be *easy*, but I'm sure I can do *that* much."

Joffe seemed mollified by the suggestion, and put his pipe back into the right side of his mouth. "Alright then, I suppose that will have to do. Now, let me get back to work here... I want to make sure I've got the flammables right."

"Thanks for helpin' out here, Marco," Sunay said, offering a smile. Joffe's worries had become *her* worries, and the perfect little plan she had conjured now seemed a lot less perfect... which was a very bad feeling to have now that they were *long* past the point of no return.

"It's my job," the mage replied with a shrug. "Congratulations on all the promotions. The little girl is all grown up."

"Don't even start with me," the foxgirl growled.

Marco laughed. "I wouldn't *dare* stir the ire of the legendary Fire Fox!"

She punched him the stomach so hard that he doubled over and coughed. "Call me that one more time and we'll see how good ya cast magic with one hand, got it?"

He grinned as he regained his breath. "Understood."

She huffed and walked away, Marco taking stride behind her as she exited the "city" and went out onto the narrow sandy shore of the island. She could barely see the ships approaching, and with that came the nerves that she had been expecting earlier. "I wish Admiral Ahmin was here. He always knew what he was doin'. I'm sailin' blind here... with a million things that could go wrong and ruin everythin'."

"He was sailing as blind as anyone," Marco advised. "He was only brilliant at making it *seem* like he had everything under control. He certainly didn't have everything planned on Sacili. *You* were the one that broke that stalemate. You'll handle things here."

Sunay set her jaw, and said, "Yer right, but I'll never admit that in public, ya got me?"

"Got you." Marco patted her on the shoulder, and he said, "Probably want the fleet to move into position, right?"

"Yeah. I should get to it. Thanks, Marco."

The mage smiled warmly. "Anytime."

It was a pep talk she needed, because there really wasn't time to drown herself in concerns. The foxgirl left the beach and returned to the shanty town proper, crossing into the courtyard and finding the messenger enclave on the east side. "Get the word out. I want the anchors set within the hour. Everyone *not* on anchor duty needs to break dock and wait at the east side of the island. Everyone should know what their duties are. Get moving, get it done fast. Got it?"

The runners scattered in all directions through the courtyard, and Sunay took the opportunity to get to her own ship. The *Goldbeard* was going to remain moored just off the coast, her broadsides parallel to the island. That was effectively her "Plan B" if somehow the Reahtans managed to force their way through the two layers of hell waiting for them... by making the beach a kill zone.

She ran up the gangplank, stopping halfway since she was right on the level with the third deck anyway. "All squared away in here? How are the firin' teams?"

"Down to forty-five second reloads. Got a good rotation set up, too. If the Reahtans get this far, dey are gonna be facin' a steady stream."

"Good deal," Sunay said. "I'll go find Joffe and make sure he gets his butt in there."

Gurgn nodded, pulling himself back into the ship and issuing orders. Sunay meanwhile ran up to the deck to find Juno.

The spidergirl was decked out for war, with thin leather armor padded in essential places and five knives sheathed down the outside of each thigh. Sunay sighed at the sight, as she had been reluctant to put both the captain *and* the first mate on the front lines of the coming fight. "You don't look like yer ready to man the deck," Sunay said tiredly.

Juno grinned broadly. "Spit on mah knives an' everythin' too."

The foxgirl finally relented. "Alright, ya can join me in the strike teams. I'm sure Garth can man the deck until we get back. Just don't be gettin' yerself killed, got it?"

"Yay!" Juno chirped happily, quite literally *skipping* towards the gangplank.

"If ya find Joffe before I do, make sure he's ready to light our bonfire!" Sunay shouted to the retreating spidergirl, Juno flipping her hand in a wave to acknowledge the order. The foxgirl turned to Garth, and said, "I promise *one* o' us will be back before ya have to make any decisions or anythin'."

The deckhand laughed. "I think I can manage to look stupid while waitin' for everythin' else to happen."

"Good man. That's why I like ya."

Sunay left the ship, and went through the courtyard to the west shore, where she and her chosen "front line" would wait the coming of the Reahtans. Joffe was on the shore out front, with Marco directly behind, his hands curling around a light blue tome. Rosaria sided up to Sunay's left, and updated the foxgirl on what else had been learned. "The anchors are set, and Leonas is leading them towards their waiting point. Meanwhile, it seems that the Reahtans have loaded their ships as full as they can. Two hundred ships at the very least, and we're figuring at least twenty people to a ship."

"They're throwin' their whole damn navy at us," Sunay said. "Excellent."

"That's still four thousand men to account for," Rosaria replied.

"And we'll account for every single damn one of 'em if we have to."

The captain of the *Ispania* set herself in position at Sunay's side, the fingers of her left hand gently running along the hilt of her cutlass. "I suppose we shall."

"Surprised yer joining us up front," Sunay commented.

"We all have our parts to play," the woman replied. "Mine is here. Besides, I am hardly the most eager person here. Your first mate looks ready to swim out and meet our enemy herself."

Juno did indeed look very anxious, rocking on her feet and her tongue flicking over her lips. The spidergirl cocked a half grin and answered, "I was *literally* born ta kill Reahtans. I'm lookin' forward to puttin' dat upbringin' ta good use!"

"Well, the goal is to *avoid* having to go toe to toe with these lunatics as much as possible," Sunay reminded. "Our job is to just make it *look* good while everything else whittles them down." She then called out, "How's it goin' with the smoke, Joffe?"

"As ready as it'll ever be!" the craftsman called back.

Joffe never really explained well just what this smoke was, or if he did, Sunay's eyes glazed over at the explanation. All she could accurately remember was that it was a combination of... something... that created a thick white smoke heavier than air... but not heavier than water. It had been quite hectic to get the amount of supplies needed in such a short time, and at the end of it all requiring emergency supply coming via Administrator order.

"Then let it rip! Marco, get ready to give us some wind if we need it!"

Joffe frowned, but complied, yanking a cord that started a chain reaction in the line of boxes that wrapped along the entire western half of the coast. As Joffe had claimed, the smoke wasn't particularly dense, but it rolled out to sea easily enough, and lingered on the water enough to shroud the anchors that were strung along by long ropes starting a quarter mile out and running all the way up to the coast, while the breeze Marco was able to conjure helped push it further out to sea. *That* part Sunay had been able to understand. As the ships ran into the ropes, the tension would bring the anchors up and rip into the flimsy hulls of the Reahtan naval vessels.

Presuming it worked. The stakes that were driven into the waters off the coast might just be ripped out by the ships, making all the anchors worthless. The anchors themselves might not even do significant damage. But if it *did* work there was going to be a lot of Reahtans tired after having to swim to shore.

"Alright everyone! Back to the city!" Sunay yelled, and the crowd retreated towards Morganstown proper. The crux of this entire plot centered around appearances. The pirates needed to *look* like they were taken by surprise in order to properly lure their enemies into Sunay's little house of horrors.

Once the group had properly taken their places inside the city, Sunay scampered up to the third level to try and get a good look at the approaching navy, putting a spyglass up to her right eye. She did so just as the first round of ships sailed into the smoke. *That* part worked perfectly. She couldn't see the lines and anchors, and that was *also* working perfectly.

But the worry that it wasn't going to work perfectly didn't abate until she saw several ships in the first row jerk violently upward. The Reahtan formation was so tight that the vessels up to six rows behind didn't have time to react, and as a result, nearly fifty of the ships were torn apart on the trap, men hastily jumping overboard as their boats took on water and sank.

Now, a smart commander would promptly order their ships to try and sail around, but Sunay knew that the man assigned to lead the invasion was *anything* but smart. Legionnaire Minimus Maximus, a man with battle prowess near unparalleled, the agility of ten men, the strength of twenty, and the brain of half of one. He was a single-minded fellow, knowing of only one way through any task: head on and swinging.

As a result, the rear guard had little support as the Gold Pirates used their remaining ships appropriated from the Reahtans and slightly modified with iron plates on the prows, ramming the rear ships, forcing them into the grinder, and making sure that there was no means for escape while completely ruining the remainder of the Reahtan Navy.

The absolute minimum had been accomplished. Now it was time to send an enduring message to the young and aggressive empire. The Gold Pirates owned the seas.

The foxgirl sprinted back down to the ground level, and ordered her strike team to charge the Reahtans as they stumbled to shore. And they did, at first in small numbers, easily cut down and overwhelmed. No one was enjoying the slaughter more than Juno. The spidergirl bounced almost happily around the battlefield, biting and stabbing any enemy in sight, the men predictably crumpling within seconds upon exposure to Juno's lethal venom.

Sunay's fighters held the line even as the numbers balanced, as the Reahtan sailors were still exhausted from swimming and demoralized from the wreck of their entire fleet. The pirates were able to hold their position for nearly a half hour... until Legionnaire Minimus Maximus made it ashore.

If the Legionnaire was at all fatigued, he didn't show it, and Sunay swore his eyes were glowing red with rage, visible through his mop of black hair plastered to his face. Minimus pushed the hair away, revealing that his eyes *were* in fact red, and he almost thoughtlessly kicked one of Sunay's pirates away as he stood to his full height and drew his weapon from where it had been strapped to his back.

The axe head alone was damn near bigger than Sunay's torso, curving down a third of the shaft, leaving a large gap in the middle before the bottom of the blade joined the shaft once more. The foxgirl realized that the gap was actually meant as a handhold when Minimus took the greataxe and swiped horizontally in a half circle, killing three of the pirates and one of his own men in a single blow, cleaving them so cleanly and swiftly that none of the bodies might as well have even been there.

That one swipe had been so devastating that Rosaria hadn't even been in the kill zone, and the blade took her left arm clean off on its return. Sunay's eyes bulged in horror while Rosaria quickly took stock of the limb that was no longer there, and with clarity of mind that the foxgirl found astonishing, ordered Sunay and her kin to, "Run! Retreat!"

The Ispania's captain stayed, for what little distraction she served, while Sunay led the rest into the city and towards the courtyard. No wonder that man was content facing everything head on. He wasn't human. He was some sort of bear, lion, buffalo chimera that had skinned several humans and was wearing that humanity as a disguise.

Juno frequently looked back, and said, "All ah'd need is one bite."

"Yeah, good luck getting it right *now*," Sunay countered. "Let's see how he and his little friends fire walk, shall we?"

Sunay lit the wick, so to speak, with a waiting torch she grabbed as she was running. With any luck, the framework of Morganstown was as flimsy as it felt, and the whole damn thing would turn into a raging bonfire and collapse on itself quickly enough. Juno followed suit on the other side of the courtyard, and it looked like Joffe had done his work well, as the entire first floor was engulfed in flames by the time they were on the other side, with the Reahtans led by Minimus entering just as the pirates were about ready to leave.

The timing was exactly perfect... as Sunay wanted her and her kin to be completely clear before the whole thing went down. While most of the structure collapsed inward, fragments tumbling from the highest floors made it a mad dash to get to the eastern shore and onto the *Goldbeard* as the first floor buckled and set off a chain reaction, the entire city of Morganstown collapsing on itself with the dry tinder of the upper floors smoldering and slowly building the flames.

It went down sooner than Sunay had wanted, and thus hadn't trapped the majority of the Reahtans that had made it ashore. But it at least caught that freak of nature Legionnaire. Sunay liked her odds against the rest even as they worked their way through the burning remains, especially as they emerged into the range of the *Goldbeard's* cannons.

Joffe had developed several different types of payload for his cannons, though Sunay didn't quite understand why he called the small ball clusters grape shot, as the individual balls were more the size of grape*fruit*. They were designed to disable sails, but both he and Sunay figured they could also be used for infantry targets due to their wide spread, as getting hit with one of the "grapes" was just as deadly as getting hit by one of the "rounds."

And that theory was remarkably accurate, as with remarkable routine, the cannons started firing on the approaching forces one at a time, each one spitting a rain of iron into the kill zone. By the time the tenth had fired, the first was ready to go, giving the steady stream of death that Gurgn had promised. Limbs torn off, bodies twisted and split in half, it was a mercy more than anything to take a grape to the head, which many did.

In the meantime, Sunay and the *Goldbeard's* crew took to defending the deck, grabbing bows and arrows to pick off any attempts at climbing the hull... not that they'd have much luck with that. Then the Reahtans surprised Sunay with ingenuity she had not been expecting.

The soldiers began pulling out remains from the fire that hadn't been severely burned yet, and began charging the ship, using the long planks as shields from arrows and then as makeshift gangplanks to gain access to the *Goldbeard's* deck. While the tactic was clever, Sunay and her crew adjusted quickly, pushing the planks away as much as possible, shooting the soldiers as they tried to navigate the climb, or in the case of Juno, crawling along the *underside* and wreaking havoc with men already trying to maintain balance.

Sunay's plan had been *brilliant* to counter the numbers advantage; what had been thousands of Reahtan soldiers had been whittled down to handfuls now being pressed by the rest of the Gold Pirate crews that had begun sending their men ashore.

But numbers, and possibly even rationality, mattered little to Legionnaire Minimus Maximus.

He emerged from a portion of the ruined city that no human had any business surviving, through the densest portion of the fire, the tunic under his armor still literally smoking, and his axe lightly glowing from exposure to the heat. While *it* cooled quickly, the Legionnaire did not. He charged, overwhelming squads of pirates single-handedly even after he became the only Reahtan willing or able to continue fighting.

He had grabbed a plank dropped by an earlier attempt and was heading straight for the *Goldbeard*, when he took a ball of grape shot directly to the chest. Somehow, it didn't rip him in half, but did knock him down and send him sprawling. Sunay boggled, there was no way that beast could have survived a direct hit from a damned *cannon*...

168

right?

Gurgn surprised her, coming up from below decks, his face impassive and his voice flat. "That's not gonna stop 'im. That man is too stupid to know when he's supposed to be dead. Everyone, make some room. You too ma'am. Jus' try to stay outta the way. Juno, hide up in the riggings. When I call for ya, bite 'im."

"Gotcha!" the spider girl said, shimmying up the main mast and disappearing into the ropes and sails above. Sunay looked back towards the shore, where Legionnaire Minimus was indeed pulling himself up to his feet, then howled in rage once standing. He then charged again, shrugging off arrows as he drove the plank into the *Goldbeard's* hull, right above where the second deck would be, embedding the plank *into* the ship.

The Legionnaire charged with reckless abandon up his makeshift plank, and jumped the remaining distance to the deck railing, pulling himself up and over so quickly that no one on board could have stopped him even if they had wanted to.

Minimus didn't look nearly as large up close. Still huge, but she was used to a tigerman that was a head taller and wider than even that. It dropped a blanket over her astonishment until she reminded herself that he could probably kill a normal human being with a heavy breath.

Gurgn stepped forward, making sure that he caught the Legionnaire's attention. Minimus's eyes narrowed, and he growled, "You."

"Me," Gurgn answered.

"I was told you died."

"In the eyes of Reaht, I did, and I was glad to let it go," the rowmaster replied, the cockneyed accent he normally used dropping away like he had never learned those poor habits. "If you're the sort of man to lead my homeland to battle, then I don't want anything to do with it anyway."

"You're jealous that I proved to be beyond your teaching!"

"You learned nothing beyond how to swing a weapon. My teaching was lost on you."

"That's all I needed to learn, you fossil!" Minimus bellowed, swinging down his axe with a chop that Sunay feared would split the deck in half.

Gurgn sidestepped the attack, but barely, and Sunay did not like the odds of the rowmaster's cutlass against the implement of death that Minimus yanked free of the deck with more than enough time to parry away Gurgn's counter.

Minimus snarled, swinging again and drawing blood across Gurgn's chest. Any closer and it would have likely been fatal. "You are old and you are slow," the Legionnaire taunted. "If you are the best your kin has to offer, I will feast heartily while this vessel burns in the night."

Minimus delivered another strike, this one biting into Gurgn's shoulder, cleaving the shoulderblade and sinking halfway into Gurgn's arm. Sunay yelped in fright, then watched as the rowmaster used his other arm... to hold the weapon in place.

"I am fast and as strong as I need to be," Gurgn declared, before he yelled, "Juno! Now!"

If Minimus hadn't been focused on trying to wrench his axe away from Gurgn, he probably would have been able to react in time to the spidergirl dropping down from above, landing on his shoulder, and sinking her fangs directly into the base of his neck. The Legionnaire bellowed, releasing his axe to grab Juno by the back of her neck, rip her away and throw her with disturbing force into the raised section below the helm.

Gurgn took the opportunity to drive Minimus's own axe into the Legionnaire's abdomen, crashing against the breastplate, cutting into the armor and scoring a bloody gash from the chop. Now in a blood rage, Minimus yanked the axe free, cuffed Gurgn away with a backhanded slap, and delivered the finishing blow that cleanly slashed off Gurgn's head.

Sunay almost forgot the danger as she prepared to get revenge, and was saved from being cut down herself by Juno. The spidergirl tripped up the foxgirl, and said with level, cold, murderous intent, "Leave this one to me, won'tcha?"

Juno normally was so lighthearted, even in the face of danger, that Sunay wasn't sure how to respond to the icy glare, defiant posture, and twisted gleam in her first mate's eyes. Juno didn't give her a chance to respond, taking deliberate strides towards Minimus, her full attention focused on the barbaric legionnaire.

"Yer not only not dead, you're still standin' and swingin' that tree trunk around," Juno observed. "Impressive. But if ya think yer gonna last much longer, ya got another thing comin'. Ya got one chance to get outta here and cut yer losses. Otherwise, I ain't gonna promise nothin'."

Minimus felt the wound in his neck, and Sunay could see uncertainty for a brief moment. "I've seen animals like you, woman. I do not fear you."

Juno's lips drew into a malevolent grin. "Oh, don't worry. You will."

The spidergirl dropped unnaturally low, like her knees dislocated and spread out from her hips in an unnatural direction, avoiding Minimus's cleaving strike, and giving Juno an opening to strike with two of her poisoned daggers, one to each thigh, scoring broad gashes along the front from flank to groin.

"Two more," she taunted as she stepped away from his counterattack. "Even if it ain't gonna kill ya right away, I know yer gonna feel it real soon."

It certainly seemed like he did to Sunay's eyes. Even if he was still defiant, and still attacking, the blows were slowing, his right hand that was supplying the bulk of his strikes' power was slipping from the gap in the blade earlier with each swing, and his left arm was starting to tremble.

Another bite on his right bicep was followed by Minimus stumbling to one knee, and another bite to the neck as he tried to stand again.

Still the legionnaire tried to resist, though now his strength was almost entirely gone. He fell to his hands and knees, then dropped to his elbows, unable to even lift his head. Blood dripped from his mouth and gut onto the deck, and Sunay was able to regain her composure. "Finish the bastard, Juno. Then the rest of you dump him overboard to rot like he deserves."

The spidergirl shook her head. "Nuh uh. Gurgn's got the right of it. The fool is too dumb to die. I got a better idea."

She ran to the railing, where the Gold Pirates had once again asserted control of the shore. "Ey! There still any Reahtans alive?" Juno called out.

Leonas had taken charge, and he answered, "Twenty-seven eventually surrendered, we were going to suggest a committee to determine what to do with them. Why?"

"Because I want ya to give 'em one of the ships we stole from 'em, and send 'em back to Reaht with their Legionnaire!"

To Sunay's ears, that sounded like absolute madness, but seeing dawning comprehension spread across Leonas's face suggested that there was more to it. Seeing Sunay's confusion, Juno explained, "Killin' 'im just gives 'im the honorable death he wants. It means he gets revered by the people o' Reaht as one of their martyred champions. But send 'im back to Reaht in defeat... and he gets none o'dat. He becomes shamed and diminished, and he'll never be able to influence anyone ever again. It's a fate *worse* than death for a Reahtan."

Sunay really didn't want to hear it. She could see Gurgn's headless body, Garth nervously trying to figure just what to do while Bolin nervously regarded the rowmaster's head five feet away from the helm. Sunay wanted this Legionnaire cut in a hundred pieces and roasted over an open flame.

"Cap'n, *I* don't even wanna kill 'im right now," Juno explained. "*That* should tell you something."

The foxgirl growled threateningly under her breath. Sunay wanted to send a message, not butcher people who couldn't fight back. And sending this man back in shame would definitely send the message she wanted. Even if she *loathed* the idea.

"I'll be down below," she spat. "Get it done before I come back up and change mah mind."

The foxgirl sulked in her cabin as the hours passed, getting updates of the dead from Juno and Garth, adding to the weight of those she watched die. Members of her own crew, like Marcy, the night rigger killed during the initial exchanges on the west side of the shore. Gurgn. Crew from other ships, killed in the fighting. Leaders like Captain Rosaria.

Sunay got a message in her cabinet from Bonny, stained with tears, that relayed news that Rackham had overdone himself in the pincer attack that crushed the Reahtan ships. Trying to be a younger man than he was and getting overwhelmed by four soldiers.

So many dead that by the time she got word from Admiral Roberts commending her for her victory against all odds that the foxgirl didn't think it was much of a victory. How could it be? Ahmin never had this many people die. Especially among his own crew. He took so much burden on himself to prevent that.

There was a rap on her door, and Sunay grumbled, "Go away unless yer here to tell me that Legionnaire is out of cannon range."

"The surviving Reahtans sailed away long ago, ma'am," Marco informed. "I'm here to tell you that we're about ready to pay respects to our fallen. It's not something you should be absent for."

Sunay groaned. No, she shouldn't. "A'ight. I'ma comin'. Keep yer drawers on."

Evidently, the misery was evident on her face as she joined Marco in the hall. "That's an awfully sour expression for a woman who just turned the world on its head," the mage commented as he led the way, Sunay sulking behind him.

"Hard to celebrate a ton o' dead," she replied.

Marco nodded. "Forty-two, by our count. Which *does* seem like a lot until you consider we were facing a force that numbered close to five *thousand* men."

"Ahmin never lost that many," Sunay said dourly.

Marco rolled his eyes. "Ahmin also never faced those odds in the thirty-five years he served with the Gold Pirates. He joined an organization that had already established control of the seas, and the worst encounters he ever faced were ones like Sacili, controlled raids against smaller forces. It's not a fair comparison, and you know it."

He reached behind himself, and pulled Sunay under his arm. "No one feels like celebrating right now. We will honor our dead, we will take our time, and when the time is right *then* we will celebrate our victory. But even until then, do *not* forget that in *two battles*, you led us to break the back of an entire *navy*. Any accolades that will be rained upon you will be well deserved."

The foxgirl flashed a smile, hoping that it would at least put an end to a topic she *really* didn't want to discuss. "Mebbe. But I'll worry about that when we get to that point."

Marco patted her shoulder warmly, then let her slink back behind him as they emerged on the deck, then down the gangplank to shore. The pirates had found one more fallen, bringing the number to forty-three, all laying on beds of tinder and covered in as white of sheets as could be found on pirate vessels.

The various captains took their turns speaking for their crew, or for their fallen colleagues, setting each bed to flame as they finished each speech. From Bonny's tearful remembrance of Rackham's love for, "wine, war, and women, in that order" to Leonas remembering Rosaria's "grace and elegence in words, deeds, and combat", or coming to the brink of breaking down regretting his first mate's promising career cut short, each one felt like a punch to her gut.

Sunay went through her own time at the head of the procession as if on auto-pilot, the words coming without her expressly thinking about them, almost like someone else was writing them and putting them in her head at just the right moment. They weren't bad, they weren't out of place, but she felt increasingly detached from it. It extended beyond the forty-three of her kin dead. Her spirit also buckled under the weight of the uncounted thousands burning unceremoniously in the remains of Morganstown.

There was a break in her very self, the first cracks of strain that came of realizing she couldn't do this forever.

Even if she could live forever, the stress wouldn't allow it to be as a Gold Pirate.

And then she got to Gurgn, and words failed her. She opened her mouth, and things refused to happen. There was just nothing she could say to properly capture the life of the *Goldbeard's* elder statesman.

It was Juno that showed mercy on her captain, the spidergirl's eyes glistening with moistness and gently trying to pry Sunay's fingers off the burning ember as she said, "May I, Cap'n? Please?"

Sunay conceded the floor gladly. She knew that Juno had been much closer to Gurgn than anyone else, though had never really had the guts to dig into the reasons why. Had Juno been willing to offer those reasons before now, she would have done so without prodding.

But she did today. "Thirty-one years ago, I was born in a cave northwest of here, on the coast of what is now Reaht. Twenty-one years ago, a man wrapped 'is arms around me, and pulled me outta dat cave, and into a new life. It wasn't a perfect life, it wasn't a normal one, but it was a better one than to be an instrument of death.

"That man was the one I'm honoring. Many years ago, before I was even born, Gurgn was a legionnaire for the empire we just put into its place. He initially saw me as the direct result of a people driven to desperation due to the empire he helped build."

Juno wiped away the forming tears, and said, "He was a man who felt Reaht was about honor and true equality based on the merit of your deeds. And he felt he failed that empire, and felt that he failed me. But he didn't, no matter what he woulda said. He... he and... damnit, I'm gonna say 'is damned name... he and Ahmin were the fathers I never 'ad the chance to 'ave. And now, I've lost 'em both."

Sunay's heart wrenched. It was as hard to hear the words than if she had been the one to try and say them. Juno meanwhile forced to keep her composure. "When Gurgn learned that Minimus Maximus was in charge of the attack, he told me that dis would be 'is 'Final March.' If ya've been 'round Reaht long enough, ya know what dat means. It's when a warrior knows he's facin' 'is last fight. Win or lose. Unlike anyone else 'ere, Gurgn knew 'e was gonna die today. He made 'is 'Final March' so that I and you and all o' ya could have so many more."

Sunay now understood Juno's reactions to the aftermath of Minimus's assault. She and Gurgn no doubt had gone over exactly how it would happen and what they both should do in response.

"So, no matter 'ow much I wanna, I ain't gonna cry today," Juno finished. "Not 'cause it'd be weak, but because it would be disrespectful. He died the way he wanted, and that ain't somethin' to cry about. And I'll march on, knowing that it's because of da man that marched with me fer twenty years."

She knelt down and touched the ember to the tinder, "And you better damn well keep marchin' until you reach the city o' gold, old man. I better not catch up wit' ya until yer there, got it?"

Juno ceded the floor to the next in line, but the rest of the ceremony died into the background as Sunay hugged Juno tightly.

"I promised I wasn't gonna cry..." Juno whimpered as the foxgirl felt moisture pooling on her shoulder.

Sunay was sure Juno's shoulder was going to be equally as wet. "Sometimes ya can't fight it. Don't try."

Chapter Nine: There and Back Again

"Juno, what year is it?"

The spidergirl looked up at Sunay like she had grown a second head. "Twenty-one and eleven."

Sunay nodded. She knew that of course, but hearing it helped the number sink in. "I've been doin' this for sixteen years, and sometimes it feels like yesterday."

Juno nodded. "Yeah, it does, don't it?"

Then the foxgirl frowned. "And then sometimes it feels like a hundred, like today."

The spidergirl asked, "Why ya say that?" even though Juno already had a pretty good idea.

The events in Reaht Harbor and Morganstown still weighed heavy on Sunay, even two years later. Even if she had done the nigh impossible in setting the seas to rights, that weight still hadn't eased much. She didn't want to live her life like Rackham, fighting and drinking until she forgot she wasn't able to do either.

It felt terrible and horrible to think that way, with the responsibility she had, but at the same time, she knew that this feeling wasn't going to go away. It hadn't since the battle two years ago, and if anything, that tug to take a new road in life was getting *stronger*. Some of the older crew liked to call these feelings, 'land sickness', yearning to get back on solid ground after years spent mostly on the seas.

Instead, Sunay offered a non-committal shrug and a lie. "I dunno. Just feel old sometimes."

Juno laughed. "If you feel old, how d'ya think *I* feel? I should be like... a million... or somethin'."

Sunay shook her head playfully, and slouched against the railing, looking out towards the coast that was finally in view. "Maybe so. Feh, don't mind me. I dunno why I'm feeling all blahs. It'll pass, I'm sure."

Balco cried out from the crow's nest, "Port of Roma! Five miles!"

"Bring us in, Bolin!" Sunay ordered. "Our route should be clear!"

Roma represented an anomaly when it came to Reaht, a city-state that was able to throw *out* the Reahtans and force them to fall back. Without naval support, it was up to a week of travel through blistering desert conditions to reach Roma, and without that naval support not even Reaht could hold their gains. Roma quickly declared itself a free city-state, and Reaht lost their major port for any further movements west. The eastern empire was still expanding northward along the eastern shores of the continent, but that was a problem for the Gold Pirates' land agents.

A problem that they seemed to be trying to recruit her for... though the specific problem was one they wanted to discuss privately. Normally, this sort of secrecy would have her setting the *Goldbeard's* sail to full in the exact opposite direction, but she had enough good experiences with the land agents in Reaht that she was willing to hear them out at the very least.

"I think ya know the drill by now, right?" Sunay called out to her crew on the deck as she walked along the railing to the rowboats. "No settin' the boat on fire until I get back this time."

"Awww... but we wanted t' surprise ya again!" Juno whimpered.

Roma *had* a harbor large enough for the *Goldbeard* to dock, but Sunay rather wanted to be in and out quickly, without teasing the crew with possible shore leave. So the foxgirl left by rowboat, paddling the half mile from where the ship anchored and towards the docks. Roma itself was basically a harbor and maybe two streets for homes and shops. It was the sort of town where merchant vessels sailed into to resupply then got out as quickly as possible.

As a result, Sunay's destination was easy to find. There was only one inn for the city, and Sunay doubted it was ever anywhere near capacity at any day the entire year. It certainly wasn't as Sunay walked in, the entry room effectively the same as the dining room, and where she was met by her "contact."

Sunay's eyes widened, and her lips curled upward before she yipped happily, and threw herself into Laron's embrace, kissing him soundly before pushing away slightly to ask, "What are *you* doing here?"

"I... negotiated with some of the Reahtan agents to help them make this little surprise," Laron replied, turning to lead Sunay to the table he had reserved.

Beef steaks were waiting, nice and rare just like Sunay liked it, the blood leaking from the meat the moment she took a knife. "I had almost forgotten how much I missed this..." the foxgirl said between bites while she greedily gobbled down the meat while ignoring the side of grapes and cucumber.

Laron poured out some red wine, which was one thing Sunay

loved about Reaht. They knew their alcohol. Not that weak "fortifying" crud from Aramathea, or the piss-water beers and ales of Avalon. This was hearty, fruity and could knock you flat very easily if you weren't careful.

There was obviously a question that needed to be asked, but steak came first. Laron understood this. He knew he'd always be second in Sunay's heart to a good slab of meat, and couldn't blame her for it. But when that steak was done, Sunay asked the question that needed to be asked. "Alright... what brings you all this way?"

The foxgirl suspected she already knew, as there was really only one thing that would prompt Laron to cross the entire continent to present this news in person. As she suspected, he answered, "Two months ago, I finalized my land purchase. A beautiful strip of land on the coast of the sea, right between the farmlands and the city of Lourdis proper."

Laron reached down under the table, then unrolled what turned out to be two separate sheets of parchment. The first was an artist's sketch of the property that Laron had described. And it was pretty much exactly as he said it was, a stretch of land that contained part of the shoreline before it turned into a rocky cluster turning towards the northwest. The second was an overhead map of his property with boundaries marked. It definitely looked like a sizable holding, in fact a little *too* large.

"How much money did you save up, for Coders' sake? This is like... fifty acres!"

"Fifty-three," Laron confirmed with a smile. "I was able to leverage the right people, as well as agree to maintain the nearby shoreline for when the harbor expands. It's more than enough land for the trading post I want to build, a home, and suitable farmland on the northern half to sustain us... and a family."

He said that last bit after a pregnant pause, trying to gauge Sunay's expression. This was a day she knew was coming, but at the same time, it wasn't a day she ever prepared for. It was one of those things that had always seemed "a ways off," and now it was right in front of her.

Sunay gulped nervously. "So... that's that, huh? Ya got yer land, like ya said ya would, and now it's my turn to hold up my end of the deal, huh?"

Laron reached over to touch her hand, then looked hurt when she instinctively jerked away. "You... you don't have to do anything right now. I know you've had a lot on your mind. I've been hearing more and more about the adventures of the Fire Fox the closer I've come to Reaht. I'm sure you've had more tasks than you can count on your plate."

Damn it, he was being *too understanding* here. And that made her feel even *worse*. "I'm sorry," Sunay whimpered, "I've just been so bogged down by everythin' that this has just all come up on me at once. Geez, ya'd think I'd know how to handle surprises by now."

"Sunay... Sunay... you don't have to drop everything right now," Laron insisted. "I'm not going anywhere right away. I don't even need to... Sunay!"

His surprised exclamation came because Sunay had abruptly jumped to her feet and ran out of the inn, blindly running trying to find some secluded hole to hide in while she sorted out the tsunami of thoughts crashing into her head.

She'd be lying if she didn't admit that this was *exactly* what she was thinking about as the *Goldbeard* approached Roma. About the weight on her shoulders, about the years on the seas, about how what she would have wanted most right then and there was a reason to finally step away from the whole thing and have something resembling a peaceful life. That Laron would come, sweep her off her feet, and take her away.

As terrified as she no doubt looked when Laron had showed her everything, his news had been everything she wanted to hear, and if she had been able to set aside all the logistics of her position, she would probably have been on a ship or cart heading straight to Lourdis within the hour.

But the problem was the whole logistics of everything.

Had she been *smart*, she would have been planned for this transition long ahead of time. Juno was a more than capable first mate, and would be an excellent captain. But the spidergirl *hated* the responsibility she already had, and would only accept a promotion to captain reluctantly, and would not suffer it for long before she either quit or had a breakdown. Sunay probably shouldn't have pushed her into the first mate's position to *begin* with, but it had been important for Sunay to set someone established on the ship considering the foxgirl's rapid rise through the ranks.

Meanwhile, Garth had all the tools to be an *excellent* captain and leader, and Sunay had noted such repeatedly, giving him more and more responsibility. But the truth was he didn't even have any experience as a first mate, and that was experience that Sunay felt was necessary in order to be put in the captain's cabin. She had entertained letting him get that experience on another ship, but had feared that he'd never come back when the time came for Sunay to step down.

And she *didn't* want to simply hand over the role to someone from another ship. They were a family more than a crew at this point, and it would just feel wrong to walk away from that family and let some complete stranger take to ordering them around.

But she couldn't keep stringing Laron around for the years it would take for her to properly fix this chain of command. They were already in their thirties, for Coders' sake! It's been sixteen years since they've met, and she'd spent the last ten or so stringing him along with vague promises. That wasn't right *either*.

Maybe the Void could swallow up *everything* tomorrow and she'd never have to face the consequences of her decision.

That'd work.

Then she felt a hand slap over her mouth, another grab her by the waist, and pulled her inside what had looked like an otherwise non-descript house she had just passed without much thought. Whoever this fellow was, he was strong... able to effortlessly lift her off her feet and toss her across the room to land on a Reahtan style sofa, so large that she was able to fit from head to foot without even bumping into the slanted armrest or dangle off the open end at her feet.

She was about to angrily demand the meaning of this, when her jaw dropped from the *second* shock to her system that day. "You!"

He had certainly seen better days. His mask was gone, revealing a small scar across the left side of his lips, and his hair was flecked with the white that came with age. His clothes were in good repair, at least, so didn't seem like he was slinking from hovel to hovel desperately trying to evade any and all eyes, but it was clear that the years could have been nicer to former Admiral Ahmin.

"Yes. Me," Ahmin said dryly, standing over Sunay as she sat up. "You look well, Sunay."

"I wish I could say the same about you. What in the Coders' name are ya *doing*? Ya completely dropped off the map! Yer wanted by yer own people! Hell, I should be reporting you right now!"

"*I'm* supposed to be chiding *you* here," Ahmin replied. "You have a *golden* opportunity to get out of this organization, and you need to take it. *Now*."

"What? Why?"

"The Gold Pirates aren't what they once were. The Administrators... they aren't who they used to be."

Sunay's eyes narrowed, "Are you insane? There hasn't been a

single change in Administrators since you left."

Ahmin grit his teeth and snarled, "I didn't say they are different *people*. I said they aren't who they used to be. They've changed... they've been slowly changing ever since the events at South Gibraltar. Maybe even before that. Rola's still good, as far as I understand. She's stayed away from all of them and has been actively avoiding any further contact, but every other leader in the organization, land and sea, is potentially compromised."

"Compromised? By *who?*"

"The Dark One. The Minister. Whatever you want to call him. He's the one who's twisted all of it. The Daynes. The Void... it's all him."

Sunay said angrily, "There *isn't* a 'Dark One'. Morgana killed her apprentice. I saw his damn headless body in Tortuga."

"So it's not Mohraine. But there *is* an influence. You *met* that man, remember?"

Sunay did, quite keenly. "That doesn't mean The Minister has anything to do with anything else," she replied, even though she didn't entirely believe it as she said it. "It could just be one nut who thought he could get a whole bunch o' people to get eaten up."

Ahmin called her on it, "You don't believe that either."

"Alright, I don't," she shot back. "But the alternative is to believe that the organization I've spent half my life with is now some sort of twisted shell of itself and is now controlled by a man who has done absolutely *nothing* different than normal from my perspective for... reasons!"

She had known Ahmin to be an intense individual at times, but she had *never* seen such a fervor in his eyes or his voice before. "The purpose is to weaken the biggest line of defense that could be reasonably mustered against him in a short amount of time. You've seen it, I know you have. You *saw* the defeat in the fleet here in Reaht before you whipped them into shape. You saw how the Reahtans had been pushing them around."

"Yeah, and Admiral Roberts himself ordered me here to whip 'em into shape," she said, while conveniently leaving out the part that Rola suspected it was to separate the wolf spirit from the foxgirl.

Ahmin's eyes darted nervously towards the door, and he snarled at it. "I don't have time to argue this. If you still trust me even the slightest bit, then you go back to your boyfriend, you accept his proposal, have your crew send you off to Lourdis, and save every single one of their lives. Things are going to go bad very soon, and I don't know how many I can save. *Please* don't make me worry about you and your crew."

He then left, towards the rear of the house, and in considerable haste, leaving Sunay's mind spinning. Rola had mentioned something about what Ahmin was talking about, but she hadn't seemed to give it too much merit, as least as far as it concerned her.

But... what if he was right?

She slowly stood up, wincing as her neck and back protested the movement. She considered following Ahmin's path to the rear of the house, but decided that she wouldn't have any luck tailing him if he didn't want to be found. An entire coordinated effort from land agents all around the continent had no luck... she wasn't going to fare any better by herself.

She had gotten about ten steps out the door when she was quickly escorted out of sight into an alley between houses by *two* strange men, though once they were properly secluded they stepped away and she could see the fairly obvious yellow scarves draped over their necks.

They were twins, in both dress and appearance, like proper Reahtans in burgundy red tunics and faded brown canvas pants, tanned, toned if thin, black hair and brown eyes. They were even the same height, though her initial impression that they were both men was incorrect.

"Captain Sunay..." the brother on the left said.

"... we are glad you are well," the female twin on the right finished.

"And who are you?" the foxgirl asked warily.

She didn't get an answer, at least not one she found suitable. "We are agents tasked..." the boy started.

"...with tracking rogue admiral Ahmin." his sister added.

This wasn't unnerving at all. Sunay fought back a nervous gulp and said, "Good to see ya folks on that."

"We learned of his presence in this city..."

"... and thought it suspicious that you came here."

Don't tell them!

Sunay blinked repeatedly and looked right and left initially to try and find who had spoken before she remembered. She hadn't heard the "Chosen" voice in her head speak that strongly in over sixteen years. She had followed those instincts dutifully since, and knew that it hadn't intentionally led her astray yet.

But don't lie, either! They'll know!

"The man found me," Sunay replied, sorting out her thoughts to form a careful, if somewhat misleading, truth. "He was insane, I think. Ranting about... something. I dunno exactly what."

She could feel the twins eyes on her, intensely staring like they could see inside her.

"We don't think..." the brother said.

"... you're being entirely honest," the sister finished.

"What could you..."

"... possibly be hiding?"

Both agents took an aggressive step forward, and Sunay steeled herself with her hand grabbing the hilt of one of her knives. "Hey! We're on the same side here. Back up."

Then Sunay felt it... felt the Void's presence. Not very strong, but enough to set her stomach churning. The twin siblings stopped in their tracks, eyes locked forward as if looking straight *through* Sunay and off into space. It was a very brief moment that felt far longer than it really was, but when the pair had refocused on the world, they both took one very long stride backwards.

"We apologize, Captain..."

"... we did not intend to upset you."

"If you think of anything..."

"... forward it to the Eastern Free Provinces Administrator."

The twins bowed simultaneously, then returned to the road without further word, their steps in nigh perfect time with each other. Sunay gave them a *long* head start before she emerged back onto the main street, hoping that she never saw them again.

The foxgirl was *again* bumrushed, but this was followed by a familiar and welcome smell. Laron's arms wrapped around her and pushed her head against his shoulder. "When I learned that those two were in town, and looking for you, I tried to find you as fast I could. What happened?"

"Who *are* those two?" Sunay asked, not even attempting to push away.

"Zhan and Jaina, as I'm told. They are investigators who operate directly under the Eastern Free Provinces Administrator," Laron replied. "Even the agents *here* are scared witless even *talking* about those two above hushed tones. Why were they looking for you?"

Sunay shook her head as she finally pulled away, "They thought I would lead 'em to Ahmin. They didn't believe me when I told 'em I had nothing to do with him for years. Coders, I just want to get out of this place."

Not yet.

The Chosen voice occurred at about the same time as the buzz of new orders, which seemed to be in disagreement with Ahmin's very strong suggestion to get away from any and all Gold Pirate activity as soon as possible.

Laron saw the foxgirl's glazed over eyes and felt her stiffen, then asked ruefully, "Duty calls?"

Sunay tried to shake all the discomfort out of her body. "Yeah, duty calls," she grumbled, then met Laron's eyes. He definitely looked disappointed, and resigned to what he thought was inevitable. The foxgirl grinned wanly, then said, "Still got that other earring?"

Laron nodded slowly.

"Well then, lemme have it, ya goof."

While Sunay removed one of the gold loops in her left ear, the man dug into the pocket of his trousers, then pulled out a black velvet box and handed it to her. Sunay popped it open, saw the immaculate jewels and links of gold, then very gently picked it up between thumb and forefinger. Handing the box back to Laron, she then put the earring in the now open peircing and said, "This is gonna be my last mission. After this... we're goin' to Lourdis, got it?"

The man's face lit up brightly. "Then I'll wait for you here. The crew will no doubt want to send you off, and it'd be easier to sail by your ship rather than try and negotiate alternate travel."

She kissed him once on his right cheek. "I'm gonna hold ya to that, boy. Don't go anywhere or do anythin' stupid."

Sunay sprinted back to her rowboat as fast as her legs could churn, and paddled back out to the *Goldbeard* in a record time. She held up a warning hand to Juno as she scampered below decks, promising to answer questions later. She skipped down the steps two at a time, then nearly ran down Vax, the rowmaster promoted to replace Gurgn, as she crossed the hall to her cabin.

She was expecting the mirror, so was a shade bit surprised to receive written orders. Roberts had a reputation of giving orders personally, at least to her and the *Goldbeard*. It was a bit of a bother, as she had been hoping to inform Roberts personally of her engagement.

Well, if he could write her, than *she* could write *him*. Sunay composed her letter informing him that she was getting married and that she was tendering her resignation effective at the end of this last mission. If he didn't like that, well he could be present when he gave orders!

Sunay returned to the deck, unable to hide the smile on her face. She cheerfully shouted out, "Bolin, set our course to ninety-three until we clear Vargas's Point, then to thirty-eight. Our destination is the Isle of Donne."

"What's goin' on there?" Juno asked.

"Dunno. Admiral Roberts got reports that the Void is movin' in that direction. We're to investigate."

"Jus' investigate?"

Sunay nodded. "Just investigate for now. If the Void is an impendin' threat, we're allowed to help 'em evacuate, but otherwise, we're to leave the island alone and keep our distance from Dominus Augustus."

Juno nodded. The *Goldbeard* itself had been mixed up with the triad of archmages enough that the spidergirl knew exactly why Admiral Roberts wasn't keen on sticking their noses into further business with that triad. Or quartet, to be more accurate, with the recent addition of the mage keep in Kuith.

Bolin noted quickly, "We don't have much of a current right now, and the winds are strong comin' in from the east. This is gonna be a slow trip."

Winds from that direction *were* odd for this part of the continent, and did little to dissuade any concerns that weirdness was awaiting them in the Eastern Forever Sea and the Isle of Donne. "Then it's gonna be a slow trip. Vax and his team are gonna have to pull the bulk of the weight. Let's get to it."

With the orders settled, it was time for Sunay to break the news. "And there is one order of business I have to say. It probably won't come as a surprise to any of ya, but it has to be said to make it official and all o' that. This is gonna be my last mission. I'm gettin' married after this and settlin' down with Laron in Lourdis."

She expected the reaction she got from the deck crew, sadness coupled with elation. "About time!" Juno declared, clapping the foxgirl on the back soundly. "Dat's some great news!"

"Ya'd think so, until I tell ya yer gonna be the actin' captain until Admiral Roberts sends over a replacement."

Juno shrugged. "I think I can survive a short run in charge. If not, and I bite everyone here, eh. At least it'll be quick for 'em, right?"

If Juno was expecting laughter, she would have been disappointed by the nervous chuckles while the crew sorted out if that had been a joke or not. Sunay knew it wouldn't be a good long term solution, but honestly, she had reached the conclusion that there wasn't going to be much of a long term for this crew at all.

Because the more she let Ahmin's advice settle, the more she began to think he was more right than she wanted to admit at the time. "Yer gonna see me off, right?" she asked Juno with a smile.

"Yeah... yeah..." the spidergirl answered, returning the grin. "We'll save ya some money and sail the two o' ya to Lourdis."

Sunay barked out as she noticed the deck crew neglecting their stations, "But first things first, folks. We still got a job to do at the Isle of Donne."

~ ~ ~ ~ ~

Sunay felt something had gone horribly wrong long before the island was supposed to come in sight. It was merely confirmation when the island never came into sight at all.

The Isle of Donne was gone, likely swallowed up by the Void. Sunay knew that much. She could feel the lingering sickness of dire water. It *had* been there. Which was where it got *really* strange... because the Void *wasn't* there now.

This was new behavior that the Void had never exhibited. It advanced, it devoured everything in its path... but it never retreated. Yet Juno heading up into the crow's nest on Sunay's order confirmed what she felt. Dire water had been here, but it was gone now.

"What in the Coders' forsaken hell happened here?" Sunay grumbled as Juno shuffled back to the deck.

"I don't get it, and I don't doubt ya neither," Juno said. "You say dire water's been here, it's been here. And I can't think of nuthin' else that can make an entire island go poof. But that's just normal water out there, Cap'n."

"But not even the Void can make an entire island disappear that quickly," Sunay added. "It took almost a year for South Gibraltar to collapse even after we learned it was advancing. This all happened within two weeks."

Then she heard Balco cry out, "Man at sea! One hundred and forty at one half mile!"

The foxgirl shook her head, still amazed at the things the

186

Goldbeard's lookout could find. "Still any idea how Balco can find a man bobbin' in open water at a half mile?" she asked Juno.

"I can't even find my shoes in my cabin half the time," Juno answered.

Sunay smirked, and called out, "Bolin!"

The helmsman didn't even let Sunay finish. "Already on it, ma'am!" he declared, and they felt the ship shift in the water from his turn not even a beat later. As they got closer to their target, Balco kept them abreast of the man so that the *Goldbeard* didn't inadvertently run the poor sot over.

Balco was also able to make other observations as the distance rapidly closed. "Cap'n! He's a Reahtan soldier!"

The foxgirl sighed and cursed under her breath. What the hell was a Reahtan soldier doing out here? "Juno, get up in the rigging," she ordered. "Just in case we need ya to bite 'im."

Juno snapped a salute and said, "Aye aye," before taking a running jump onto the main mast and zipping upwards. Seconds later, Garth was able to spot the man along the port side, and lowered a rope for the Reahtan to grab onto. "Tie it around your waist if you don't have the strength to hold!" the deckhand shouted.

"I have the strength. Now pull," called the voice from the sea. If the volume was any indication, he wasn't lying.

Judging from the hands that eventually grasped the railing, he was a big fellow. Did they make 'em small in Reaht? It was followed by a figure that was very much *not* Reahtan in appearance, copper red hair that fluffed out into a ridiculous bang as he shook the water off, along with very pale skin and eyes that Sunay couldn't quite decide whether they were green or blue.

"Well, you ain't exactly what I was expectin'," Sunay remarked.

The Reahtan soldier eyed her warily, and quickly made a shockingly correct identification: "You're the Fire Fox!"

"That's what I'm told," Sunay replied darkly.

"Where is the spiderwoman that is part of your crew?" he demanded as he stepped forward aggressively. "I have vengeance to deliver!"

He reached over his back, presumably where his weapon was supposed to be, and cringed in reminder that he must have lost it at some point. Sunay then ordered, "Juno. Move in. Don't kill 'im... yet."

The spidergirl dropped down, landing directly behind the Reahtan, and nudged him in the back of his armor with two of her

187

daggers. "I've given these blades a nice dip in mah poison," Juno warned, gently poking him for effect. "Ya move... poke poke! Ya don't tell mah cap'n what she wants to know... poke poke!"

Sunay added the carrot to the stick. "But if ya cooperate, I'll give ya one of my rowboats here, some supplies to help ya on yer way, and everyone lives to see another day. How does that sound, friend?"

He growled angrily, and his fists clenched in rage, but he made no other movements and eventually relaxed long enough to grumble, "Very well, woman. Ask what you wish."

"Let's start off with the basics," the foxgirl said, pacing slowly in front of the soldier. "Who are ya?"

"Largo. Gladiator of Reaht."

"I'm gonna guess that ya weren't out here for a relaxin' swim. I'm also gonna guess that means you were here on the island that is supposed to be out that way." She pointed behind her in the general direction of where the Isle of Donne once was. "That means that you have a much better idea about what happened than I do. And I kinda need to know."

Largo grit his teeth, but a slight reminding jab against his armor courtesy of Juno loosened his tongue. "I was part of a specially formed legion led by Legionnaire Minimus Maximus..."

Sunay grinned. "Well *that* name sounds familiar, don't it, Juno?"

"Uh huh," the spidergirl replied. "Explains why he wanted to get even wit' me."

Sunay gestured to Largo, and said, "Continue, friend."

Largo took a deep, steadying breath. "Reports from our governor on the Isle of Donne had stopped coming. Requests sent by pigeon from our forces never returned. After a week of silence, our legion was sent to investigate."

"Makin' sense so far," Sunay encouraged.

"We learned quickly that the island had been plagued by undead. They overwhelmed us upon landing, we only luckily managed to make it inside the Dominus's tower. Inside, we found several undead creatures, tainted by something."

"The Void," Sunay remarked. That fit what she knew of Dominus's Augustus's purpose. Had he lost control of the Void he had been working with to create his Void-touched creatures? But why would the Void just vanish after the fact? Morgana's fight with her apprentice had lingered *years* after that incident.

"Whatever you want you want to call it, the undead hordes and the tigerman tried to halt our progress..."

Sunay's eyes bulged. "Tigerman? What tigerman?"

Largo shrugged. "The tiger chimera who repeatedly tried to block us from going further in the tower. Kept telling us it was in our best interests to leave and other such nonsense."

"Sounds like he had the right of it," Sunay retorted coldly. Ahmin had been at the Isle of Donne. Why? What had he been searching for? And where was he now? "And what happened to the tigerman? Do you know?"

"The next I saw him was at the top of the tower. At that point, only the Legionnaire and I lived. The Dominus had been turned, as undead as the rest of his tower. The Dominus then turned the Legionnaire, promising him a return to his former glory. It was a lie, of course. I don't understand why the Legionnaire thought it was anything but. The tigerman returned, and kept my former leader busy while I dealt with the Dominus."

"You against an archmage?" Sunay questioned. "And ah... the tigerman... thought that was a good idea?"

"The Dominus attempted no spellcasting," Largo replied. "He only tried to lure me with false promises and lies. I easily dispatched the undead horror, and at that point, even the Legionnaire collapsed. Then the tigerman started mumbling about a 'Dark One' and how I alone had the power to fight him."

Sunay found that highly doubtful. "Is that right?"

"The tigerman told me to find the 'Dark One.' He might have said more, but that was when the island started to collapse. He grabbed me, told me I better swim fast, and threw me out of the window and into the sea. I've tried to take his advice."

"Ya didn't travel very far. How long ago was this?"

"Just two days prior. I am not an accomplished swimmer."

"Yer too stupid to die, like the Legionnaire, I swear," Juno grumbled. "Two days treadin' water in *this* armor? Don't you guys think of takin' it *off* before tryin' t' swim?"

Largo seemed aghast by the idea, "If we cannot swim..."

"Yeah, yeah..." Juno interrupted. "It was a rhetorical question, idiot."

Sunay had turned away from Largo, and gave her orders. "Garth, prepare a rowboat for our friend. Juno, once he's clear, meet me in my cabin. Garth, you'll have the deck until we return."

Sunay went below decks, lost in a swirl of thoughts, all of which were really bad omens. About Ahmin... about the Gold Pirates...

About the whole damn *world*.

The foxgirl dropped into her desk chair, her head down in her hands, and was still in that position by the time she heard the door open and Juno step inside. Once the spidergirl closed the door behind her, she said, "Ya know, every single person on the deck knew who the tigerman was. Ya don't need t' keep it secret."

Sunay shook her head. "Ain't about Ahmin... not directly, at least."

Juno's entire body slumped in sadness. "Ya don't think... that he's gone too, do ya?"

"Who knows? Ahmin's been able to get to and away from places awfully quickly. I wouldn't bet money on him bein' dead *or* alive." She finally looked up at Juno and added, "This is what Ahmin warned me about. And I don't like the implications."

"How so?"

"Ya know how we got slowed by unusual winds?"

"Yah."

"That collapse happened two days ago. Right when we *should* have arrived there."

All six of Juno's eyes widened to near circles. "Ya don't think... how could...?"

"Admiral Roberts' orders came by paper. Not personally like they usually do." At this point, Sunay didn't care that she was revealing privileged information to her first mate. "It was odd from the start, and Ahmin warned me in Roma that the Gold Pirates have been compromised by a 'Dark One.' No doubt the same 'Dark One' he told that Reahtan about. So yeah... I kinda do think that someone, not necessarily Admiral Roberts, tried to set us up to get swallowed up by the Void."

"But... why?"

"I dunno. Maybe it's our association with Rola or Ahmin, who defied their fellow Administrators. Maybe we've somehow avoided the same taint that the rest of our kin haven't. Could be something else entirely. What I *do* know is that I'm not intending to let you or this crew sail back out there after you drop me and Laron off at Lourdis."

"Then... what *are* we gonna do?"

"I'll think of that when we get to that point," Sunay said reluctantly. She hated not having even the semblance of a plan. But for now, the best plan was getting away from here as soon and as quickly as possible. "Just have Bolin set us a course for Roma, and once we've picked up Laron, have him head straight for Lourdis. As

190

few stops as possible."

Juno nodded. She didn't fully understand what this was all about, but she didn't doubt Sunay any. "Aye, aye." The spidergirl made to leave, then stopped before opening the door, offering one last bit of advice: "No matter what, Sunay... we'll follow ya. Wherever the seas take us."

~ ~ ~ ~ ~

Sunay got more evidence that she was making the right decision as they entered Aramathean waters. Sunay asked for Juno and Laron to be present to witness the coming communication just so that they could confirm she wasn't crazy and was approaching this problem rationally.

The foxgirl told them to stay out of sight as word from Admiral Roberts came, but it turned out to be unnecessary as said word came in the form of another written letter.

"Yep. Definitely odd," Sunay said as she ripped open the envelope to look at the contents.

"How is this supposed t' go?" Juno queried.

"Rola had a small mirror that could connect her directly to any agent or Administrator she was associated with. She certainly *could* communicate through letters, and did if she had very time-sensitive orders to make but was otherwise indisposed, but she found it much more effective to talk to them directly."

Meanwhile, Sunay absorbed the letter's contents.

Captain Sunay,

> *All ships and crew are ordered immediately to report to staging grounds at Pearl Point for an urgent priority mission on the keep at Kuith. Your presence is mandatory, and no excuses will be permitted in this matter. Sail to the designated staging grounds immediately. You have three weeks.*

"Like hell..." Sunay snarled angrily, penning her reply. Even *if* she felt any obligation to obey those orders, three weeks would not be *nearly* enough time to sail from their position in Aramathean waters, across the South Forever Sea, then north along the East Forever Sea to damn near the Icy Expanse. That, along with her reminder that she had given *plenty* of due notice of her impending marriage and the customs that allowed the *Goldbeard* and its crew to take her to her last port were all added in the reply that Sunay sent with a slam of her cabinet door.

Laron tried to sooth the smoldering foxgirl until the response came and did little to quench those angry fires.

> *Captain Sunay,*
>
> *Your request for a termination of your duties has been denied, and the request for transport from your crew is also denied. Report to the established staging grounds in three weeks time. This is final.*

The foxgirl crumpled the letter in her first so hard that she started drawing blood on her left palm. "*Denied?* You don't... you can't... t' hell with this fool!"

Sunay went back to pen and paper, and she didn't even try to hide her disdain in the letter she composed.

> *Admiral Roberts,*
>
> *Denial is not a power you have to give here, jackass. You had plenty of time to issue a replacement for my position, as well as plenty of time to determine if my crew was needed long before we left Reahtan waters. That you foolishly did not do so is not my or my crew's problem.*
> *So take your denial and shove it directly up your ass. If you want the Goldbeard to report to your stupid staging area, you are welcome to come to Lourdis and take it. Otherwise, go find the nearest signpost and sit on it. This is final, you arrogant piece of* ~~XXXXX~~ *filth.*

She had crossed the last expletive after Laron massaged her shoulders and suggested that she had already made her point. Sunay agreed, if only because seeing the heavily scribbled out portion really left little doubt to her original intent anyway. She again slammed the cabinet door shut with her reply, and said resolutely, "There ain't no way we're reportin' anywhere. I don't care *what* they say next."

What they had to say next didn't take long.

Captain Sunay,

> *You are correct. I apologize for my aggressive behavior. Have your first mate report to me after you have been safely brought to your destination.*

Perhaps oddly, that *didn't* ease Sunay's mind at all. "Okay... this *can't* be right." Following a hunch, she uncrumpled one of the older letters, then laid them both down on her desk, confirming her suspicions. "Look at this. It's different handwriting. Whoever wrote this second letter tried to mimic the first, but he didn't quite do it right."

Laron agreed. "The 't' is different, as are the slants on the stems."

"So, do ya think Roberts wrote this one... or th' first two?" Juno asked.

"Ya know... I'd put my money on neither," Sunay said, looking up over her left shoulder at Laron. "When was the last you heard from Rola?"

"Two days before you returned to Roma. She told me she had to go dark while she sorted out her own house. She said she would be waiting for us in Lourdis, so I don't think it was particularly threatening to her. But yes, she was certainly concerned about something wrong within her own ranks."

"So that's that, eh?" Juno said. "We've just all gone rogue?"

"Well... not officially," Sunay corrected, "but yeah."

"I'm sorry," Juno said. "And here ya were all ready to settle down and be a good little housewife and all."

Sunay sputtered, "Yeah, uh huh. We'll sort out that mess and where we have to go once we reach Lourdis."

Truth is, Sunay wasn't sure there was a safe place on the entire continent for them... or anyone else.

~ ~ ~ ~ ~

It was funny how life could come full circle.

Sunay's first memories were of a shack of an orphanage in the middle of a forest a handful of days from the harbor at Lourdis. And of all the multitude of places that she could have wound up at the end of her pirating days, it turned out to be here.

It was with immense relief that Rola had kept her promise. Her and Law's horse-led cart clopped up the wooden deck towards where the *Goldbeard* had dropped anchor alongside the boardwalk. With all the narrow misses and unnerving conspiracies weaving in and out of Sunay's life, that the wolf spirit and her husband seemed unharmed was a welcome discovery.

Sunay dashed down the gangplank, happily embracing Rola as the wolf spirit met her right at the bottom. The pair pulled apart, and Rola said, "Glad to see you. Did Admiral Roberts give you trouble?"

The foxgirl wasn't entirely certain how to answer that question, "At first, but he came around. I'm not entirely certain how I'm gonna keep these folks out of harm's way, though. Roberts expects the Goldbeard to be back in the action."

Rola gave this considerable thought. "We could sink it."

That was not an option. "We aren't sinkin' her," Sunay growled angrily. "She's a perfectly good boat."

The wolf spirit then offered, "Do you think the Versilles militias might be able to use it?"

Laron shook his head. "They don't have the resources for a navy at this point in time, and a ship this size is more an easy mark than a fearsome force without smaller vessels to support it."

"He's right, ya know," Juno agreed, finally finishing her walk down the gangplank. "Both you *and* Ahmin liked to worry about that little detail, remember?"

Sunay did remember that.

Rola was getting frustrated by the brainstorming, and it reflected in her voice. "Well, as long as this ship is seaworthy, Roberts is going to expect it back in service, and for all you to be on board. That seems like a very bad idea for all of you."

Sunay's gaze drifted off into space, towards the sandy coastline that eventually yielded to rocky shores. And that was when a bolt of inspiration struck her.

She pointed out and said, "Your plot is out that way, ain't it, love?"

Laron nodded, pointing inland towards what was the beginnings of construction. "Yes. You can actually see where I've broken ground on what will be our trading post. Closer to the coast, though you probably can't see it from here, is where I've already had the foundation laid for our home."

Sunay again drew his attention to the coast. "Well, I'm talkin' about right there on the beach. That's some nice, soft sediment, ain't it?

"As far as I can tell... yes."

"Hey Joffe!"

The craftsman emerged from the assembly on the deck. "Yes, ma'am?"

"Get down here! I need yer expert advice!"

Joffe did as ordered, striding down the gangplank and siding up to the foxgirl's left side. "What can I do for you?"

Sunay again pointed to the beach, and said, "Think we could rig up some supports so that the Goldbeard could beach itself there without too much damage?"

Joffe shrugged. "I'd have to get a closer look at the actual sand and how far it went before bedrock, but in theory, sure. There'd be other factors like the slope of the shelf and water depths, but those are all things that could be worked around."

"What are you thinking about, Sunay?" Laron asked.

"A pirate themed inn and tavern. Who else would know how to run it other than some genuine pirates?"

Laron gave the idea some thought, although whether he genuinely agreed or was just humoring the foxgirl was unclear. "A good oceanside view... there'd have to be some renovations to be sure... finding someplace else for the cannons... but yes... I could see that. An excellent source of secondary income at that too!"

Sunay grinned and called out to her crew, "We've got our next mission folks! Get to work!"

The foxgirl had a crazy idea, but it was just crazy enough to work. Though as Sunay retreated to her cabin to put that idea into action she steadily lost that initial confidence.

Admiral Roberts still was not responding to attempts to talk to him in person. This was probably a good thing, as Sunay wasn't sure she'd be able to pass off the lie believably. Even in letter form Sunay wasn't sure anyone, much less the Admiral, would buy it. Yes, the tensions in Versilles were high, and yes, the militias of the newly freed province occasionally skirmished with expeditionary Avalonian forces that were testing the opponent's military strength. But the odds that the *Goldbeard* would get caught up in the fighting and managed to get so severely damaged that it needed to be beached while repairs were made seemed a bit too much for Roberts to fall for.

Rationally, she should have had the ship sunk, and claimed the loss. But the foxgirl just didn't like the idea of the ship being torn apart for salvage at best, or left abandoned at worst. Even if it was a burden, it was a burden she didn't want to just get rid of. The

Goldbeard was almost as much family as the rest of the crew.

Once she closed the door of her cabinet with her report, the only thing she could do was wait and see.

Rola patted her on the shoulder and said flippantly, "If it doesn't work... I could still sink it."

"Are you plannin' on bein' *on it?*" the foxgirl retorted grumpily.

The wolf spirit laughed, and gave Sunay's shoulders a playful squeeze.

The sounds of working outside as the crew helped Joffe with his rig that would bring the *Goldbeard* ashore drifted to Sunay's ears. This crazy scheme had to work, because despite how much Sunay hated the idea, otherwise the end result would have to be sinking the Goldbeard and having her crew go into hiding under Rola's authority. No one deserved *that*.

Much like the other communications with what was assumed to be Admiral Roberts, the reply came quickly. So at least the tension didn't get much chance to rise past the boiling point. The response, like the others, was fairly brief, and unsettling in its acceptance.

Captain Sunay,

I extend apologies for the unfortunate circumstances. As the fleet is committed at this point to our missions on Kuith, there are little resources we can offer to expedite repairs. Inform your first mate that I will communicate with her when the opportunity arises. Make sure you have transferred command to him in that time. I will consider this your last message as a captain. Enjoy your life, Sunay. You have earned it.

Rola's eyebrows raised, likely for the same reasons that Sunay was dubious. "Admiral Roberts would know your first mate is a girl, wouldn't he?"

"Yeah," Sunay confirmed.

"And considering the way he talks, I can't imagine he writes much better."

"Nope."

"And this is what you've been dealing with since meeting Laron in Roma?"

"Yep."

Rola plucked the letter from Sunay's hands, reading it carefully like she was trying to find a secret message scrawled between the lines. "If you don't mind, I'd like to look into this."

"I'd rather you didn't," Sunay replied nervously. "You've already been targeted once, likely by whatever has caused *this* mess."

"And will likely be targeted again, regardless of what I do," the wolf spirit answered unrepentantly. "Oh, do settle yourself. I can be discreet when I need to be. You, meanwhile, have operations to oversee."

Rola patted Sunay on the head playfully, and showed herself out. Sunay slowly exhaled, her lips flapping tiredly. Rola was right, and that wasn't something that the foxgirl ever liked admitting to.

~ ~ ~ ~ ~

It would be another six months before the wolf spirit found her way to the foxgirl's door. By that point, the Groundbeard Inn had opened its "doors" to moderate success. The rooms were never full, and the dining room was never packed, but it was doing alright for itself as a side business to Laron's trading post, which *was* flourishing considering its prime location next to the harbor.

Sunay was the only one manning the dining room that night, as it had been slow and Juno saw the opportunity to spend the night fraternizing with Donovan. Sunay hadn't exactly insisted Juno stay. The foxgirl was the better cook, and there had been all of two people still there eating, the last of which had moved to leave by the time the sun had been setting.

"Have a good night, Victor!" Sunay said with a friendly wave.

It might have been odd for a tavern to be empty by nightfall, but Sunay had liked the idea of her inn being something more family friendly, welcoming to young and old, more for weary travelers than salty sailors. The Gold Pirates had always been a different breed when on the seas... it made sense they'd seek a different clientele on land.

Especially since Sunay suspected there were going to be little foxgirls and foxboys running around within a year.

That didn't mean the bar at the Gold Inn didn't have its liquor. Because it did. It had a *magnificent* selection from around the world, in fact. Mellow white wines from Hermia, in the heart of Imperial Aramathea's vineyards, deep reds from Bolone in Reaht, amber ales from Winter's Cape you could lose yourself in. Those who *did* find their way to the Gold Inn after dark were in for a treat.

Which was a perfect time for the wolf spirit to finally make her return. There was no fanfare or loud greeting to Rola's entrance, which Sunay decided could have only been an ill omen. That unease was only reinforced by the wolf spirit's flat ears and low dragging tail as she pulled out a stool and slouched into it, head down. "I need something *very* hard. You're probably going to need one too."

Yep. This was *very* bad news. Sunay took out two tall clear crystal glasses, and set them on the bar in front of Rola. "Ice?" she asked.

Rola nodded slowly, and Sunay opened the cold compartment underneath the bar. At this point in the evening, it was more water surrounding a half melted block, but Sunay found that made it easier to chip off the chunks she needed to drop into the glasses. Then she went to the bar, and knew instantly the brew of choice. Blue Mirror Spirit, a distilled liquor fashioned first by the Daynes after occupying Avalonian lands during the first campaigns.

Only a handful of the Daynes were left in the aftermath of the second campaigns, and even fewer still that remembered the process of distilling that they used. As a result their Blue Mirror Spirit was increasingly rare and carried an ever increasing price tag. Which was a shame, because it was one of the most potent alcohols the foxgirl had ever sipped on.

And make no mistake, this was an alcohol that could only be sipped.

Unless your name was Rola, it seemed, because she downed half the glass in one shot, tilting up her head only long enough to drink before slouching back down.

Sunay decided to try and prod discussion first. "So... what's the news?"

"It's gone," Rola said darkly.

That was little help, honestly. "What's... gone?" the foxgirl asked.

"Take your pick. Kuith. Reaht. The entire eastern coast. The Gold Pirates..."

It was the last bit that made Sunay yelp, "Whattya mean the Gold Pirates are gone?"

Rola finally looked up, eyes red with crying or lack of sleep or both. "The fleet was lost when Kuith collapsed into the void last month. Reaht followed soon after, along with the land agents that had been holding at the staging area. The other administrators went dark along with the communication network. As far as I know... you, your crew, and the few agents under my authority that I was able to keep under my service are all that remains with any ties to the Gold Pirates."

Rola finished the glass. "The single most powerful force of stability in the world is utterly crippled, and the 'Dark One' is more powerful than ever." The wolf spirit laughed bitterly, and added, "And we don't even know who he is... hell, we don't even know if he is a he at all."

Sunay stopped sipping. Rola had the right of it. Sunay finished her glass, choked down the burn, and played the waiting game before the alcohol took effect. "So... what do we do now?"

"I don't know," Rola answered honestly. "Maybe nothing is the answer. Live our lives the best we can, and pray to the Coders that it'll all work out somehow. I know that's not much of a plan, but it's the best I can think of."

Sunay drew in a slow breath, and poured out two more glasses of Blue Mirror Spirit. "Well, in that case, I think this is the best way we can spend this night."

Rola finally flashed a tired smile. "I like how you think, my little fire fox."

The two women started on their second glasses, and Rola finally started burying her fugue under genteel conversation. She gestured lazily towards Sunay's stomach, and said, "Decided on any names?"

The foxgirl's eyes narrowed, knowing it was *far* too soon for her to be showing. She eventually shook it off. How Rola knew, or if it was just an educated guess, was unimportant. "I dunno just yet," the foxgirl finally said. "A smart guy told me that I should be expectin' four or five..."

The End

199

Other works by Thomas Knapp

The Broken Prophecy

The Sixth Prophet

The Tower of Kartage

For more information, visit http://www.tkocreations.com

Other works by Fred Gallagher

MegaTokyo: Volumes 1-3

MegaTokyo Omnibus Vol. 1

Available from Dark Horse Comics

MegaTokyo: Volumes 4-6

Available from DC Comics

For more information, visit http://www.megatokyo.com or
http://www.megagear.com